OUT OF SIGHT

A Novel

ERIC SMALL

MIDDLETOWN PUBLISHING GROUP

St. Augustine, Florida

Middletown Publishing Group
St. Augustine, FL

Out of Sight - Eric Small -- 1st ed.

Dedication

For the 53,435.

Acknowledgments:

I can't imagine writing and completing this book without my wife Denele's love, support and encouragement, not to mention her stellar editorial and proofreading assistance.

My eternal gratitude to my mother Sally, my brother Steve, and my sister Nancy for their ongoing love and support, and to my late father Richard, whose love of books and reading had much to do with my own love of words.

My eternal gratitude to Howard Kaplan, MD, without whom I'd know little about complex eye disease.

Author image used by permission from Lifetouch Portrait Studios, Inc. Stork Photography

Cover image: Photo 202275340 / Penn Yan © Beautynature | Dreamstime.com

Preface

"My dear fellow, who will let you?"

"That's not the point. The point is, who will stop me?"

From *The Fountainhead*. Ayn Rand. 1943

1

Thomas Edison Orwell checked his notebook, squinted at the dilapidated house, and muttered something approximating satisfaction. The location perfectly suited his needs, and he knew he could fix it up into a first-class place for his new endeavor.

He called the realtor holding the listing and made a low-ball offer. As the house had languished on the market for years, he figured he could get it for a song. He might have to add a little negotiation dance into the mix, but he doubted it.

His guess proved accurate. The realtor called him back in twenty minutes with a counter-offer, and he knew he had them. He offered about one-half of one percent to his original offer to give them something to save face with, and the owner accepted it, he assumed with an enormous sigh of relief. The place was a disaster, after all.

As the offer was all cash, a quick closing date resulted in his ownership of a giant white elephant. And a wonderful project to keep him out of trouble.

He called his wife, Brenda, to give her the um, good news, and she just grunted. Edison, the name he preferred, took that for an expression of unmitigated joy at his acquisition. Okay, no he didn't. But Bren was on board with his project, he knew that. She'd consented to Edison using her money for the purchase. He had no savings of his own. His next call was to his good friend, and skilled carpenter, Morris Goodwin.

"It's a go, Mo," he said, chuckling at his unintended rhyme.

"So you said, Ed," he replied. Mo was fast on the uptake.

"Let's start right away," Edison told him.

"Um, how about tomorrow? I'm kind of busy right now."

"Oops, sorry. What's her name?"

Edison received his answer when Mo yelled, "I'll be right back, Gloria."

"Tomorrow it is," Edison said in haste.

"I'll call Dave first thing in the morning," Mo said before he hung up.

***

Edison peered out his bedroom window at the gloomy late November sky. Winter arrived early in the tiny town of Standard, New York. An unremarkable Thanksgiving had passed, and the early days of December often portended the arrival of sleet, slush, and snow. An involuntary shiver racked his body. Not for the first time, Ed wondered why he and Brenda had chosen this remote town in which to settle. Or more accurately, to resettle. But he knew why. Burned into the very core of his soul, he knew.

No one ever referred to him as Tom or Thomas. From early childhood, people called him Edison or Ed. His parents, God rest their souls, had named him after Thomas Alva Edison, the brilliant inventor and New Jersey resident, who remains both a Menlo Park, New Jersey and American icon.

Edison grew up in Edison, New Jersey, a town, like him, named after the great genius. Truthfully, he grew tired of the Edison from Edison stuff. He held onto his name anyway, but often changed it to Ed. Only a few people asked him his relation to Edison, and even fewer dunces asked about his familial relationship to George Orwell, which was only the *nom de plume* of Eric Blair.

Edison Orwell was neither an inventor nor a renowned author. He had long served as a bureaucrat in government service, in a cubicle, performing a nondescript function in a job he hated. But it paid the bills. Well, it helped. Most of what they owned was because of Brenda's inherited money and earnings as a college professor. And after the troubles… well Bren owned everything. She still did.

Edison was seventy-three years old. He stood five foot ten in his stocking feet. He was a little overweight at 185 pounds, but muscle formed a fair chunk of those pounds, as he engaged in physical activity regularly. Not just exercise, but doing stuff like fixing up old houses. His round face included deep set dark brown eyes and slightly larger than average lips, with a nose flattened by an injury. Ed's forehead and face contained more than his fair share of creases and lines, creating an effect of him always looking worried. Close to the truth.

He closed the blinds, plunging the room into semi-darkness, gave an enormous sigh, and headed downstairs to where Brenda was preparing breakfast.

2

Edison, Mo, and Dave stared at the old building.

"Needs a lot of work," Mo said, stating the obvious.

"No way that old shack meets Code. Might have to rewire the whole place," Dave, the electrician speculated.

"We'll have to enlist some of the other guys," Edison said, "but I think we can get it done, say… by end of April."

"It's almost December now," Mo replied. "Only if we work day and night, and bring in all the old union guys would we have a chance, and a remote one at that, to get it done by, say… the end of June."

"Oh, don't be so negative. You haven't even seen the inside. It's beautiful in there."

The three men entered the building, and Edison fell through the floorboards. Undaunted, he pointed at the ceiling.

"Look at the crown molding," he said, while extricating his leg from the broken wood.

"Look at those floorboards," Mo said, his voice dripping with sarcasm. "Seriously, Ed, this place is a mess, inside and out."

Dave stepped gingerly while looking around. "You know," he said, "this place isn't half bad. It needs a new floor, but look at these electrical outlets. I'll bet my last dollar that someone already upgraded the wiring."

The two other men inspected the outlets.

"You're the expert, Dave, but they sure look new to me, too," Mo agreed.

"Okay, let's look around and assess what needs fixing and who we think should join this merry band of ours. But carefully, guys," Edison said, rubbing his leg.

They spent the rest of the morning making observations and taking notes. At about 11:30, Edison called a break, suggesting they grab a late breakfast at Pete's Eats, a local diner they frequented.

"Too early for a cold beer," he intoned, wiping his sweaty brow, "but I'm famished."

The other men agreed, and they all piled into Mo's Chevy S-10 for the short ride to Pete's.

Darla, the familiar hostess at Pete's Eats, greeted them at the door, and seated them in their regular booth on the left side. They rarely came here now, only about five times a week, down from their previous seven. Much too busy doing… not much. At least in Edison's case. Mo and Dave worked part time. But they intended to devote significant hours to Edison's project. Just as soon as he filled them in on what he had in mind other than fixing up an old building.

"A Junior/Senior Center," Edison pronounced, folding his arms on his chest in evident satisfaction.

Mo and Dave both leaned forward, as if gauging their friend's sanity. Mo ventured a question.

"Um, Ed, what's a junior senior? Someone say, fifty-one? Not yet eligible for Medicare, but old enough for AARP membership?" Mo asked.

Edison laughed. "Not a junior senior, a combined Senior Center and a safe place for young children and teenagers. Think kids teaching us how to tweet, post photos on Instagram, and play video games, and we teach them about life."

"Hey, I like that," Dave said. "I can teach them how to become electricians, and Mo can teach carpentry. And Edison, you can… um… teach whatever you did in your government job."

"I was thinking I could offer good, sound practical advice," Edison said, "but the government thing might work, too."

"Eddie O is getting into the guru business," Mo declared. "We all are. Hey, I'm on board."

"Me too," Dave agreed.

"It will take hard work, and a big-time commitment," Edison warned. "And money."

"We won't charge for our labor. Right, Mo?" Dave said with a snicker.

"Nope. Not a penny. It's for the kids."

"Guys, you know what I mean."

They both nodded and assured Edison they'd ante up as much as they could.

At that moment, their regular server, Dolly, who was hovering near their table, and as usual, listening to their conversation, spoke up.

"I like the idea," she said. "I'd go there myself."

Dolly, who was pushing eighty, looked a hundred, but also had the sharpness and agility of a teenager, added, "How can I help?"

Edison told her he'd keep her informed, and she hustled off to fill their orders.

"Is Bren on board with this?" Mo asked.

"Absolutely. It was her idea."

***

"It was not my idea, Eddie," Brenda told him when he returned home.

"Did you or did you not tell me I should do something with my time other than go to the diner in the morning and drink beer at night? That maybe helping young people or elderly folks might help with my, um, problems? Didn't you suggest that? And you approved the purchase of the property."

Brenda sighed. "I did."

"So, isn't this idea just an extension of that?"

"I suppose. And I even like it, Ed, I do. But it sounds expensive, way beyond the minuscule purchase price for that eyesore on Apple Street."

"I have two investors already," Ed said.

"Mo and Dave. Need I say more?"

"They might not be the keepers of Fort Knox, but they can help. And they have skills."

"They do," Bren said. "And they're both hard workers. Or at least used to be. Oh, Eddie, I think it's a wonderful idea, you know that, but be careful with the family funds, okay?"

"You know I will," he said, leaning over to kiss her. "And I expect you to serve as a deputy wise man."

"Wise woman," she corrected. "And I'm not your deputy. I'm your long-suffering wife. And may I suggest something?"

"Um, okay. Shoot."

"Recast your idea."

"How so?"

"No offense, but you don't know shit about adolescents."

"I do so… um… maybe not. But what's with the 'no offense, but…?' Why do people say that? Is it attempt to inoculate themselves against hurting people's feelings? Or saying 'with all due respect.' That one gets me, too. It's sort of like an inferior respect. Only that much respect as is due, and no more."

Brenda waited for Edison to finish his latest rant.

"It never even occurred to you that no teenager in his or her right mind would want to be characterized as a 'junior,' or hang out with a bunch of old people?"

"You said it was a wonderful idea," Edison accused.

"I meant that in a kind of organic way. You know, like an evolving concept. One that needs to develop, ferment like a fine wine."

"Well, I know enough not to serve alcohol to minors," Edison said, changing the subject in the vain hope that Bren would laugh.

"Seriously, Ed, you have a wonderful concept. You're putting something positive into that old place. Just keep thinking about it, okay?"

Edison just grunted.

3

"**B**ad news, Mo," Ed said when he called his friend. "The town rejected your permit application?"

"Um, no, that's not it. What permit? Oh, never mind that now. No, I mean Bren shot down the Junior Senior Center idea."

"Why? And I thought you said it was her idea."

"It was, sort of. She just wanted me to use my free time constructively, maybe to help people."

"Isn't a Junior Senior Center doing that?"

"Well, yeah. But it turns out I know squat about adolescents."

Mo laughed. "I could have told you that."

"So why didn't you?"

"You were so excited about the project, neither Dave nor I wanted to puncture your balloon."

"Bren had no problem deflating it," Edison muttered, half to himself. "Wait a minute. You and Dave talked about it?"

"Sure. And we would have told you at some point. We'll still fix the place up, don't worry."

"Yeah, but what should we do with it?"

"How about just doing the same thing, but call it a community center?"

"That could work," Ed admitted. "Okay, let's do that."

"Okay. And Ed…"

"Oh what is it now?"

"Apply for a permit. And notify the town building inspector of your intentions. We can start work without either approval, but we can't open if the permits aren't in order. You don't want to piss off the local government. And you will if you ignore their byzantine processes."

"Are they honest in this town?"

Mo just guffawed and hung up.

***

"This looks pretty straightforward," Edison said to his empty home office. "Let's see, I just download the application, fill it out and bring it in, and presto, the town issues a permit. I don't know why Mo was so negative about it."

"Are you talking to yourself again?" Brenda yelled from the kitchen.

"No. I mean yes. I'm just making mental notes," he shouted back. He could almost hear her silent response that mental notes stayed in one's head. But she said nothing.

He often spoke to himself when he was thinking. It was a well-honed habit, and one that annoyed almost everyone when he was still working. Brenda tolerated it, but couldn't resist mentioning it sometimes.

He thought about Brenda. A wonderful woman, Bren. To tolerate the likes of him for over forty years made her a candidate for sainthood. Ed knew he wasn't always a joy as a husband. But he was honest and treated Brenda well. Hell, he loved her from the moment they met. They had an unbreakable bond, borne of many years together. Even after that nasty business, that bond remained. Or so Edison thought.

***

Brenda Haverford Orwell was a handsome woman, with iron grey hair and a squarish face. She stood five feet seven inches tall, with a trim figure. Her once smooth complexion now contained many faint lines — visual evidence of her seventy years of life. Her recent departure from the university left her without a sense of purpose. They had no children, so playing with the grandkids was not an option. And she abhorred the idea of looking after Edison as a full-time job.

At the moment, she was reflecting upon his idea for a community center. It might give both of them something positive to do with themselves in their joint retirement.

***

Edison completed the permit application. At least in his view. He'd left multiple blank spaces where he concluded that the information was unnecessary, intrusive, or annoying. He walked the short distance from his home to the town hall, where he proceeded to the Office of the Registrar of something or other.

Striding up to the bullet-proof glass partition, he brandished his sheaf of papers, and spoke into the small microphone embedded in the glass.

"I'm here to file this application and collect my permit."

No response. He repeated himself. Again, no response.

He knocked on the glass, and said "Hello, hello? Is anyone there?"

Still no response. Ed looked down at the papers he held, then back at the glass, and thumped his fist against the glass. That brought a thirty-something man in a button-down shirt and red tie to the window.

"A little patience, sir. We're shorthanded here, and I was busy in the back. What can I do for you?"

"I'm here to collect my permit for a community center. I bought the old Horton place, and I'm fixing it up."

"A laudable project, to be sure, sir. But we do not give permits out just on request. We have a stringent application process."

"I have my application right here," Edison said, passing the papers through an opening on the bottom of the glass.

"Great, great," the man said. "Just leave them here, and expect to hear from us in six to eight weeks."

"Why so long?" Ed inquired. It didn't bother him much, be-cause he figured it would take at least that long to complete the reno-vation, but he thought he should ask just the same.

"As I explained, we're shorthanded here. We'll review the ap-plication, make our requests for additional information, and evaluate the completed package."

"What additional information?" Ed asked. "I downloaded this application from your website and filled it out. What else do I need? It's a community center."

"Site surveys, Phase I and II environmental impact statements, Certificates of Need, and a full wetlands study, to name a few. There are other requirements, as well. Although you might get away without all the environmental stuff if your building's history is well-docu-mented in the town records."

"What's a Certificate of Need?"

"The town requires six of them. Statements from prominent town residents attesting to the benefit your project will confer upon the community."

"It's a community center. By definition, it benefits the commu-nity."

"Maybe so, but the town law requires affidavits."

"Who qualifies as a prominent town resident?"

"Well, perhaps your clergyman. Someone like him."

Edison didn't have a clergyman. He hadn't attended any reli-gious service in about fifty years. And he held his tongue at the infer-ence that a member of the clergy had to be male. He'd find other types of prominent residents. He did not know what an environmental im-pact statement was, but he'd figure that out as well. Someone would know, and how hard could it be to get one? Arguing with this guy wouldn't help. So Ed stayed pleasant.

"I wonder, sir, if you might have the time to look this applica-tion over, and give me the benefit of your guidance, to put me on the right track."

The man looked at his watch. Not a good sign. But he surprised Ed by agreeing to scan it for completeness.

But it didn't go well. The man pointed out all of Ed's omissions and handed the application back to him to "correct and resubmit."

Ed thanked the man with poor grace and trudged out of the town hall. This might be harder than he thought.

When he returned home, he filled Bren in on his experience, ending with a gigantic sigh and speculating whether he should just give up.

Bren looked at him. "Give up? That's not my Edison. You never give up."

"Bureaucracy is an immovable force. You can't fight city hall."

"You once were the bureaucracy," Bren pointed out.

"Yeah, and I knew it was fruitless to fight my organization, too."

"But people did. All the time."

"Some were successful," Ed admitted.

"It's a worthy project, honey. See it through."

4

"Getting a permit might present a problem," Ed told his friends when they reassembled in front of the building.

"You met the town building and zoning officials, I presume," Dave said.

"Yep."

"And you need about four thousand documents, environmental studies, and certificates, along with affidavits from the president, both senators, and at least three of: a priest, a minister, an imam, and a rabbi."

Ed hunched his shoulders in frustration. "Um, that's about right."

"Ignore that."

"Huh?"

"I mean it. As an electrician, I've needed approvals for about thirty years in this town. And when I first tried, oh so many years ago, I was told the same bullshit."

"So you don't bother with approvals?"

"Oh, I get them. Don't open without a full sign off from the town. That won't go well."

"So, how do you get approvals?"

Dave looked at Mo, the carpenter. "I have two separate ways. How about you?"

"I call my congressional representative, state legislator, or influential local official to see if they'll intervene, and if not, outright bribery."

"Yeah, those are mine, too. There's a third, less effective way, of course, but you have to consider it."

Ed perked up. "What's the third way?"

"Sue the bastards. Or at least get a lawyer to threaten to do so."

"Have either of you done that?"

"Not personally. But my clients have several times."

"Yeah. Mine, too."

"Did it work?"

"About ninety percent of the time. This town doesn't like litigation. They ordinarily just fold."

"So why is that a less effective way?"

"Lawyers cost money. Calling your legislator costs nothing. Bribery is still cheaper than lawyers."

"Can't you go to jail for bribery? I can't risk that."

"You can avoid that route, although it's a way of life in Standard. I don't know of anyone ever prosecuted for bribing a local official in this town. You're almost a pariah if you don't at least offer tickets to a ballgame or something."

"I think I'll try assembling the required information first. At least everything except the environmental studies. The town guy said he might allow me to skip them if this building has an established history."

"I know where you can find that out," Mo said. "Go back to the town hall and look through the land records. If you can stand the mind-bending boredom, you might hit pay dirt."

"Isn't that stuff online?" Ed asked.

"Oh sure. Carefully organized into a searchable database accessible from the comfort of your own home."

"I sense a wee bit of sarcasm."

Mo laughed. "No, this might be the last town in America to not have most records digitized."

"Maybe I'll try to get the affidavits first."

"Sure. Just call your pastor. The one you don't have."

"This is hopeless."

"No, it isn't. Have faith. Oops. Bad choice of words. But you know what I mean."

Ed knew. And it was the same advice Bren had given.

"Okay, enough of that. Let's get to work. I'll get a permit somehow."

***

Ed trudged back down to Town Hall, and down the corridor to the land records room. He tried to follow the instructions given by the records librarian, as her nameplate referred to her, but the documents flummoxed him. What did Liber mean? What is a folio number? And what was a Grantor? And more to the point, how did any of this help him get a permit to build a community center?

Ed sat at a table in the room, his head bowed and his eyes closed, willing his brain to understand the legalese. As he sat there in despair, the librarian approached him.

"What are you trying to find?"

Ed looked up and gazed at the woman.

"I'm trying to get a permit to build a community center, and a clerk in the permits department suggested the possibility of a waiver of some requirements if I knew the history of the building. But I don't have the first idea how to find that."

The woman, who wore a name card with "Doris" written on it, looked at him for a moment.

"Where are you planning to build?"

Ed told her, and she gave a low whistle.

"That old place?"

"Yes, I bought it this week. I plan to fix it up and create a spot where people of all ages can meet."

"That sounds wonderful," Doris said. "And an upgrade to that old eyesore. The town should commend you for undertaking such a project. I can help. Do you have the lot and square number for the property?"

Ed tilted his head like a dog, hearing words but not understanding.

Doris laughed. "I'll take that as a no. Don't worry, I know the property, and a thing or two about how to cut through the legalese designed to confound ordinary folks like us. She walked over to her desk, entered a few keys on her computer, muttered, "okay, okay, there it is," jotted something down, and tore off the page from the pad she'd used.

"Got it," she said to Ed, who murmured his thanks, without knowing what he was thanking her for.

"You don't want the land records. I hope you have a title insurance policy for your purchase."

Ed nodded. "Yes."

"Look at the information in that policy. What you also want is the permit history. It will give you architects, builders, construction dates, materials, alterations, and much more."

"That sounds like what the clerk was talking about," Ed said. "But he mentioned environmental and wetlands studies, as well."

"Which clerk?"

Ed gave the man's name, and the woman grimaced.

"What's wrong?"

"Oh, he's a good man. But a stickler." She paused, looked at Ed, gave a brief nod, and lowered her voice. "After submission, the application might languish anyway, but once completed, bring it to Gertie. She's much more receptive, and might not require every single last item. No guarantees, of course. And I hope so, because we don't keep that environmental stuff here."

"Where is it kept?"

"New York State Department of Environmental Conservation, known as the NY DEC, and the U.S. Environmental Protection Agency, or EPA."

"Do you know if they're online?"

"I think so. Not like the ancient style record keeping in our quaint little town of Standard. But again, talk to Gertie first." She leaned in conspiratorially. "Roger goes to lunch every day at 1:00, and Gertie is by herself in the office then."

With Doris' help, Ed checked the building's permit history, found some interesting tidbits, but nothing that would disqualify the building as a community center. Doris helped him discover that the area met the zoning requirements. So, it looked like clear sailing for his project.

5

Edison left Town Hall and strolled past the town square, taking a roundabout way home. He needed to think, and the small, tree-lined park comprising the geographical center of Standard provided both shade and a vehicle for quiet thought.

At this time of year, the trees were bereft of the colorful leaves they bore just a few scant weeks ago. Town Square radiated dazzling beauty during the autumn months, as the leaves of different varieties of maple, oak and hickory all burst out into a coat of many colors before descending to the ground in an effervescent voyage to a sea of brown.

Many piles of raked leaves dotted the square. The Town would soon haul them away to parts unknown. Ed stepped around a pile and sat on one of the many benches scattered around the park. He sighed, crossed and uncrossed his legs, and fidgeted in an effort to get comfortable on the cold, hard bench, but gave up with a silent shrug, as if ceding victory to the inanimate object.

Thus seated, Ed thought about his project. He and his friends could fix up the house, no question. But the formal process for obtaining a permit seemed daunting. Even if he cleared the preliminary review by the clerk, Doris told him it would languish. But he had to try. He struggled to his feet and walked briskly home.

Back in his house, Ed called Mo to pick him up to go back to work at the future home of the Standard Town Community Center. Ed needed a ride, because he didn't drive. He had no driver's license. The State of New Jersey had revoked it, and that prevented him from getting one in New York. Not that he wanted one. With his eye condition, only a fool would get behind the wheel of a motor vehicle. Ed sighed.

He'd been such a fool once. More than that — a raving, dangerous, stupid, inconsiderate moron.

Mo picked him up a few minutes later, and they worked the rest of the day fixing the place up. A lot of work remained, but they made some progress. After several hours, Ed called a stop to the work, wiped his sweaty brow on his sleeve, and surveyed the place with approval. It hadn't even taken shape, but he could visualize a bustling, active community center. So Mo dropped him off back home, where he and Brenda had dinner, watched the evening news, and sat quietly until bedtime.

At one time, Ed liked to read in bed, but his eye condition made it harder for him, until someone invented the e-reader. Now, by adjusting the font size to extra-large, he could read pretty well. A bit of a struggle, to be sure, but not enough to stop him. He and Bren read until they both became sleepy, and retired for the night.

The next day, at a time calculated to coincide with Gertie covering the office alone, and with application in hand, Ed trudged back to Town Hall. A short woman with gray hair, octagonal glasses, a round face and a sunny smile greeted him and asked how she could help.

Ed showed her the application and asked whether he needed to complete every single item on it.

"Oh, I doubt it," the woman said. "There's an awful lot in there that shouldn't apply to something so beneficial to the community. They designed this application for a commercial enterprise, like a grocery store, or one of those big box stores. Let me see what you have so far. Hmm. Uh huh, uh huh, yes, excellent description. Much needed in Standard. Oh, I think we can waive some of this stuff. An environmental study? It's not like that property ever had a gas station on it. It's been there for years. Everyone knows old Mrs. Horton lived in that house. And oh, my, she was called old Mrs. Horton when I was a teenager. A pleasant woman. Kept to herself, but did no one any harm." Gertie continued her trip down memory lane for a while, nattering away, while Ed just listened patiently. This woman could help. Much better than… oh crap.

The original clerk, Roger, pushed open a side door and looked over Gertie's shoulder at the application.

"I have this one, Gertie," he said to her. "Mr. Orwell met with me a couple of days ago."

Gertie looked at him, then at Edison. "Well, it's been so nice chatting with you, Mr. Orwell. I'm sure Roger will take good care of you. Good luck with your project." And with that, Ed's hopes for approval of a skinny application went "poof."

What could he do? He listened to the clerk drone on about the five hundred things he needed to do before the Town would even consider the request. And even then, only forwarded it to the Zoning Board, which couldn't even approve it, just offer a recommendation to the Town Board. Pursuing the project was fruitless, at least following the path the clerk laid out.

He needed another path. Lawyers were out of the question. Ed hated lawyers with a passion. After his experiences, it would take a lot for him to visit an attorney for any reason. And this did not even come close to making the cut. No, he needed something else. He could write to his U.S. Senator, or congressional representative, and maybe get some attention to his project. Maybe if nothing else worked. Who did he know in the Town with any influence?

No one. He and Bren were recent arrivals. He didn't even know who served on the Town Board, or even who the Mayor was, although he was pretty sure both existed. Maybe Mo or Dave knew someone. He called Mo first.

"I know everyone on the Town Board," Mo told him. "But they won't help you. They never help anyone. They just refer you back to either the Town Clerk or the Zoning Board. And they just say you need to follow the clearly stated application process."

Ed called Dave and received the same information.

"What about the Mayor? And, um, who is the Mayor?"

"Rufus P. Winkle. And he might help you, if you catch him sober, and grease his palm with cold, hard cash."

"I don't want to do anything illegal," Ed said. "He's the Mayor. Doesn't he want what's good for the town?"

Dave gave a dry laugh. "Rufus wants what's best for Rufus."

"How long has he been the Mayor?"

"Going on twelve years."

"How does he get elected?"

"No one ever opposes him. And truthfully, Rufus doesn't do much harm. Not much good, either, but no one thinks he's ever embezzled town funds, and people like him."

"Do you?"

"I'm not a fan."

Ed hung up with Dave and sat down in his easy chair to think. No lawyers, no bribery. Who cared about the town enough to help push the community center project through?

Religious groups came to mind, but Ed had a level of unease about dealing with anything having to do with organized religion. That's not to say he was an atheist, because he was not. Ed believed in a higher power. Not a white-bearded man in the sky, but some kind of force in the universe. But not one that controlled everything. If that was the case… well, no omnipotent, benevolent force would have let the terrible event happen at all. When the trouble had occurred, Edison had thought about God, not to ask forgiveness, but to express sorrow that he'd let God down. There was no redemption, just eternal shame.

No, Ed wouldn't call religious leaders. He settled on his State representative, Jack Smiley, and placed a call to his office.

To Edison's surprise, the man himself came to the phone.

"Edison Orwell? May I call you Ed?"

Without waiting for a reply, State Senator Jack Smiley continued talking. "What can I do for you, Ed? Anything for a constituent, I always say. You are a constituent, right?"

Edison assured him he was, and that he lived in Standard.

"My hometown," Smiley said. "Love the place. Live in Meeker Falls now, but I never forget where I came from."

Smiley took a breath, and Edison jumped in and told him what he had in mind. He started to tell Smiley that the workforce to fix the place up was all volunteer and self-funded, but stopped when Smiley spoke again.

"Great idea, Ed. You bought old Mrs. Horton's house. What a fine woman she was, God rest her soul. She must have been a hundred years old when she passed on to a better place. Jack paused, and Edison imagined he was crossing himself, or mouthing a silent prayer for Mrs. Horton's soul. Ed had never met the woman, who passed away many years before he and Brenda moved to Standard. Her old home had deteriorated from neglect by her heirs, who Ed supposed were happy to rid themselves of the place.

"I have to warn you," Jack said after the brief interlude. "It's a worthy project, but I doubt I can get the State to fund any more than, say half a million, maybe a full million, but no more than that."

Ed hadn't asked for any money. But he wasn't about to turn it down, either.

Jack continued. "Lots of money is available to take care of urban blight, but most of it goes to those big cities. It's about time some pork, um, funds, go to the little guys."

"Urban blight? In Standard? This is just a bucolic little village of 4200 people. Can you make that work?"

"Trust me, son. I can convince a mule to run like a horse. But maybe not urban blight in Standard. Hmm. A community development grant. That should do. I'll get you the money, don't you worry. The Jack Smiley Community Center will be a reality within the year. You can bet on it."

Ed had just wanted help to get the approvals. That part of the issue proved not to be a problem to Jack, who just laughed.

"Oh, good grief, is Roger at it again? Don't answer that. I've known him since the fourth grade. A bit of a weenie then and still a stick in the mud. I'll just pencil whip your application, and you can get on with it. Jack Smiley gives you his word on that. And can I count on your vote in November?"

Ed assured of his vote, thanked him, and hung up. And if Ed could successfully jump up in the air and click his heels, he'd do just that. Edison was not a cheerful man, but today, maybe a brief smile crept into the corners of his mouth.

6

Edison stood inside the doorway of the Jack Smiley Community Center, greeting townspeople as they streamed into the completely renovated former home of Old Mrs. Horton. A photo of the grand lady adorned what was termed a Town Memories wall just inside the entrance. Various other photos, some of local dignitaries, including State Senator Jack Smiley, formed a tidy mosaic. No pictures of Edison, Brenda, Mo or Dave appeared on the wall. All declined inclusion, seeking to remain in the background.

But everyone knew this was Edison's brainchild, not the least because he owned the building, but also because everyone had seen him, Dave, and Mo working there.

Even Jack Smiley, the consummate politico, mentioned Ed's tireless work in his long-winded dedication speech. Ed credited Senator Smiley for securing funding for the project.

And that money had helped. The place was beautiful. Ed, Dave and Mo, and a few other friends had supplied the skilled labor, and toil and sweat, but they had little money to pay for the games in the video game room, the sleek line of computers in the library nook, or the new furniture spread throughout the place. Not Ed's original concept of a Junior Senior Center, but without question it served as a fine meeting place for young and old alike.

About the library. The Standard Town library occupied a modest building on the other side of the small village, and you could walk between the Community Center and the library with little effort. That had Ed thinking. Why not collaborate? He'd broached the idea to the town librarian, Kara Cornish, and she'd enthusiastically agreed. The library furnished a couple of bookcases full of the latest novels, which one could read at the Community Center or at home. The readers would return them to the library, which would regularly replenish a new stock of books, to provide for some turnover. Once a week, someone, whether it was Ed, Brenda, Dave or Mo, or someone else, would pick the books up. As Kara loved encouraging reading, the arrangement was a perfect fit. And returning the books to the library brought people into the library itself, where they might find new reading material.

With Brenda's help, and a freshly minted volunteer staff, the Community Center had developed a full slate of programs — from arts and crafts, to computer help, to tax preparation help, as well as storytelling. This last one was a little different. Facilitators encouraged people to take part in a round table type discussion, where each participant added to a story begun by a moderator. It had attracted exactly no participants when launched, but now had dozens of willing storytellers clamoring for inclusion.

Ed envisioned the central lounge, with its comfortable easy chairs and sofas, as a location for quiet conversation and discussion. He expected mostly old geezers like himself to occupy the space, and maybe that's how it started. But it soon transmuted into a cacophony of voices, both young and old, loud and quiet, but rarely angry. It had become the social center for the Town of Standard.

That's not to say the Community Center had no quiet space to think or have a regular conversation. The solarium, with its comfortable chairs and tables, and beautiful view, served that purpose admirably. Many times, during an animated conversation in the center lounge, someone would point in the solarium's direction, which signaled a desire to discuss a particular issue privately. And off they'd go.

One day, Edison walked over to the Town Library to fetch the latest selection of books Kara intended to provide for the Community

Center. Ed liked Kara, and the two of them would often sit down at one of the library's big tables and enjoy a cup of tea together. This day was no exception, and when Ed arrived, Kara already had the teapot boiling.

Ed gave a slight wave as he entered the building, which was empty except for Kara.

"What do you have for us today?" he asked, his usual greeting.

"Oh, a few mystery novels, a couple of classics, and two books on the bestseller list. The usual stuff."

Kara looked around at the empty library. "You're taking my customers, Ed," she accused. Her comment had earmarks of lightheartedness, but they both knew she was right.

"I know," Ed said with a sigh. "We thought requiring the return of the books here would get more people into the library, not less. And with the internet providing access to information for kids' schoolwork, and e-books keeping people out of the physical library space, it can't be helping this place stay vibrant."

"Not your fault, or your responsibility," Kara said.

"It is my fault. No Community Center, people come here instead."

"Our business waned even before the Community Center, but I must admit, many of the programs you have over there, we used to have here."

"So let's fix that," Ed said.

"What do you have in mind?"

Ed told her, and she smiled. "It might work."

"Worth a try, anyway."

Edison put his teacup in the little sink behind the big counter, picked up his sack of books, and headed back to the Community Center.

Ed had wanted to do something good for the townspeople, and maybe he had. But at what cost? By opening a community center, he'd put a fine woman at risk of unemployment, and had drawn needed funds and talent away from the library. Ed sighed. He couldn't do anything right. Oh, he knew everything has unintended consequences. Hell, some things had inevitable consequences. Some that he couldn't fix, not now, not ever. He dropped his head in shame at the thought, and whispered to himself, "Oh, why, why, why, was I such a stupid fool?"

Upon his return to the Community Center, Ed placed the books on a shelf and surveyed the room. Two kids, about seven years old, sat with a woman who was obviously the mother of one or both of them. The children were both reading. The woman smiled at him, then went back to reading her own book. It was nice to see the Community Center library being used, but the sight made Ed feel guilty. He'd thought their little reading nook would be an excellent addition to the Community Center, and serve as a counterpoint to the game room, and he was right. But maybe too much so. No one visited the library anymore, except to return books in the outdoor slot allocated for that purpose.

He was not a librarian, nor were any of the volunteers at the Center. He knew Kara would gladly spend some of her free time at the Center. Indeed, she'd already done so. But this only further distanced people from the actual library. So Ed's idea to fix that was simple. If people didn't go to the library, he and Kara would bring the library to the Center.

He knew that he and Kara would have to convince an always skeptical Town Board that seemed to never hear a proposal they couldn't deny. But he thought he had the perfect pitch. Saving money. There was a large, unused, in real estate broker lingo, bonus room that would serve nicely as an adjunct to the actual library. Here was the saving of money part — he'd lease the space to the town for one dollar. They wouldn't close the actual library, of course, but it would be open only three days a week, with Kara splitting her time between the two library buildings. They'd save money on heat and electricity at the main library building, and the library would have loads of customers built right into the Community Center. Most of all, it wouldn't waste Kara's talents. A win, win, right?

Of course, the best of intentions sometimes go horribly awry, and with Edison, such disasters were almost an article of faith.

7

Edison walked home. He arrived to the pleasant aroma of roast chicken. He kissed Brenda before peering through the oven window at his dinner.

"Smells great, honey. When's dinner?"

Brenda smiled at him. "Soon. Go wash up and set the table while I start on these nice fresh green beans."

"Fresh green beans? Where'd they come from?"

"Cleavon's. He's been getting in a lot of fresh vegetables lately."

Ed nodded and headed down the hall to the bathroom. When he returned, he retrieved the flatware from a drawer in the long hutch, and placed them carefully on the table.

Bren put chicken, green beans and a baked potato on Ed's plate, then duplicated the procedure for herself, and they both sat down at the kitchen table.

"How'd things go at the Center today?"

Ed told her and said he'd walked over to the library.

"How's Kara?"

Ed sighed. "She's a great old lady, but I'm afraid we've taken away most of her patrons."

Bren gave a slight laugh. "That old lady is many years younger than us. But I agree, she's a terrific person."

Bren paused and cast a steady, knowing gaze on her husband. "You have an idea."

"I do," he said, and told her.

Bren thought about it. "What does Kara think?"

"She seemed to like it. She mostly sits in an empty building as things stand now. And it's possible that having an adjunct to the actual library in the Community Center will correspond to people going to the primary library as well."

Bren looked doubtful. "I don't know, honey. Maybe you should get rid of the library in the Community Center instead."

Ed pressed his palms to his temples. "I know. I know. It's a far better way to help Kara. But it's pretty popular, especially with the young parents and their children. Maybe they should go to the library instead."

Bren nodded. "Of course, they might not. Tough issue. Think about it a little before you approach the Town Board. If there is a way to screw everyone, our beloved Town Board will find it. And they are still chafing over how you circumvented them to get the Community Center. They won't be eager to help you."

Ed ran a palm across his forehead, wiping off imaginary sweat. "Yeah, isn't that the truth?"

Edison had no chance to consider either the adjunct idea or closing the Community Center library. Looking at the local newspaper the next morning, he came across the calendar for the Town Board. Prominently on the agenda was consideration of a motion to close the town library. As he considered this, he heard the phone. It was Kara.

"Did you see the agenda for the Town Board?"

Ed told he'd just seen it.

"I knew this was coming. We have very few patrons now that people can get the latest bestsellers right at the Community Center."

"But the library is the source of those books. We're just making it a little easier to get a few. The library has stacks of them. And we're not helping kids with their research projects. You are. Closing the library makes no sense."

"Tell that to our bean-counting Town Board. They see cost-savings in everything."

"I will. A few books on a bookshelf in a Community Center is not a library. And only morons would equate the two."

"Edison, please don't call them morons. At least not to their faces."

"I'll be the picture of quiet solicitude, I promise."

And he was, at least for the first three minutes of his allotted presentation time. The Mayor cut him off in the middle of a sentence, telling him his time was up, and calling the next three-minute presenter.

"I was just about to point out the many benefits of public libraries that a community center can't possibly provide," Ed whispered to Brenda.

The Mayor heard his comment and glared at him.

Edison glared back, and the Mayor stopped the proceedings and threatened to have Ed removed as a disruptive presence.

"I disrupted nothing, you ignoramus."

The Mayor motioned to the security guard, who approached, and caught Edison's eye and, with a single index finger, pointed at the door. Not wanting to create a scene, Ed rose and shuffled to the door. Bren rose to follow him, but he waved her back. He whispered, "Don't miss your chance to speak."

He'd lost his cool, and maybe cost Kara her job. What was the matter with him? He couldn't get anything right. Even the Community Center, which he'd intended to do something positive, had backfired. What was he thinking? Arranging easy availability of books at the Community Center to encourage reading and bring more visitors to the actual library. People, at least in Standard, were lazy. If they could get a book more easily at the Community Center, why would they make a needless trip to the library? Just because they had a vast selection of books, periodicals, reference materials and a wonderful librarian? Nah, lots going on at the "CC," as people called it.

Now, the townspeople's indolence could cause the loss of a valuable resource. The Town Board was that stupid. He was sure of it from listening to them drone on before taking public comments in a contrived effort to show that they gave a flying… fruitcake about the community.

But the Town Board didn't close the library. They considered it, but deferred any decision after hearing several townspeople, including Brenda, make calm, impassioned pleas for its continued existence. That helped, but Kara's quiet, dignified, yet full-throated defense of the co-existence of the Town Library and the Community Center turned the tide. Kara commanded the respect of most folks in Standard, and even the parsimonious Town Board was hard-pressed to ignore her candid appraisal of the merits of each of the two facilities. As she pointed out, a community center is more than just a meeting place with some books, and a library is more than just books with a meeting place. For one, the primary purpose is socializing, for the other, it's reading. Social Studies and English classes are both valuable. But they're not the same thing, nor are they interchangeable. Both the CC and the Town Library offer much more, and they co-exist wonderfully. Take away the library, and the Town of Standard will have a gaping hole to fill, as the next library is all the way in Meeker Falls.

The crowd murmured nervously as she referred to the hated football rival. No way the Town Board would decide right then. Not after that. But they didn't reject the idea. They just deferred decision until the next month's meeting. It saved the library, at least for a while.

Bren reported the news to Edison when she returned home, and he thanked her.

"So, I didn't screw it up for Kara. That's good."

"You tried to help, honey," Bren said and kissed him on the head. "You always try to do the right thing."

Edison looked at her for a moment. "Trying isn't the same as succeeding."

Bren's eyes blazed. "No, it's not. But it's a hell of a lot better than ignoring good advice and wantonly exposing yourself and others to danger."

Bren was a kind soul. And she didn't remind Edison of his monumental error of judgment and good sense often. It festered under the surface all the time, and he knew it. He felt the shame multiple times each day and was aware he'd affected people outside his family. How could he not? But sometimes he forgot how much his stupidity hurt Brenda as well. So, he just gave a weak nod, muttered something to the effect of "I know, I know, you're right of course," then excused himself and went upstairs to the bedroom, where he sat in the dark, brooding.

***

"Wake up, honey."

Brenda shook his shoulder, and Ed, startled, reached back to remove the source of his discomfort.

"You fell asleep in your chair, and were whimpering," Bren told him. "I heard you all the way downstairs."

Ed looked up at her, took her hand in his, and said, "I'm so sorry, honey. I've caused you nothing but misery."

"That's not true at all. You made a mistake. A costly one to be sure, but you owned it, and have tried your best to make it right."

Ed grimaced. "I haven't done a good job of that, have I?"

"You might try talking to people with similar problems. Maybe you can help them, and prevent the same horrible thing from happening to someone else."

Ed thought about that. He'd kind of thought of it before. The whole community center thing was a subterfuge for his personal interest in using it to communicate with young people. To help them avoid his path. But he'd gotten it wrong. It wasn't young people he needed to talk to. It was older folks like himself. People dealing with the physical challenges that he'd handled so poorly.

He resolved right there and then to return to his original purpose. He'd identify people similarly situated and tell them… oh shit. They wouldn't like it. And the younger they were, the less they'd like it. They'd ignore him or tell him he hadn't been careful. And it was true. But Ed didn't think anyone could be careful enough to prevent an inevitable disaster. But he had to try. Lives depended on it. He thanked Bren and tried to rise from his chair. And sat down immediately. He felt each side, then moved his palm around the back of his neck and rubbed it. Gently, because it hurt like hell. He'd snoozed in an easy chair in front of the television frequently, without incident. This wasn't an easy chair. He felt stuck to the chair, like a prisoner awaiting execution. Well, not quite, but it sure felt constricting, because all of his limbs were asleep. He stamped his feet to wake them up, with some success. And his neck felt a little less stiff. He lurched forward to escape, and… fell face first onto the floor. Bren, who'd tried to help him extricate himself, had instinctively stood back when he lurched forward, so she could not catch him. But she extended a hand, which Ed took as he righted himself, and, with Bren's help, hoisted himself to his feet, gasping with exhaustion at the effort. Bren looked at him with concern.

"Are you okay?"

Ed nodded, but even that hurt.

"Let's just go to bed," Bren said. "Tomorrow's another day."

Ed wondered why people said that. Tomorrow's another day seemed redundant. But he gave Bren a weak smile, and she helped him to the bathroom to get ready for bed.

8

The next morning, deep in thought, Brenda Haverford Orwell knit her brow. She hadn't slept well. Edison's discomfort troubled her. Every time she thought he'd let his huge mistake pass, he'd regurgitate it. Brenda understood, as his gross error in judgment had caused such harm, but they'd both hoped that moving to Standard might serve as a new beginning.

Brenda gave it some thought. Was she still angry? She thought not, but she understood Edison's profound sadness and self-loathing. Hell, she was sad, too. She'd lost a great deal, not just from Edison's idiocy, but also from his aggressive assumption of responsibility, shedding all of his assets in an insatiable quest to assuage his profound remorse. He'd ignored all legal advice, and might even be in jail if she hadn't drawn the line at that.

She'd given up a job as a tenured university professor to move to Standard, and had nowhere nearby at which to continue teaching. So she retired from a position she loved, and she and Edison lived comfortably on their two pensions, and her savings. Nothing cost much in Standard, so by local standards, they were relatively well-to-do. They'd also sold their home in New Jersey, but half of that money went to pay the legal judgment against Edison. She'd refused to use any of her funds. She understood why Edison ignored the lawyers' advice and didn't fight entry of the judgment. But his actions affected her profoundly. She gave up her teaching job and her house. They had to leave the city of her birth and the state she'd always called home.

Friends, family, and everything familiar no longer formed parts of her life. Standard was a lovely little town, for sure, and they'd both made new friends and had fresh places they frequented. In the new Community Center, Ed's brainchild, she even had a place to teach. But Standard was not, and she feared, never would be home. And Ed, it seemed, might never get to a point where his actions did not constantly wrack him with guilt. They'd moved away, but the sad fact is that you take yourself with you.

Brenda sighed, fussed with her skirt, and stood. She had to head over to the Community Center for the book club. She and Kara served as co-facilitators, and the club was wildly popular.

"Ed," she called up the stairs. "Let's get a move on. I have to be at the CC in fifteen minutes."

"Are you walking or driving?"

"It's a beautiful day. Let's walk."

"Okay, I'll be right there."

Edison finished brushing his teeth, ran three fingers through his thinning hair, put away his shaving gear, and headed downstairs. Ed locked the door behind him, a long-established habit that was completely unnecessary in Standard, took Brenda's hand, and they walked to the Community Center.

Kara greeted them inside the front door. She and Ed exchanged a brief pleasantry, and Brenda and Kara headed off to one of the side rooms for the book club, while Edison stood for a while in the center lounge, looking for a familiar face. He laughed quietly to himself. That was a silly thought. Everyone here had a familiar face. It was hard not to recognize almost everyone in town, and knowing those in the smaller subset of the CC was a given. What Ed was actually looking for was one of his good friends, like Dave or Mo, or even another old geezer like himself to talk to. He soon found someone. Not Dave or Mo, or one of his other friends, but an intelligent-looking man Ed judged to be about seventy. He wore horn-rimmed glassed perched low on his nose, the universal sign of age-related blown near vision. He was reading, or trying to read, one of the many small print flyers strewn on a long table set aside for that purpose. And he was a stranger, maybe new to town. Ed approached him, hand extended, and introduced himself.

The man looked up, startled, and asked Ed to wait a minute while he put the reading glasses in a case, and retrieved another pair, this time wire rimmed. He peered at Edison, tried to take his hand to shake it, and they missed. Not by much, but Ed ended up shaking only a few of his fingers. Ed wasn't sure, because his own vision was poor, but he had the distinct impression that it was the other man who'd missed. They both gave a nervous laugh, and the man introduced himself as Harrison Crutch, and for Ed to call him Harry.

Ed took a moment to look Harry over. He had a round, friendly, wrinkled face and a bulbous nose with a few tiny white hairs springing out. Pure white- haired temples flanked his balding dome. Upon his nose sat his wire-rimmed glasses, through which Harry squinted at Edison.

Edison could have been looking in the mirror, at least regarding the squinting. Ed did a lot of that himself. If lenses for glasses hadn't experienced such tremendous advances, Ed suspected he and Harry would stare through five- inch-thick glasses so heavy people almost couldn't wear them.

Ed wasn't sure how to approach the delicate subject of vision, so he just plunged right in.

"Glaucoma?" he asked.

Harry nodded. "You?"

"Yep. Mostly untreated until it got pretty advanced."

"Yeah, me too. Ignored it until the missus, God rest her soul, insisted I get an eye exam. She noticed it. They can do a lot now. No cure and not perfect, but there's treatment."

"Yeah, I can't do everything I used to, and what I still can do takes extra effort."

"It does," Harry agreed. "Like reading the tiny print on those flyers." He pointed at the nearby table.

The tough topic behind them, Ed and Harry engaged in pleasant conversation, before Harry noticed the immense clock on the wall and said he had to get home. He reached into his pocket and retrieved a set of car keys, and gave Ed a friendly wave as he headed for the door. Ed looked at him in astonishment, and discreetly followed him outside, only to watch Harry open the door to a Ford Taurus, get behind the wheel, and drive away.

When Brenda finished her class, she found Edison, and they walked through the park headed for home. Brenda saw Ed's grim face and asked him about it. Ed told her about Harry.

"Oh dear," Brenda said. "Did you confront him?"

"No. I was too stunned. I hoped I was mistaken, and they weren't car keys, but then I saw him drive off."

Brenda took a moment to eye Edison, to gauge what was going through his mind. She knew the main reason why Harry had upset him. But she scanned the profile of Edison's face for something else. She knew Edison always felt a deep-seated guilt for what he'd done. He couldn't forget it even for a moment. It had become part of him. And Brenda accepted that. She doubted she could have forgiven herself, either. She forgave him. Not for the damage he'd done to others. It was not her place to do that. No, she forgave Edison for the damage he'd done to her, uprooting her from a comfortable life in the bosom of her hometown, with friends and family nearby.

But walking with Edison, she was thankful they'd moved to a place that didn't require a car. They owned one, but she was the only one to drive it, and even that mostly for grocery shopping. Pretty much everything was within walking distance.

Brenda knew from experience with her parents and Edison that people equate driving with independence. Children with aging parents who still drive often want to take away their parents' car keys, and have a vague idea that they are limiting their mobility, but consider the hazard presented by an unsafe elderly driver to supersede any diminished ability to get around. And they arrogantly believe that old people don't need to go places, anyway. The former is unquestionably true. The latter not so much.

Loss of mobility creates an uncomfortable dependence upon others, which is tough enough for someone of advanced age. So, Brenda had a good understanding of how the inability to drive affected someone much younger, like Edison, or that stranger Harry. That tremendous loss of freedom could cause many people, young or old, to fall into a deep depression. Brenda was acutely aware of this, so she walked with him as much as possible, and drove the car only when absolutely necessary.

At the moment, she was studying Edison's face for signs of depression. Oh, Edison suffered from depression, she knew that. But he seemed at peace with his inability to drive. At least until he saw Harry, who apparently had a similar vision impairment as Edison. Was Edison envious of Harry? That he could drive and Edison could not?

She received her answer without asking the question.

"That man is a menace! He's going to kill someone," or…, Ed had a catch in his throat… "have a terrible accident. No way he can see well enough to be behind the wheel of a car. If he's like me, he's terribly subject to glare, has little or no peripheral vision, and the world is often blurry. And he's driving a car."

Brenda listened without commenting. She was glad Edison was expressing outward rage. Lord knows, he'd worn himself out expressing it inward.

"Are you going to do something?" Brenda was a little worried about what he'd do. He'd had enough trouble with law enforcement. They didn't need more.

"I don't know. I have to think."

"Think before you act, honey. That's a good idea."

They reached home. When they had changed into more comfortable clothes, Brenda fixed them both sandwiches, and they sat down to lunch.

9

Before they finished lunch, Ed's phone chirped.
"My phone sounds like a dying bird," he grumbled.

"You can change it," Brenda said. "But after you answer."

Ed looked down at the caller ID. "It's Kara."

Kara didn't bother to say hello. "They're putting the library consolidation back on the agenda for the upcoming board meeting."

"Oh shit," Ed said.

"Exactly."

"It's not ideal, but it might be time to put my idea into motion," Edison said.

"If I could think of anything else, I'd suggest it. Did Bren have any ideas?"

"She had one before. Close the CC library nook. But I guess it's too late now. But I'll ask her if she has any new ideas."

"Thanks, Ed."

"We'll figure something out," Ed assured her, in as confident a voice as he could muster. Privately, he had doubts. It was a five-member board, with three members appearing hostile to the town footing the bill for a library.

"When's the meeting?"

Kara told him. It was in three weeks. So they had that much time to figure out a way to save the library. Ed felt responsible for Kara's debacle. Hell, he was responsible. Without his concept of a community center, no one would have considered, or even thought of eliminating the library. But absent a miracle, the Standard Town Library was a thing of the past.

But miracles happen. They are rare, always a surprise, and frequently offer only an opportunity, rather than a complete answer. But a slight chance is far superior to no hope. And just such a miracle occurred in the little town of Standard, a mere two days after Ed's conversation with Kara. A slight crack in the anti-library armor. No, no one changed his or her mind. But the three Town Board members opposed to funding the library suddenly became two. One member of the Town Board resigned, citing health reasons. The resignation appeared to lock the Board in a two to two tie, which doomed the resolution to defund the library, at least for the present. And the next Board Member might not support the resolution.

Ed wondered who that would be. Under the town charter, they would hold a special election in thirty days. Ed had no idea who might run. It might be a good idea to figure that out and gauge the candidate's support or lack of support for the library.

Mo always had his ear to the ground about the Town, so Ed called him.

"Cyrus Boondoggle," Mo told him when Ed asked who he thought would run.

"Really? A guy named Boondoggle?"

Mo laughed. "No, but people call him that. His name is Cyrus Boone. He heads up the Zoning Board."

"Do you think he'd support the resolution to dissolve the library?"

"No question. He's tried to screw the library in the past, with crazy zoning proposals that would make it almost impossible to park there. He might have done the same thing to the CC if you hadn't convinced Senator Smiley to throw his support behind it."

"What's his beef with libraries and community centers?"

"Oh, Cyrus is cut from the same cloth as the rest of the old-timers in this town. They hate anything you might call progress."

"I get the Community Center as change, but a library?"

Mo looked at him. "You know Kara, right?"

"You know I do."

"Is she a stand-still kind of librarian, forever stuck in the Dewey Decimal System?"

"Um, no. She's more like a visionary."

"Yes, sir. That's our Kara. She's tried all kinds of new ways to get people to read, and most of all, to learn."

"Cyrus Boone hates reading?"

"I think Cyrus just fell in love with his elementary school librarian in the nineteen sixties, and hates anyone who is not like her."

"He'd vote to eliminate the library."

"In a nanosecond. He'll raise both hands, and yell aye, aye."

"Is anyone running against him?"

"No. Understand this town. He's next in line. He's paid his dues, or so people think, so first vacancy goes to the head of the Zoning Board."

"Isn't there an election?"

"Sure. One where people vote for a single candidate."

"But that's un-American."

"Well, it's Standard procedure in the ever-unchanging hamlet we call home." Mo emphasized Standard in his answer.

"Has anyone ever run against the sole candidate?"

"Not that I recall," Mo said.

"And you've lived here for...."

"Seventy-two years."

"And you're...."

"Seventy-two."

Ed shook his head in despair. "We're screwed."

"I wouldn't say that. We can try to convince the other two board members who've expressed support for shutting down the library."

"Really? Is there any chance of that?"

"I doubt it, but we can try, or just give up."

"I have to try. I owe it to Kara. It's my fault for pushing the community center. Without that, she'd have no problem."

Edison heard Mo's tone change. "You think it's your fault? That everything would be hunky-dory for the library if you hadn't pushed for a wonderful addition to our town?"

"Yeah. I do. A lot of what we do at the CC, Kara was already doing at the library."

"Don't take this on yourself. We all pushed for the CC, and so did Kara. And the two of you worked out a cooperative arrangement with an eye towards getting more people into the library, so it could fulfill its core purpose—giving people access to books, magazines, research material, help on their science projects, and so much more. There's a good reason for both places to co-exist, and you and Kara proved it. Just because some dickheads drunk with small town power want to obstruct anything good in this town doesn't mean that you're responsible for the library issue. Those board members have an eye on the library property for some reason, and you had nothing to do with it."

Ed listened to his impassioned friend with new respect. It was the longest speech he'd ever heard from the usually taciturn carpenter.

Ed asked around, but found little reason to believe that the two board members would change their votes. They expected to go forward in thirty days, as soon as they swore in Cyrus Boone.

***

Ed gathered his council of war. He, Brenda, Kara, Kara's husband Stan, Dave, Dave's wife Wilma, and Mo sat around the Orwell kitchen table to plot strategy.

Having called the meeting, Edison began. "One of us needs to run for Town Board."

Even though they all expected to hear something as quixotic as this from Edison, they exuded a quiet murmur, anyway.

Stan spoke up. "Has anyone told you how Standard handles Town Board elections?"

"Yeah, I did," Mo said. "But maybe it's time to change that. A lot of new people moving into Standard. They might be amenable to living in the United States of America, which not only permits elections, it encourages them."

"Are you willing to run?" Dave asked.

"Me, hell no. I was thinking maybe Brenda."

Bren laughed uproariously at that. "Not happening."

Edison looked around the table and encountered averted eyes. "Look, someone has to step up."

"Your idea, Edison," Kara almost whispered.

"Me? I'm a grumpy old man. People know that about me. I might only get the votes of the people around this table. Every single one of you is more popular than me. And we need someone who can win."

"The CC is very popular. And you're its architect. People regard you more highly than you think," Stan said.

"Winning is very unlikely, honey," Brenda added. "But not trying guarantees defeat. You're our best chance."

Edison threw up his hands in surrender. "Okay, I'll do it. How do we go about this?"

Kara explained the process, including the forms to fill out, the petitions to get signed, and the technical details of running for the Town Board.

Stan offered to serve as Edison's campaign manager.

"We'll have your name plastered all around this town as soon as you're eligible to run."

Cyrus Daniel Boone plucked a toothpick from the small cup on his desk and worked the wooden prong between his front teeth. He stared out the window for a moment, then tossed the toothpick in his wastepaper basket. He struggled to lift his heavy frame to his feet and lumbered to the door.

Cyrus was a big man. Three hundred pounds packed into a five-foot nine frame. He had a jowly, round face and he'd slicked back his thinning hair with homemade pomade. He looked like a bulldog who'd stuck his head in a can of beeswax.

Bulldog described him well, as he showed great tenacity in attaining his ends. And at the moment, his long-sought goal dangled deliciously in front of him, with not a single obstacle to its achievement.

Cyrus boarded the golf cart he used to get around town. Sure, it was eminently walkable, but walking took effort, and smelled suspiciously like exercise, which he abhorred. He traveled the short distance between the building housing the Zoning Board and the Town Hall, where he intended to file his application to fill the vacant seat on the Town Board. Cyrus chuckled to himself. He didn't really need to apply. Under longstanding custom, the head of the Zoning Board was next in line for the Town Board. The election was just a formality, necessary to create the impression that the process was fair and democratic. No one had ever run for the Town Board against the next in line. Until now.

When he arrived at Town Hall, a clerk advised him he had an opponent, and there would be a formal election, as required by the Town Code, in thirty days.

"Who's the rotten bastard?" Cyrus boomed, in a tone that residents might hear all the way to Meeker Falls.

The clerk told him. "Orwell? That cockroach? I'll kick his ass." He stormed out of the office, went outside, and hurriedly boarded his golf cart to find his hated opponent.

He found Edison standing outside the Community Center talking to Jack Smiley, who had become a friend during the process leading up to the opening of the CC. Jack had appreciated Edison letting him take all the credit. It was a win-win for Ed. He'd avoided the lime-light, which he hated, and it gave a powerful politician a parochial in-terest in the CC. That resulted in State money coming in to support its operations. And anyway, the two men liked each other.

Ed's interest in running for the Town Board had surprised Jack, who by now knew about Ed's desire to not be the center of attention. He'd voiced no objection to Ed's challenge of the *status quo*, telling Ed that "the Town of Standard could use shaking up." The consum-mate politician might have voiced a different view if Ed was not facing off against Cyrus Boone, who he very much disliked, calling him lazy and corrupt. When Ed asked him how he knew this, Jack had just given a tight smile, and said nothing more.

Cyrus wriggled out of the golf cart and stomped over to the two men.

"Smiley, I should have known. You put him up to this." Cyrus' bellowing attracted interested onlookers, who stopped their conversa-tions to watch the coming spectacle.

Ed and Smiley looked up from their chat, which centered on the sad status of the New York Knicks. Smiley spoke first.

"Cyrus Boone, you noxious nincompoop. I had nothing to do with Ed's candidacy. I will say it's high time that Standard had a real election. People are excited about it. It's the best thing to happen here since…" He looked back at the building… "this here Community Cen-ter." He paused for dramatic effect, as if speaking on the Senate floor. "And what do you know, Edison Orwell is at the center of both."

Cyrus looked at Smiley with visible disgust. "He doesn't have a chance, you know."

Ed watched and listened for a few moments, then quietly said, "You know I'm standing right here."

The two other men whirled to face him.

"I don't want to be the center of attention. Everyone who knows me is well aware of that. I don't have Jack's gift for eloquence."

He looked at Cyrus and held up a single finger to stop Cyrus from interjecting. "Nor do I have your passion for political advancement. I'm not doing this to hurt you or anyone else. I just think I can help this town in a way that you can't." He lowered his finger and nodded at Cyrus. "Now yell and scream at me. It won't be the first time, and I daresay it won't be the last."

Several people had craned their necks to overhear the conversation, and Edison's comments precipitated a loud murmur. Cyrus began speaking, looked around, muttered a curse, and stormed off.

A few people came up to Ed and told him they'd vote for him over that blowhard. One man came within a few feet, pointed a finger at Ed and said,

"Cyrus has paid his dues in this town. Who the hell are you to be running against our fine traditions?" The man didn't wait for an answer, and walked away.

Jack looked at Edison and gave a low chuckle. "Politics. Don't you love it?"

Ed shook his head sadly. "You know I don't. What have I gotten myself into?"

"You're an idealist. That's a good thing." Jack affected a dreamy look. "I used to be that way. A long, long time ago."

"It must have worked for you," Ed told him. "Look where you are today."

Jack looked at Ed for a long moment. "I lost my first election," he said. "Idealism is great. Practicality is better. Combining both is the holy grail of politics."

***

Stan Cornish sat across from Kara in their little breakfast nook. The couple often lingered there, continuing to talk long after they finished breakfast. The two had married young, and were among the few high school sweethearts who stayed together after getting college degrees in separate schools. They'd married soon after their respective graduations. They were sweethearts then, and had remained so for almost forty years. The county government employed both Kara and Stan, the latter as an administrator in the county offices in Meeker Falls.

Stan was lanky. He still had most of his hair, and wore his graying locks parted to one side. His oval face exuded kindness, or at least that's what people told him. And his visual appeal matched his personality. Stan was a nice guy, and well-liked in their small town.

At present, discussion centered on Edison's candidacy.

"Do you think he has a chance?" Kara asked.

Stan swallowed a bite of scrambled eggs, put his fork down, and wiped the corners of his mouth with a napkin. He gave a slight cough, scratched his nose with an extended index finger, then rubbed his hands together.

Kara watched this performance with mounting dread. Her livelihood likely depended upon Ed winning the election, and Stan, his campaign manager, looked already defeated.

But Stan surprised her. "I do, honey. It's an uphill battle for sure, but Edison has a chance. People in this town are the most bull-headed traditionalists on the planet, and Ed's candidacy is upsetting their world. They're used to one way of doing things. Cyrus is next up, ergo he's the next board member. But there are two things, at least, that Ed has going for him."

Kara waited expectantly.

"One, he's not Cyrus Boondoggle. Cyrus has alienated many people by parceling out favorable zoning waivers to his friends. I doubt anyone could prove he received kickbacks, but he's not the most honest man, and people know that. He'll get the support of those who received the special treatment, but many people have not been so fortunate. So it might be payback time for them."

"What's the second thing?"

Stan leaned over and planted a kiss on Kara's lips. "You," he said.

"Me?"

"People like you. You've done way more for this town than Cyrus. And the traditionalism cuts both ways. A library is the most traditional place in any town. As you've pointed out to me, libraries go back to ancient times. Demetrius of Phaleon founded the magnificent library of ancient Alexandria, Egypt, in 283 B.C. Now that's traditional." Stan folded his hands in his lap and gave a triumphant look at Kara, proud of his closing argument.

Kara indulged him. His historical reference was a beautiful touch, she had to admit. But she had reservations.

"I'm not the candidate," she pointed out. "And we love Edison. He and Brenda are good people and loyal friends. But Ed can be prickly. He has some inner demons he never talks about. Is he the right candidate? You're the most popular man in town. Maybe we should have picked you."

Stan sighed. "We've been through this, honey. The county charter prohibits county employees from holding public office. It's an anti-corruption statute. Neither of us can run. Don't worry, Ed will be fine."

Kara made a show of crossing her fingers.

"He's our last hope."

10

The last hope had his doubts. Lots of them.

"What the hell am I doing, Bren? I can't run for office. I have the personality of a tick."

"That's a little harsh, dear. A mosquito, maybe, but not a tick."

"You're not helping."

"Oh, come on, Eddie. You're plenty personable. People just need to get to know you, that's all."

"How are people going to get to know me in time for the election?"

"Many people already know you. You're the guy who brought them a community center. You're there most days, and I've seen you schmoozing with many of the visitors. Like it or not, you're the next best thing to a celebrity in this town."

Ed hung his head. "Yeah, that's me. A celebrity."

Brenda reached over and touched his arm. "You're a decent guy. And a much better person than Cyrus."

Ed responded through tightly pursed lips. "That's a pretty low bar. He's a corrupt moron."

"And you're going to stop him. But more to the point, you're going to help Kara."

"I hope I do. I'm responsible for her troubles."

"No, you're not, honey. From what I hear, that library property is much in demand. But no one can develop the land while the library sits there. You didn't cause that, and the CC created more interest in reading than ever existed before. Your plan with Kara for the exchange of books was brilliant. Kara told me just that just yesterday. She doesn't blame you, so why do you blame yourself?"

Ed sighed. "I guess I've just gotten used to blaming myself for everything."

Brenda's troubled eyes exhibited concern. "We moved here to get away from the daily reminder of that."

"It's not working. I still think about it most days, and dream about it most nights."

"And every moment of every day, you've tried to make amends for it. Maybe this is another way of doing that."

"Maybe. Kara is a good person. I'll help her any way I can. I just wonder if this is the best way."

"I think it's the only way. Now get out there and start campaigning!"

"I need the signatures first," Ed reminded her.

"Oh, Stan is taking care of that. He's coordinating a petition drive. You'll have the necessary signatures."

"How can he be so sure?"

"Townspeople have a higher opinion of you than you think. And they hate Cyrus as much as we expected. That's a wonderful combination."

Resigned to the inevitable, Ed wearily lifted himself out of his chair, kissed his wife, opened the closet, and grabbed his coat. With a little wave over his shoulder, he walked out and plodded to the CC to begin his campaign for a seat on the Town Board.

***

In the small, windowless office of Dave's Electrical Contractors, Inc., David Larson pondered how best to help Edison. A charisma transplant being out of the question, Dave explored other ideas. His personal interest in the election went beyond just wanting to help Edison, and by extension, his good friend, Kara Cornish. No, Dave had good reason to dislike, if not hate, Cyrus Boone and his crony, Mayor

Winkle. Dave had sought what he thought was a simple zoning variance for a small addition to his little office on the outskirts of Standard. He'd done the requisite paperwork, and made the application, but had failed to pay the expected bribes. He knew the lay of the land. Dave had lived in Standard for a long, long time. But he had a moral objection to paying small town government extortion. The head of the Zoning Board was the now Mayor Rufus Winkle, and his deputy was Cyrus Boone. The two men, as corrupt as they come, made sure he never got the variance. Dave never expanded his office. And he held a grudge against Winkle and Boone ever since.

Maybe they did me a favor, he thought. Expansion is not always a good idea. Dave had done just fine. Fortunately, his license came from the county, not the town, or he'd never be able to conduct business in Standard. As it was, he was the only licensed electrical contractor in town, and had plenty of business. Regardless of whether expansion was a good idea, failing to pay a bribe should not have stopped it.

Dave put the election out of his mind for a moment. He had a job to get to. His blue eyes glanced at the papers on his desk. He lifted his six foot four, two- hundred-pound frame out of his chair and headed for the door.

***

Mayor Winkle's rotund ass was plastered to his chair. He drummed his fingers on the oak surface of his desk while staring into space. A problem vexed him. He ran his hand across the surface of his head, half-expecting to find the tousled locks of his youth rather than the shiny bald dome he encountered. A pallid round face topped the Mayor's bulging torso, sagging chin, a pug nose and closely set dark brown eyes. Bushy brows formed the only growth on his skull.

The Mayor stopped drumming and fidgeting and considered the problem. He reached for his reading glasses, propped them on his nose, and scanned a document marked "Confidential." The Mayor finished reading the executive summary at the top of the first page, sighed, and put it down. He'd read the complete document multiple times, and it had the same expiration date every time, with no permitted extensions. The offer was good for only a short time. An acceptable deadline until the unforeseen event that troubled him now. Tossing the papers back on his desk, the Mayor mumbled an expletive, and reached for the bottle he kept in the bottom drawer of his desk. He poured a double shot of Old Crow, which he threw back in a single gulp. He gave a small gasp and slammed the glass back on the desk.

"Cheap ass bourbon," he muttered. "But it gets the job done."

Fortified by some of Kentucky's worst, Mayor Winkle arrived at a decision. He would squash the candidacy of that interfering screwball Edison Orwell like a stinkbug. Happy with comparing that officious interloper with a smell requiring eradication, Winkle considered how to derail his campaign. And quick. They needed to close on the deal two days after the election. A plan gradually came into focus, and he picked up the phone and made a call.

***

Ed's best friend, Morris "Mo" Goodwin, was hard at work fashioning a covered enclosure for Edison or one of his supporters to stand in while distributing campaign material. Volunteers would distribute most literature person to person, of course, but Mo was a skilled carpenter, and he thought it might come in handy to have a fixed location to hand out lawn signs and campaign materials. If you can, why not make even a local election as professional as possible? As it had never happened before, the election was shaping up as the social event of the year. It seemed like everyone wanted to get involved, and discussion in Pete's Eats often centered on it. The dispute between the traditionalists and those who yearned for something new in "this stagnant town" was fervent, but mostly genial. In Standard, everyone was your neighbor. No one wanted to alienate the people they saw every day.

Mo thought about how he met Edison. They were waiting on line together to buy "to go" coffees at Pete's Eats. Pete's was busy most mornings for people going to work, and Mo went there every day to pick up a coffee and a bear claw, before heading to what he called his office. That office was a small bungalow in downtown Standard, where Mo lived. As a free-lance carpenter, he had no place of business, but plenty of work.

He was also something of a womanizer, going from one girl-friend to another. Seventy-two years old, twice-divorced Mo had no in-terest in marriage again, but plenty of interest in women. As a long-time resident of Standard, he knew almost everyone, but had few close men friends. He recognized Edison as a newcomer the minute he saw Ed fall in behind him at Pete's. Ed wasn't sure of the procedures at Pete's, and that was clear to Mo, who viewed him nervously eyeing the large chalkboard menu hung behind the cash register.

"Whaddya want?" Mo asked him with a friendly grin.

Ed looked at him, then glanced at the chalkboard. "Just a damn cup of coffee. Plain, unadulterated coffee. No latte, no milk, no choco-late sauce, or frickin' fruit on it. Coffee. And I don't see that up there."

Mo couldn't help it. He cracked up laughing, extended his hand and introduced himself to the cranky new guy.

When Ed shook his hand, Mo told him to just say coffee, black. "In fact, just mimic what I say. I'm getting the same thing. You want it to go, right?"

Ed nodded. "I thought I'd sit outside at one of those tables." He pointed out the window to the front of Pete's.

Mo bought his coffee, dropped a few coins in the tip jar, and headed toward the door. But he paused just outside, and waited for Ed to come out. He liked the old curmudgeon.

Ed came out of Pete's with his steaming Styrofoam cup of cof-fee and saw Mo waiting for him. Nodding at one table, he asked Mo if he wanted to sit down for a bit. Mo accepted, and the two men chatted for a while, while sipping their black coffees.

Mo chuckled to himself while thinking about that first meeting. He guessed most people would have just glared at the impolite old guy and moved on. But Mo took an instant liking to his honest, albeit crotchety, demeanor, and the two men became friends.

Mo's dad, who died several years before, had been a master carpenter, and had passed much of his knowledge to Mo. Mo hated sloppy work of any kind and was a perfectionist in his carpentry. He'd lost so many assistants that he finally gave up and just worked alone. He could depend on himself, he knew that. Mo had a son named Lester from his first marriage, but all of his attempts to share the family trade had fallen on deaf ears. But he couldn't argue with Lester about it once he saw just how awful the boy was with his hands, and impatient with measuring. The adage, measure twice, cut once was anathema to Lester, who usually measured once, cut about six times. But Mo had to admit, the kid had turned out just fine as an English professor at SUNY. He married a woman Mo liked. No kids yet, but Mo was optimistic about the possibility of grandchildren in his future.

He figured he'd want to be called something like Mo Mo. Anything but the formal "Grandfather" that he'd endured.

Whoa, was he ever getting ahead of himself! He almost lost sight of his carpentry. He finished the structure and stood back to admire it. Pretty good, he thought. A nip here, a tuck there, and we'll have a fine campaign stand. "Almost time to sand it smooth," he murmured to the empty room. Mo was a fanatic about smooth finishes. When he finished sanding, the final product would feel like silk.

Mo spent the rest of the day refining the campaign stand, then called Stan to tell him it was ready.

As Ed's campaign manager, Stan handled everything. And the brain-trust of Brenda, Kara, Dave, Wilma, and Mo intended to leave almost nothing in the process to Ed. They didn't say it out loud, but they feared Ed would be his own worst enemy in getting elected. They all thought he would shine as a member of the Town Board, which badly needed shaking up by an honest man like Ed. But it was too important to let Edison screw up his own election.

11

Edison mostly limited his campaigning to shaking hands at the CC and talking to people at Pete's. And that was going fine, as he annoyed only one or two people a day, at a lower rate than usual.

Until one day at the CC, when Edison snapped. Standing outside at the door to the CC, he spotted Harry, the almost blind guy, park his car unevenly, taking up two spaces.

Ed's blood boiled. His eyes twitched, his shoulders tensed. His posture resembled that of a tiger ready to pounce. He fixed a steely glare at the parking area, as the unsuspecting Harry unlatched his seat belt, removed the key from the ignition, and wriggled out of the car seat. He slammed the car door and proceeded to the front steps of the CC, where Edison, coiled and ready, awaited his approach. When Harry spotted Edison, he raised his right hand to give a friendly wave, and Edison lit into him.

"What is the matter with you? You're endangering everyone by driving that car, seeing, or should I say not seeing, a goddamn thing in front and to the sides of you. You're going to hurt or kill someone, just like… so many other crazy, stupid, selfish assholes on the road. And look at your car," Edison added, pointing to the parking area. "You can't even see well enough to fit your fucking killing machine in one space."

Edison's raised voice made a bunch of people stop to watch and listen to the developing drama.

Harry looked shocked at the venom coming from Edison, but he quickly recovered.

"Who the hell are you to judge my driving skill? The State of New York gave me a license. They're the only body that has a right to judge my driving. You have a hell of a nerve saying anything. You haven't seen me drive. I've never, um, only twice had an accident. Never hurt a soul. Who hasn't had a fender bender once in a while? Oh, probably the great sanctimonious Edison Orwell. You know what? Go fuck yourself." He turned around, stormed to his car.

As he did so, Edison called out to him, "How many close calls have you had where you almost killed someone?"

Harry did not respond. He opened the driver's side door and gave Edison the finger before boarding his vehicle and driving off.

"He's going to hurt someone," Ed said quietly, mostly to himself, but others overheard. A few people nodded, but most people seemed shocked at his vehemence and viewed Ed as just an angry old man. Ed didn't notice either group of people. He walked off and headed home.

After he left, people inside the CC and those on the front steps gathered to talk about the event. All agreed that the tone was horrible. That even if Ed was right, and most seemed to agree that Harry shouldn't be driving, Ed could have adopted a differed tactic to get his point across. Like talking to Harry man to man, rather than berating him in front of a group of people.

And one thing was certain. The incident didn't help Edison politically. When the talk turned to the election, few of the people who overheard the argument thought Edison would be a good fit on the Town Board. The Board needed calmer voices, most people said. A loose cannon like Ed need not apply.

***

A short time after the so-called "shout out at the CC," word of the verbal altercation reached the ears of one Cyrus Boone. At his desk, Cyrus leaned forward and placed his sagging chin in his two ham-like hands. It was his thinking pose, and he tried to figure out how best to capitalize on Edison's meltdown. The obvious spreading the word of Edison's instability was a given. He and his allies would do that for sure. But he wondered if it presented the opportunity for a knockout punch. From what he'd heard, Edison was visibly angry at the prospect of Harry's poor driving. Standard was not a big, high traffic city. Even if that guy Harry's driving was horrendous, he was in the approximate median of driving skill in the town. Standard had a ton of terrible drivers, but where could they go? The town was so small that the speeds were minimal, and accidents were almost always fender-benders. Something that happened with great regularity in the town. No, there was a reason. Cyrus wondered what it was and guessed it had something to do with a drunken driver who'd hurt someone in Ed's family.

"Where's he from again?" Cyrus asked himself out loud. "I remember, New Jersey. Edison from Edison, New Jersey."

He grabbed an old-fashioned Rolodex on his desk, rifled through it, came to a name, and gave a grunt of satisfaction. That's my guy, he said to himself, and picked up his desk phone and punched in a number.

***

Ed tossed and turned that night. He couldn't get comfortable. Next to him, a sound asleep Brenda exuded a soft snore. Ed thought about getting up, but all his doubts and self-loathing flooded over him like a toxic rain. Oh why, why, why did we move to this backward little town in the middle of nowhere? But he knew. From his very core, he knew.

At some point, he drifted off into a restless sleep, but the anguish followed him into his dreams. In his recurrent nightmare, a speeding locomotive barreled in his direction, with the conductor either not seeing, or unable to stop for a little girl who'd wandered onto the tracks. Ed was waiting in his car for the train to pass, and viewed the scene with mounting horror. He bolted out of his car to extricate the little girl from the train's path, but never reached her, as Brenda held him back.

Holding and gently shaking his arm, Brenda said, "Ed, wake up. You're having a nightmare again."

"No, don't stop me. I can make it. Just a few more steps and I can get her to safety."

"Ed, you're having a nightmare."

Sweat poured down Ed's forehead, and he was shaking uncontrollably as he gradually woke up.

"It's always so real."

"I know, honey. Why don't you get out of bed, go to the bathroom, maybe splash some water on your face, and settle down a bit."

Ed searched around for his alarm clock. It usually sat on a little side table next to him, in plain sight, but it was gone.

"It's about 2:30, honey. And if you're looking for your alarm clock, check under the bed. That's usually where it falls when you thrash about and knock it over."

Ed got up, kneeled down, and sure enough, his battery powered alarm clock (works even in a power failure) was under the bed. He retrieved it and verified that the time was the middle of the night. He plodded to the bathroom, picked up the toilet seat, and aimed, then waited for a stream to come out. After completing that arduous chore, Ed splashed water on his face, towel dried, and returned to bed where Bren was already asleep.

Ed propped a pillow on the headboard and sat up for a long while, staring into space and thinking. He wasn't sure their move upstate changed anything at all, but he decided he was better off in Standard than New Jersey, even if he couldn't truly escape the demons that plagued him. He thought about that for a moment and sighed. The demons aren't plaguing me. I'm the demon. It didn't happen to me. I did it. Me. Only me.

He looked over at Brenda. What a wonderful woman he didn't deserve. She left everything behind. Her whole life was in New Jersey, but she'd uprooted to come… here.

Edison tried to sleep, but Morpheus never arrived. He counted sheep—that never worked before and it didn't work this night, either. He tried counting backwards from one hundred by sevens, but his exhaustion prevented him from continuing after getting to eighty-six. Tired, but not sleepy. There is a difference. But he must have drifted off, because the growing light coming from the bedroom window roused him. He looked over, and Bren was already up.

She peered into the bedroom. "Are you up, honey? Rough night, huh?"

Ed nodded. "Yeah. I slept very little after waking up from that nightmare."

"I tried to stay awake until you got back from the bathroom, but I guess I fell back asleep. Are you okay?"

"Yeah. I guess so. Do you think they'll ever stop?"

Brenda studied him. His posture, once pristine, had devolved into a slouch. Almost as if his troubles had bent him. She gave an honest answer.

"I don't know. Maybe not. Those events were traumatic." She paused. "To everyone."

Ed lowered his head. "I know."

"Oh, I know you do. I'm not a psychologist, and you know I think you should go see one, but I've tried to look at life's events, good and bad, as being the sum of all parts making me the person I am. Some things I regret, whether they are words I said or actions I took, and even things totally beyond my control that I dearly wish never happened. Other things I remember as joyous—things to celebrate— all filed neatly away as indelible parts of me and in my mind. I accept the good and the bad as inextricable parts of who I am."

"Acceptance is hard," Ed said.

"Yes, it is."

12

Edison and Brenda were eating breakfast when Kara called. She was obviously upset, and wasted no time with a hello or other pleasantry.

"What were you thinking?" she demanded.

"Um, about what?"

"You know perfectly well what I'm talking about. Screaming at that nice Harry Crutch right on the front steps of the CC."

"Oh, you heard about that, huh?"

"Everyone heard about it. Even people who weren't there think they were, and talk about it like they heard it all themselves. This is bad, Edison. Terrible."

"The man's as blind as… I am, and is still driving."

"Oh, I know that. But it's not like he's hurt anyone, and no one has heard about any accidents he's had. And why would New York State let him renew his license if he couldn't pass an eye test? Maybe you're just overreacting."

Ed sighed. He knew he was doing no such thing. But he could have approached the issue in a more diplomatic way. Public shaming, especially with a raised voice and angry words sprinkled with profanity, almost never accomplishes its intended goal. Edison knew enough not to argue with Kara, so after his initial weak protest, he kept his mouth shut and listened.

"We need damage control. Fast. You lost a lot of votes with that… spectacle. We need to win at least some of them back."

"Okay, I'll do whatever you say."

"I'm going to put Stan on the line. He's your campaign manager. He'll tell you his plan of action."

The next voice Edison heard was that of Stan Cornish.

"First thing, you need to apologize to Harry. Publicly."

Ed grimaced, which Brenda saw, but of course Stan didn't. But Stan caught the pause.

"I mean it, Ed. It's the only way. And only part of what needs to be done. And why do you have a reluctance to apologize? You were unhinged. Even more than your usual prickliness. And at such a nice man as Harry Crutch. Makes no sense."

"Look, Stan. You're my friend. So is Kara. I'd do anything for either of you. And I don't expect you to understand. Lord knows, I've done little to tell you any background so that my actions might have some context. Let's just agree that maybe, just maybe, I have some rational reason for what I did yesterday. That said, I will apologize to Harry for my tone, which was unacceptable, and frankly, had little chance of achieving the desired effect. It was more venting than constructive conversation. And I will endeavor to not make the same mistake again."

"Okay, Ed. I'll give you the benefit of the doubt. I owe you at least that. And I will accept you at your word. But please don't give Harry a half-assed non-apology. Please."

Ed assured him he'd give a genuine apology, and they disconnected.

***

"Really? That's useful. Keep digging. Yes, send me a bill and I'll pay it right away. Yes, put in an estimate of the additional work. No, don't send it here." Cyrus gave the person on the other side of the phone the post office address he used for specific clandestine purposes, such as this one.

He disconnected. The information was promising, and might serve as a knockout punch to both the officious interloper having the temerity to oppose him, but also Edison's friend and protector, that blowhard state senator. Cyrus permitted himself a silent gloat. If the information panned out, how would that oh so appearance conscious state legislator feel about his close association with someone having that history?

***

When he arrived at the CC, Edison noticed Harry's Ford Taurus parked in front, askew as always. He looked back at the front steps and spotted the man himself chatting with someone near the entrance. Ed took a deep breath and charged up the steps.

Harry saw him coming and put up his hands, palms facing Edison, in a show of defending himself against further assault.

"Please put down your hands, Harry. I'm here to apologize."

Harry looked over at a gathering group and put down his hands.

"Okay," he said. "Let's hear it. Publicly, like you berated me."

"Harry, I'm sorry I yelled at you yesterday. Such juvenile behavior is both un-called for and unacceptable. My concern for your safety and that of others overrode my good sense. I truly regret raising my voice and speaking to you like that. It won't happen again." Ed looked around. "With anyone," he added, and put out his hand, which Harry took with a brief show of reluctance. They shook hands, and the murmuring crowd dispersed.

***

Kara called him later that afternoon.

"I heard your apology, and at first I worried you included a kind of excuse in it, even though the behavior was inexcusable."

"At first? You changed your mind?"

"Not just me. Everyone. At least from what I overheard. People know Harry shouldn't drive. He's a danger to all of us on the road, even in an uncrowded place like this one. We all travel outside Standard, including Harry. He's not just driving like that in our little town, but on the highway, too. People were upset that you screamed and shouted profanity at Harry. They hated that. But given your apology for that part of it, while including a concern for his safety and that of others, changed their view. They admire you for having the courage to speak to Harry about it. They just hated the manner in which you did it. I think you hit a home run, Edison. Thank you."

***

"How about a walk?" Ed said to Brenda. "It's a beautiful day, sunny and bright. I can hear the birds chirping, and the squirrels making all kinds of racket outside. I was going to go out and make sure they weren't trying to get into our attic again, but when I poked my head outside, I saw how nice it is."

He looked over at Brenda, who was sitting at her little desk, working on something. She looked up and smiled.

"Edison Orwell, is that really you?"

Ed's instinct was a negative reaction to the question, but he resisted the impulse and managed a half smile.

"Of course, I'll take a walk with you. This can wait," Brenda said.

Ed peered over her shoulder. "Whatcha working on?"

"Oh, just notes for the book club that Kara and I facilitate."

"What's the book?"

"*Ethan Frome*."

"An oldie, but a goodie. Edith Wharton, if my often-faulty memory serves."

"Spot on, honey." She rose from her chair, went to the front closet, and took out a light jacket, and handed it to Edison. It's still a little chilly. You don't want to catch cold."

"What are you going to wear?"

Brenda picked up the cardigan sweater she had draped over the chair. "This will do for me," she said.

"That's what you use when you get cold in the house in the evenings," Ed replied. "Maybe you should wear something warmer yourself."

"This will be fine." She gave a sly smile. "If I get cold, I'll just let you do the gentlemanly thing and drape your coat over my shoulders."

Ed looked at her to see if she was serious. He decided he wasn't sure, then almost slapped his forehead, retrieving a latent memory. He used to do exactly that… not that long ago. What had happened to him?

"I certainly will," he said, a little more formally than he intended. He hoped there wasn't a pause between her comment and his response, but nothing to be done about that now.

Brenda waited for Edison to don his jacket, and they left the house. Brenda accepted Edison's proffered arm, and they strolled towards the town square and the central park. They walked in silence for a while, then Brenda broached the subject of the Town Board.

"I know you're running to stop the closure of the library, but assuming you accomplish that, what are your other visions for this town?"

They continued walking slowly, as Edison formulated his response. He rubbed the back of his neck with his free hand and tapped the side of his pants a few times. Finally, he announced his comprehensive plan for the town.

"I got nothing."

Brenda's eyes widened and darted around to see if anyone had heard Ed's comment. She saw no one within earshot, thank God. She stopped, let go of his arm, and looked him straight in the eyes.

"You better find something fast. Serving on the Town Board is a sacred responsibility. You will have a duty to the people of this town, and more to the point, people are going to ask you my exact question. And by the way, maybe you should read the flyer Stan is handing out.

It lays out your four main issues. Eddie, please take this seriously. We're all counting on you."

"I promise I'll study and not let anyone down this time. Can't we just have a nice, quiet walk?"

Brenda sighed. "Yes, of course. I'm sorry. We should talk about this later, back home. I was enjoying the walk, so let's continue." She took his arm again, but they both knew their conversation had broken the magic. They went through the motions of a walk around the central park, commented a few times about buds on the trees, the few places where crocuses had sprouted, and pointed to half green trees. They breathed in the fresh Spring air, and not for the first time, noted how much cleaner Standard was than their previous suburban home.

They completed their little circle and walked back home to their two-story Cape Cod-style house. It sat on a full acre, and had a mostly green front lawn, at least at this time of year, and had woods adjoining a small backyard. Homes flanked both sides of theirs, each also sitting on a full acre. Lots of space between the homes.

Theirs was white with black shutters, and a brick red door. Dave and Wilma occupied the saltbox on one side and the Wassermans, Howard and Gabrielle, lived on the other side. Ed and Brenda interacted very little with the Wassermans, often giving a simple wave, and not stopping to talk. But today, Howard waited for them near the split-rail fence which served as a makeshift property line. As they approached, Howard waved them over.

13

As Edison and Brenda approached, Howard uttered a single word.

"Garbage."

"Huh?"

"Where do you stand on garbage?"

Ed refrained from saying the obvious — that it was stuff you didn't want anymore, and it often was stinky. He knew Howard meant something else, though, but he wished he'd just come out and say it.

"Where do you stand on the question of garbage collection in the neighborhoods? There's regular collection in the village, but not here. We all have to *schlep* a week's worth of garbage to the Town Dump. We've done it for years, but Gabby and I aren't getting any younger, you know." He eyed Ed and Brenda. "And neither are you."

Ed glanced at Brenda. "Um, garbage collection would be nice, for sure."

"So, you're for it?"

Bren gave him a warning. She could do that without words, just by a slight stiffening of her body. Proceed with caution is what it always meant.

"I said it would be nice. But without studying things like cost and effect on our tax base, and whether it would be a separate assessment on each homeowner, I wouldn't say I'm for or against it right now."

Ed saw Howard's countenance show signs of disappointment or disgust. He couldn't be sure.

"I'm not on the Town Board, Howard. I don't have any access to that information. All I'm saying is that none of us want to pay a fortune to have that convenience. And we don't yet know what it will cost."

Howard seemed mollified by that.

"Yeah, the last thing we need is to pay through the nose for something like that. But the village is doing it. I wonder how that's getting paid for? It's Statue of Liberty Sanitation, I think."

Ed nodded. "I've seen their trucks. It's them. Lady of Liberty icon painted on their sides."

"Maybe we could find out who's paying for that. I don't know if it's the city or the county."

"I don't know either." Ed wondered where the Mayor lived. He guessed he lived in the village, which would explain a lot. But he didn't say it out loud. He resolved to look into it. Kara or Stan might know who paid the bill.

"I'll see what I can find out. And if I'm elected to the Town Board, I'll have access to that information right away."

"Gabby and I are both voting for you. But I have to tell you, it's an uphill battle. Things rarely change in this town. It's more Standstill than Standard. And a word of advice.

Ed cocked his head with his good ear facing Howard.

"Start campaigning. And I don't mean just at the CC. Go to Pete's Eats and do something other than drink your coffee with your head down, or just talking to Mo and Dave. And you have to campaign at the Town Dump. It's customary and is a great place to meet and greet everyone in this town. At least those who don't live in the village. Those people you see all the time, anyway. No, the Town Dump is where all the neighborhood folks like us go regularly. It's almost as big a social center as the CC."

Ed thanked him, shook his proffered hand. Bren did the same, and everyone returned home.

"What do you make of that?" Edison asked when they were inside. "And thanks for the heads up."

"You're welcome. Don't take political positions without knowing the facts. And you recovered nicely. That cost stuff even made Howard think. And he seems rabidly in favor of trash collection. And it would be nice...."

"It sure would. But I meant it. None of us want to overpay or have our nice small-town tax bill skyrocket because we want big city services. Next thing Howard will want is a subway system."

"I don't think so, dear."

"No, but you know what I mean."

Ed took Brenda's advice to read the flyer Stan was already handing out. A little miffed that Stan hadn't bothered to ask him for input, his attitude was something less than stellar as he located the one Brenda had picked up. Scanning the bullet points neatly set forth on the single page, he saw that he favored fiscal responsibility, economic fairness, promotion of reading and education through a robust library, and a fully democratic town election process.

Ed thought about those positions, and couldn't find fault in any of them. The first two were pretty non-specific. Plenty of wiggle room for a... oh my God... politician. The last two truly jived with the impetus and means for his candidacy. He wanted to save the library, and the only way to do that was to challenge the formerly undemocratic local election process.

Contrary to his initial aggravation, Stan had impressed him, and he picked up his phone to call him.

"I like my position statement," Ed said when Stan answered.

"You should. We discussed it before I printed it up. You just read it?"

"Well, yes. When did we talk about this?"

Stan told him, and Ed slapped his forehead. "Oh, yeah, I remember. It was loud in the CC that day, but I remember the conversation."

"It's always loud there. We should have moved into the solarium, but I wanted to get going."

"I'm glad you did," Ed assured him, "And thank you."

Stan ended the call, and Edison sat at his kitchen table for a while. He remembered the conversation now, but he'd completely forgotten. He wondered about whether he often had memory loss, and he asked Brenda when she came into the kitchen.

Brenda just laughed. "Nope. As far as I can tell, your memory is just fine. I forget stuff too. You might remember things too much."

While he considered Brenda's comment, Stan called him back.

"Cyrus has demanded a debate."

"What? Can he do that?"

"It's never occurred before in Standard, but we've never had an election, either. There's no law about it, and you can decline, but I don't think you should. People will assume you're afraid to talk about the issues."

"I am afraid to talk about the issues, other than the library, of course."

"Don't say that again. Please. I recommend we accept, provided we have input into who asks the questions. And Ed, don't worry. Kara and I will prep you. You'll be fully familiar with local issues when we're done."

Ed hated this. He wanted to say, no, no, no, I won't do it. It's a trap Cyrus is setting. But he thought about Kara, and his part in putting her job in jeopardy, and he agreed.

"Okay, I'll do it. But you know Cyrus has some ulterior motive. This is a trap somehow."

"Yeah, no question. But we'll just have to deal with whatever he slings. Hang in there, Ed. We have your back." Stan disconnected, so he didn't hear Ed grumble, "You mean I'll have to deal with whatever Cyrus sends my way."

***

After Ed headed out to the CC, Brenda sat down at the kitchen table. She needed to think about her current life. She and Ed had moved to Standard to get away from the constant reminder of the troubles, and it had seemed to work for a while. But she wondered about whether it still made sense. It was true she and Ed had adapted well to the extraordinary change in scenery. She looked out the window at the gorgeous upstate New York landscape and sighed. The incredible Autumn foliage and beautiful vistas of their current location dwarfed any landscape in their former home. And the current Spring brought an unmatched revitalizing energy.

But it entailed more than beauty. They'd uprooted from a long-standing life in New Jersey. That was home. This was not. Brenda couldn't, just couldn't view Standard as home.

She thought about their life here. They both had good friends and shared a pleasant living space. Probably a nicer home than they ever could afford in New Jersey. And Standard was a lovely town, which had become more and more familiar as time passed. But there remained a deep-seated suspicion of newcomers, defined as anyone living in the town for less than twenty years. Brenda shook her head in disgust at such parochial behavior.

She reached for her coffee cup, and before picking it up, reflexively extended the fingers of her right hand, and slowly closed them in an almost mechanical movement, like closing a rusty folding chair. The onset of arthritis primarily affected her middle finger, but that was a harbinger of things to come. Brenda felt her sore knee for a moment while she sipped her coffee and stared aimlessly out the window. Her thoughts turned to Edison. She loved him, she knew that, and they had a forty-six-year marriage under their belts. But Ed wasn't the same man she'd married. He'd changed so much after …what they euphemistically called the "troubles."

Tears filled her eyes as she remembered the old Edison. A straightforward, direct to the point man, honest to the core, outgoing and kind. She thought about that. The first two—honest and direct, Ed clung to for dear life. Those characteristics defined him, and they remained unaltered. But those very traits caused him more pain. His brutally honest and direct assessment of himself governed almost everything he did. People rightfully credited him with creating the CC, but Brenda knew his guilt-ridden conscience drove it, and almost everything he did. He kept trying to give back, to make amends for his lapse in judgment.

But it affected her profoundly. She was tired and missed her old life in New Jersey. She looked down at the envelope she'd just opened from the university at which she'd attained a full professorship, and fingered the letter, idly rubbing the paper between her thumb and forefinger as if willing a genie to appear and tell her what to do.

Discussing it with Edison was out of the question. Nor should she mention it to anyone in Standard. She thought of her friends in New Jersey and sighed. She supposed she shouldn't call them either. This was a good time to call her sister, but she didn't pick up the phone. At one time, she and Edison talked about everything. But they didn't do that anymore, not since the troubles. He was so wrapped up in self-loathing, and anything he could do to distract himself from that, he had no time for deep discussion with her. He was so distressed at how he'd caused her pain that he'd give an instinctively wrong answer, anyway. Oh, how she yearned for the equal terms they once possessed. Nothing surpasses love shared equally. Nothing.

14

Brenda dreaded sharing the contents of the letter with her husband, but non-disclosure was not a realistic option. Unless… she just ignored it and let things remain unchanged. It wasn't a terrible life, she thought. If she was honest with herself, it had many good points. They weren't getting any younger, and the living arrangements suited a retired couple well. They could walk almost everywhere, and they lived in a friendly neighborhood. The CC afforded her an opportunity to teach, albeit in a limited way. And she loved teaching. She'd done it for going on fifty years. Her thoughts flew back to the letter on the table. She knew she had to talk to Edison about it, not the least because it affected both of them. Unless… it didn't.

***

When Edison returned home for lunch, Brenda was overly solicitous, offering to make him a sandwich, then giving him multiple options for its contents.

"I can fix you turkey. Or would you rather have roast beef? We have roast beef. Oh, maybe you'd like ham. I have some nice Virginia ham in the fridge. Maybe you want soup instead? We have some cans of that chicken noodle you like. Do you want that?"

Edison watched Brenda's nervous twitching with growing concern. "Anything is fine, honey. Thank you. But what's wrong? Something has you all aflutter. And while you often make me a sandwich, more often you point to the fridge and tell me to make one myself.

Nicely, of course, but nowhere near as nice as you're being right now." Ed paused. "Wait a minute. Is something wrong with you? Did you hear something from Doc Smithers? Did you even visit him?"

Brenda looked at him. "Nothing's wrong with me. At least not that I know. I haven't seen the doctor."

"Is something wrong with me?"

"No, nothing's wrong with you." Brenda kept the obvious psychological problems with Edison to herself.

"Honey, what on Earth is going on?"

"Oh Eddie," she started, then stopped. This wasn't the time. "There's nothing wrong. I'm just overzealous in the lunch preparation today, that's all. I'll fix you a turkey sandwich."

Ed didn't believe her, but decided she'd eventually tell him. Nothing serious, he hoped. He did not know what he'd do without her. Edison shuddered a little before giving what he hoped was a sunny thank you.

Brenda would not tell him anything about the letter, but when they sat down to lunch, she asked, as casually as she could, about how he liked living in Standard.

Ed looked up from his sandwich. "I like it, I guess. It's pretty, and mostly quiet here, although I guess I've bitten off more than I can chew with this Town Board business. Campaigning is not my strong suit. Dealing with people isn't my strong suit, either."

Brenda listened to Edison make every issue about himself again, for what seemed like the millionth time. He'd become so self-centered. Before the troubles, he was nothing like that. Although she'd asked him how he felt, he might have reciprocated by asking her how she liked it. Instead, he inquired why she asked the question.

"Why? Do I seem unhappy here?"

Brenda tried again. "No, I guess not. Not any more than usual, I suppose. You're making a better life for yourself here than I am."

"You seem to have adjusted pretty well. I peeked into the CC classroom and watched you and Kara give your lecture a couple of days ago. I'll bet you're happy to be teaching."

Brenda nodded. Her eyes involuntarily flew to the kitchen shelf where she'd stashed the letter. And thought to herself that he didn't know the half of it.

They finished their sandwiches in what Edison thought was companionable silence. He rose, pushed his chair back to the table, returned his plate to the dishwasher, walked by her still sitting form, kissed her on the head, and announced that he intended to go to the Town Dump to campaign.

Brenda looked up. "Do you need a ride?"

"No, thank you." He glanced at his watch. "Stan is picking me up in ten minutes."

"Okay," she said, not letting her disappointment at how the conversation went creep into her voice. She'd have to broach it again. And soon. The letter contained a deadline for a response.

***

Stan picked him up, and they drove to the Town Dump. On the way, Stan warned Edison not to take specific positions other than those set out on his campaign flyer. He pointed over his shoulder at the pile of those flyers on the back seat.

"Until you're elected, those are your positions," he told Ed.

"I get it. Howard ambushed me yesterday on the garbage issue, and Bren gave me a silent warning to not take a position on it. So I'm warm on that, at least."

"Good. Talk all you want about the benefits of the library, how it coexists with the CC, all of that. You know your stuff, and you can take a logical position on it. It's the issues that you know little about that's the problem."

Ed looked down. "That's pretty much everything other than the library and the CC."

"That's not true. You know more about this town than you give yourself credit for. But you make a good point about the CC. Don't be afraid to take modest credit for it. It's very popular, and you deserve the recognition."

"Many people helped with that," Ed said. "Mo, Dave, Bren, Senator Smiley… you and Kara. I can't take credit for something that an entire group of people worked on."

Stan chuckled. "You're not much of a politician, are you?"

Ed just grunted.

"Look, take a page from your friend, Jack Smiley. He has no problem receiving kudos for the project you envisioned and success-fully brought to fruition."

"Jack got us the financing."

"And you envisioned a shining star here, bought the building, got the requisite permits, directed and took part in the work necessary to fix it up—the list goes on and on. Just accept the acclaim for it, okay? We're here. You can see several folks here emptying their weekly garbage. We'll just get out and you can start talking to them. Ask them what they want to see from their Town Board. And listen to them. Don't do a lot of talking yourself. You're on a listening tour. Listen to your constituents, and nod a lot like you sympathize with their problems and if only you were on the Town Board and could have the information necessary to consider and address them. And don't, I em-phasize don't, make any promises."

Ed looked at Stan. "Yes, sir, Captain Campaign Manager. I will comply."

"I'm serious, Ed."

"Oh, I know. Sorry for being flippant. I appreciate your help. I don't know what I'm doing, and I have doubts about doing it at all."

Stan had unfastened his seat belt, and was ready to get out of the car, but he stopped short.

"Ed, please don't say that today. We can talk about it later, but please refrain from expressing doubts about your candidacy while you're campaigning."

Ed nodded. "I won't, Stan. I promise. Let's go campaign." He opened the car door, got out, and immediately walked over to a white-haired man he didn't recognize. Hand extended, he introduced himself.

The man smiled at him, shook his hand, and advised him in response to Ed's inquiry that he didn't live in Standard. He was a home construction man emptying the refuse from his renovation work on a resident's kitchen.

Ed wished him well, and moved on to a familiar face, and performed the same politician dance. This time, the woman responded with a friendly smile, but a simple statement that she was voting for Cyrus, because, as she said, "Tradition means something in this town."

Ed thanked her for telling him that, but lingered for a moment, anyway. "I think it's great you'll be voting. It's our cherished right as Americans to exercise our freedom. Bravo to you." With that, he bid the astonished woman farewell, and moved on to the next person, a forty something man in jeans.

He didn't need to say anything. The man told him, "I'm voting for you. I'd vote for Beelzebub if he were running against that corrupt ass. And anyway, shouldn't the town allow us to vote? What's with the unopposed entitlement of these old white guys? You do some stuff on the Zoning Board, and that entitles you to run the affairs of the town? No way. We get to vote in America, and even in Standard. Thanks for running. I'm telling everyone who'll listen to vote for you."

Ed thanked him and moved on.

Stan, who'd listened to all three of Ed's encounters from a short distance away, walked over and whispered in Ed's ear that he was doing great and to keep it up. Also, that Ed should point in Stan's direction for copies of the campaign flyer. Ed nodded at Stan's comments, and moved on to the next person, a tall, skinny man who asked Ed if intended to do something about them having to go to the Town

Dump to empty their garbage, and why the neighborhoods didn't have trash collection.

Ed gave his prepared answer, saying he wanted to examine the cost and fully understand the issue before taking a firm position, and the man muttered something about politicians, and that they were all the same. Never taking a position on anything. Ed had no chance to explain that taking positions in a vacuum was not good governance.

Edison continued talking to people, extolling the benefits of the library and its wonderful librarian. Most people complimented Kara and said they loved the library. It surprised many that it was in danger. But almost no one said they went to the library regularly, or that their kids did. People went to the CC, and many picked up books there and returned them to the outdoor return slot at the library, without ever going in. Ed made a mental note to remind Kara to get rid of the outdoor return box. Make the people go into the library to return books. And maybe they should just get rid of the CC bookshelf, like Brenda suggested.

Everyone Ed spoke to was friendly, even those who intended to vote for Cyrus. One of the benefits of living in a small town. No one wanted to hold a grudge against someone they saw all the time. Ed thought about that. It might also be a downside. Everyone knew everyone else's business. He thought about his longtime home in New Jersey. That would never happen there. People had the benefit of anonymity. Lots of people. Lots and lots of people. He looked around and considered what he was doing. He was standing at the Town Dump. They had trash collection at his old home for a long time. He didn't remember a time in his life when the ubiquitous garbage trucks didn't patrol the areas like vultures seeking carrion. But here, Ed could breathe fresh air, even near a place to dump his household waste.

One thing that surprised Ed during his campaign stop at the Dump was the number of people who told him how much they detested Cyrus Boone. He'd made a ton of enemies, and Ed reflected on that. Probably because he screwed people right and left in his position of power at the Zoning Board. From what Dave told him, Cyrus and his cohort Mayor Winkle had a strict pay for play system. No greasing their palms with silver and gold, no zoning variance. Cyrus had created a lose-lose situation for someone running for office. The people who paid the bribes hated him, and the people who didn't pay the bribes and, like Dave, never got their variances hated him, too. Cyrus never expected to have to run for office. He'd expected to be anointed, like some hereditary prince.

There was a tremendous opportunity for someone, an outsider like Edison, to take on the town's traditions and run against Cyrus. He'd never win over the traditionalists, but if he didn't screw it up, he had a real chance of winning against a universally despised opponent.

Edison thought about the "if he didn't screw it up part." He messed up everything. He annoyed people, and he was a walking curmudgeon. And he had a dark secret that, should it come to light, might scotch everything. And bring down Kara.

15

He was tired of living a lie, and a part of him thought about returning to New Jersey and enduring the daily reminders. But he had a life in Standard now. He had the CC, which to his amazement, he hadn't messed up. And now he was running for the Town Board of Standard as a fine upstanding resident. If only that were true, he thought gloomily. But he brightened at the sight of none other than Morris "Mo" Goodwin unloading a trash can from the bed of his pickup.

"Spending the day around garbage, are we?" Mo teased.

"Just call me Ed the politico." He pointed to Stan, stationed a dozen yards away, poised to hand out campaign flyers to anyone willing to look. "I'm campaigning."

Mo nodded. "It's a good idea. We should do that at Pete's, too."

"Maybe tomorrow. I'm all campaigned out."

"Sure, tomorrow. Should I pick you up, or do you want to just walk and meet me there?"

Ed considered it. "I think it's going to be a nice day. I'll just walk. How about 8:30 a.m.? We can get our usual coffees, and I'll stay to campaign after. You can stay as long as you can stand it."

Mo grunted. "Not easy, is it?"

"Not for me. I'm not naturally loquacious like Jack."

"He's a talker, for sure."

Stan walked over and greeted Mo, who exchanged a few more words with both of them and then departed, hauling his trash and tipping the contents into the vast abyss before returning to his vehicle, and with a wave, driving away.

"How did it go?" Stan asked.

"Not bad. Many people don't like me so much as they hate Cyrus. And pretty much everyone expressed a preference for you over me."

Stan laughed. "I got a little of that, too. But I clarified that you're the candidate, not me, and that I'm a big supporter of yours."

"Well… thanks. Are you sure you can't run?"

Stan shushed him. "No, it's prohibited. And please don't express doubts here. Do it later. And Edison, people hating Cyrus is good news for your campaign."

Ed nodded. "Yeah, I guess so. But wouldn't it be nice if I wasn't just the 'not Cyrus' candidate?"

"Give it time. Once people get to know you, they'll, um, come to appreciate your best qualities."

"You paused," Ed accused.

As no one else remained at the Dump, they boarded Stan's car before he answered. "I did, but only because you're a little hard to get to know. Kara and I love you, but even that took time, if you recall."

Their first encounter had taken place within days after he and Brenda moved to Standard.

"Yeah, our first meeting was a doozy."

Edison recalled the day he first met Stan. Just a few days after he and Brenda moved to Standard, Edison needed nails for a job fixing up their new home. He'd walked to town and located Kelly's Hardware. Upon entry, he found a mostly empty store, with literally hundreds of little boxes of different nails, screws, washers, and other tiny items. Kelly's had everything and still did. One could find every conceivable hardware at Kelly's, but one had to look. Nails, for example, the item Edison sought, were on a particular shelf, and arranged by size, but the sizes were all reflected on the boxes themselves, in tiny print. If you didn't know where a particular size was on the shelf, you almost needed a magnifying glass to locate what you wanted. With his impaired vision, Edison had no chance. Of course, Kelly himself knew where each size of each type of item sat on his shelves, but when Edison entered, a tall man was at the counter speaking to Kelly. So Edison, with his limited eyesight, wandered over to the shelf, which he thought contained boxes of nails. He stared at the shelf for a long time without finding the size he was looking for, but neither of the two men at the counter noticed him. Edison coughed a few times and looked toward the counter, but the two men seemed deep in conversation. Their failure to notice him convinced Ed that the two men were intentionally ignoring him. He became incensed.

"Excuse me," he said loudly, and with poor grace.

The two men looked up.

"I'm looking for some nails."

"You're in the right place," the proprietor said cheerfully.

"I'm looking for sixteen gauge, one and three quarters."

"Sure, right there on the second shelf. The ones labeled 44.45."

"Huh?"

"Millimeters. The length is labeled in millimeters." The two men continued talking, and Edison seethed. He couldn't see any numbers at all. One and three quarters or 44.45 millimeters in tiny print on the boxes, it made no difference to him. Edison muttered something about not getting any help.

The proprietor looked at the other man.

"Would you give him a hand?" He pointed at a table behind him. "I need to get back to this."

Edison didn't hear the helpful request. He angrily turned back to the shelves and started pulling boxes off the shelf to pull them close to his eyes and try to find what the proprietor had told him. So, he didn't hear the tall man respond.

"Sure." The tall man walked over to where Edison was pawing at the shelves.

"Sir?"

Ed whirled around to look at the speaker and bumped into the shelf, causing dozens of boxes to topple over and dump hundreds of nails upon the two men.

Hunched over to shield himself from the metallic rain shower, Edison shouted at the lanky man, calling him a careless imbecile, among other not so carefully chosen words.

The proprietor rushed out from behind the counter and first asked whether they were okay, then looked with dismay at a floor covered with nails of different sizes all jumbled together.

But he didn't get angry. He just gave an enormous sigh, declined the tall man's offer to help clean up, and ushered the two men out of his store.

But before he did so, he reached down on the floor and picked up a handful of nails and handed them to Ed, telling him they were one and three quarters.

Ed, feeling ashamed of himself, thanked him, and left the store at the same time as the tall man.

Before they parted ways, Ed stammered an apology for his outburst, and the man extended a hand, which Ed shook.

"Stan Cornish," the man said, and smiled. "I'm not sure, but I think I'm glad to meet you."

Ed chuckled. It was hard to stay mad at this guy, and anyway, Ed knew he was totally at fault and out of line, but the guy had just brushed it off. And so had the hardware store owner, Kelly. This was some town they'd moved to.

"I know for sure I'm pleased to meet you, Stan. My name is Edison Orwell, and in case you didn't notice, I'm new in town, and I guess have a temper that I need to control."

"I'm sure it's just the stress of moving to a new place. Anyway, welcome to Standard."

Stan dropped Ed off at home. Upon pulling into the driveway, Stan stopped the car and turned to look at Edison.

"Okay," he said. "Spill it. What's on your mind?"

"I just don't know if I can go through with this. You know this isn't me, glad-handing people and talking to them as if I'm begging for their votes."

"You are asking them for their votes. Look, I get it. You're not anyone's idea of a typical politician—maybe the quintessential anti-politician, uncomfortable asking for votes. But you're great at getting things done. The CC is a prime example of what Edison Orwell can do for this town. You've already done it in the relatively short time you've lived here, and people know that. They can't name a thing that Cyrus has done, and he's lived here for forty some odd years. The same goes for Mayor Winkle. No one is sure what they do for Standard other than stop anything that resembles progress."

"Many people seem okay with that. I'm a newcomer shaking up their cherished traditions. I'm not sure I'm comfortable with it."

Stan paused and rubbed his chin with two fingers. "Look Ed," he said. "Sometimes old traditions are just that. They're comfortable, like a ten-year-old pair of sneakers. But old and comfortable doesn't always translate into good. And sometimes you need to throw out the old comfortable stuff in order to get something better. I don't know if you'll be better, but you have more of a chance of it than keeping things as they are — stagnant, and stuck in the past."

Ed persisted. "Maybe so, but am I the best person to do that? Most of the people today wanted you to run, not me. I know the County prohibits its employees from running, but the people of Standard would prefer someone other than me."

Stan sighed. "I get it, but please shed the doubts, at least while you're campaigning at Pete's tomorrow."

Ed nodded. "I will. And Mo will be there to monitor me, just like you did today."

Stan smiled. "We don't really think you need monitoring," he said.

Ed punched him lightly on the arm. "Yes, you do, but it's okay with me."

Ed got out of the car and strolled to the side door to his house. He had feigned light-heartedness, but his private doubts felt overwhelming. The CC aside, pretty much everything he'd done, he'd royally fucked up. Its potential effect on Kara tainted even his colossal success with the CC. Ed shrugged and pushed open the door.

"Bren, I'm home," he called, and heard her footsteps on the stairs.

"Hi honey," she said, and kissed him lightly. "How goes the campaign?"

Brenda kept her voice calm, but she harbored strong guilt feelings about Ed's run for Town Board. Of course, she hadn't known about the letter when she encouraged him to run, or to orchestrate the creation of the CC. She'd only received the letter two days ago, but it had raised latent feelings of discontent with their move to Standard. But how could she raise the issue with Ed after vigorously pressing him to embrace an active life for himself in their new town? She thought again about just throwing out the letter, and learning to love Standard, as… Ed had done? But she wasn't even sure of that, was she? Ed hadn't shed his guilt or his self-loathing. Standard hadn't changed that. So why even stay here? But a run for Town Board, that represented a commitment, for at least a two-year term. If they were to consider moving back to New Jersey, he needed to abort his run right away. She didn't want that. Taking on that responsibility might even help him at the same time it helped Kara. Filled with conflicting feelings, Bren almost didn't hear Ed's response to her question.

"Okay, I guess. Everyone prefers Stan to run, but I guess he can't do it."

Brenda affirmed that, and ceased ruminating, while the two of them sat down to lunch without talking about the election. She had a few weeks left to decide her professional fate, and figured she'd need every minute of that time before giving an answer.

But for the first time, Brenda considered an alternative to the two of them moving back to New Jersey. That only one of them would.

16

At the dinner table that evening, Brenda broached the subject. She fervently hoped they could have a healthy conversation, and that she could feel safe in disclosing the contents of the letter she'd received.

"Eddie, honey…" she began.

Edison looked up from his studious examination of the piece of chicken on his fork.

"Huh? What did you say?"

Brenda sighed. "I was just trying to get your attention."

Edison put the fork in his mouth, chewed the food, swallowed, took a drink from his water glass, and looked down again at his food. He then looked up at Brenda.

"Can this wait until after I finish my dinner?"

Brenda took a deep breath. It wouldn't help to bark at Edison, even though she was ready to rip his head off. They used to talk all the time at dinner, about everything. And something as important as what she had to tell him… well it wouldn't wait. Not for days. Not even to after dinner. Brenda swallowed her thoughts, and mustered a reply.

"Sure, honey. After dinner." But she wasn't sure she'd raise it. The truth was, she was a little afraid to talk about it. Not because she was afraid of him — no, Edison was never like that. He'd never laid a finger on her, and she knew he never would. His anger was mostly self-directed. He'd never hurt a living soul. And maybe that character trait made his guilt so resilient.

No, she was deathly afraid of making him feel worse—more guilty, because he was the one who'd uprooted them. It was a joint decision, but only Edison bore responsibility for their need for a change of scenery.

If she talked about the letter, she needed to do it carefully, and gradually. Ask him if he was happy in Standard. If he ever thought of moving back to New Jersey. Back home, she thought wistfully. So, she tried.

When they finished dinner, and, as customary, moved to the living room, she waited for Edison to sit down in his easy chair. She watched him wiggle his butt, obviously trying to get to the perfect spot, without success. He shrugged and picked up his reading glasses. From a basket at his side, he selected the local newspaper and squinted at it.

"Honey…" Brenda began. No response, so she said it louder, working hard to not have the volume contain an irritable edge.

Ed looked up. "Look at this! My picture's in the paper!" He turned it around so that Brenda could look at it, and she smiled at him.

"That's nice, honey. I assume it's about the election?"

"Yes, it's a short piece, only a sentence, and it describes me as an 'upstart' candidate." He thought about it. "Do you think that's good or bad?" He picked up his phone. "I gotta call Stan and ask him."

He paused. "Um, were you about to say something?"

Brenda just shook her head. "It can wait." But she thought, how can I tell him about the letter when he is becoming so involved in life in Standard?

She listened to Edison talking to Stan.

"That's good, then?" Ed said on his end of the phone. "I am challenging the establishment. Well, that's true, if you can call Cyrus Boone the establishment. Anyway, the paper isn't calling me an idiosyncratic whacko." Ed listened for a moment and gave a rare chuckle. "Okay, I set you up for that." He rang off and turned to Brenda.

"Stan says any attention is a positive. People aren't ignoring me. That would be way worse than even bad press, which this isn't."

"What did he say to your 'whacko' suggestion?"

"If the shoe fits…"

Brenda laughed. "You shouldn't say that in public."

"Nope."

"He made you laugh. That's good."

Ed looked at her. "I still laugh. I just have very little to laugh at."

Brenda just grunted, and Ed went back to reading the paper while she picked up the recent issue of The New Yorker. They talked little for the rest of the evening.

***

Mo picked Edison up at 8:20 a.m. It was a five-minute trip to Pete's Eats. They could have separately walked, but Mo had to bring some supplies to a minor job he was working later that day. Mo worked part time, only exercising his first-rate carpentry skills for people he liked. Mo never charged much, although his artisanship could have commanded premium prices. Other than the costs of wooing beautiful women, Mo had few expenses. He owned his small bungalow, and had a tidy amount of savings, which he supplemented with small-scale work.

Arriving at Pete's Eats, Mo parked his Chevy S-10 in back of the restaurant, and they walked around to the front and entered the busy eatery.

Eyeing the line, Mo turned to Ed. "Takeout or sit?"

Edison considered this. "Takeout, I think. I can talk to people as they enter and exit."

Mo pointed to the line. "And to people waiting."

Edison nodded as they took their places in line. He looked around to see if anyone was close by to talk to, but the cacophony of voices came from the multiple booths and tables in the dining area. But a man in front of them turned around and gave Edison a friendly nod.

"Lenny McDougal," he said, reminding Edison of his name. "We met at the CC."

"Of course," Ed said. "How's it going?"

"Oh, the missus and I are fine, just fine." He moved up to close the gap between him and the man in front of him. Edison and Mo did the same.

"Shaking things up in this town, are you?"

"I guess I am." Ed said, and added he didn't mean to cause trouble. "I'm just trying to do what I think is right."

They all moved up again. "Well, speaking for Jenny and me, we think a little shaking up of Stagnant is a good idea. Too much patronage going on here. So more power to you. You've got our votes." He moved up in line again, and had one more thing to say before he reached the counter to place his order.

"I just said votes. Isn't voting in Standard a novel idea?" He turned around again.

"One coffee, light, one sugar. Thanks Josie." He nodded at Ed and walked out, holding his Styrofoam cup.

Ed and Mo ordered their black coffees and took their cups outside. They found a good standing spot, where they wouldn't block the door, but where they could talk to people coming in and out.

"That went well with Lenny," Mo said.

"I'm glad he introduced himself. I didn't know who the heck he was."

"Try to remember people's names when you meet them. Trust me, Jack Smiley commits everyone's name to memory, and greets them as if they're old friends. People believe it, even if they only met in a chance encounter, or maybe never met at all."

"I'm not a politician," Ed said, as two people exited Pete's.

Ed tried. But campaigning was hard for him. He had to display a smiling exterior, and show confidence where both required enormous effort. But he got through it, mainly because Mo helped. Mo knew everyone in town, and many came up to him without being prompted. Mo reminded everyone that Edison was running for Town Board, and most people were kind about it, without committing to anything. Some told him they'd vote for him, and like Lenny McDougal, appreciated his shaking up the old process. Some told him he was making a mistake, and some even called him an officious interloper, or even more insulting, an ignorant newcomer. But those people were rare, and even they said it with a smile on their faces. No one was nasty, although many were opinionated. Ed considered that. If he were back in New Jersey, he would have heard from people with many opinions, but they would have expressed them more vehemently. He didn't think they would be violent there, just louder and angrier.

After a few hours, they called it quits. Mo had to get to his carpentry job, and Ed declined his offer to drop him off at home. He walked slowly, thinking about his two campaign days at the Dump and at Pete's. He was grateful for the opportunity to wipe the goofy, plastic facial expression off his face.

Ed could tell that about half of the town viewed his candidacy positively. He'd thought that only a few people would support his quixotic run for office. Obviously, he hadn't offended as many people as he thought. Or maybe Cyrus had ticked off more. Losing the race was not a foregone conclusion.

Ed plodded along, deep in thought. He walked toward the central park and eyed one of the hard, wooden benches. Should he do battle with it again? Discretion being the better part of valor, Ed declined the silent offer of combat and strolled on. Resuming his saturnine demeanor, Edison considered once again whether he could exit the race causing no harm. Was it too late to get a substitute candidate? Yes. He'd forgotten the filing deadline date, but he knew it had passed. He had to stick it out, Edison knew this. Accepting it was another thing altogether. And he thought once again, that acceptance is hard.

17

Reaching home, he went in the side door, and announced his arrival. To an empty house. He remembered that Brenda was at the CC teaching a class. He was happy she could do that, because she'd had to give up her teaching position, her professorship, he corrected himself, in New Jersey. Because of him. Brenda had gotten a raw deal, again solely because of his carelessness and stupidity. And she never complained. She was a wonderful person…and he was a shit. Ed sat down without turning on the lights, and put his head in his hands.

He abruptly sat up when he remembered something else — the debate. He dreaded it. He didn't want to spend five seconds with Cyrus Boone, much less what? An hour? How long was that thing supposed to last? He reached for his phone to call Stan and ask, but all he heard at the other end of the line was Stan's voicemail. Ed hated voicemail. He always felt awkward leaving a message, and his messages were mostly, um, er, um, call me. Then he would disconnect and realize he'd given neither his name nor his phone number, and would call the person or business back and leave a second message giving his name and number, then disconnecting and not knowing which message the other party received first. And wondering if they complemented each other, or were just two confusing messages. So when he got Stan's voice mail, he just hung up.

Stan and Kara had promised to coach him before the debate. And he damn well needed coaching. He knew almost nothing about

Standard. The townspeople treated him as a newcomer. It wouldn't help his election if he sounded like a just arrived know-nothing big city guy at the debate. And the debate, from what he'd gathered, was going to be one of the biggest social events of the year. It had never happened before in a local election, and it was likely that the entire town would attend. They would fill the hearing room in Town Hall to capacity, and probably overflowing that. And Ed hated public speaking. His job had not required it. He spent over thirty years in either a cubicle or a large room with many desks. A cubicle had been a step up for him. It was like his own private office.

His phone exuding its familiar sound jolted Edison out of his reverie. Stan immediately noticed his gloomy hello. He had seen the recent call from Edison, and returned it.

"What's the matter, Ed? You sound like death warmed over. Even more than usual. Did the campaigning go poorly at Pete's?"

"No, it didn't," Ed assured him. "It's those nagging doubts again."

"Can you tell me what is bothering you? What are the doubts?"

"I don't know enough about this town. You couldn't have chosen a less qualified candidate. I'm not a politician, and hate campaigning. I had to wear this plastic smile on my face all morning. That's not me."

Stan laughed, despite Ed's serious tone. "No, that's not you. Maybe we're all pushing you to campaign in the way we think campaigning should be done. The way politicians have always done it. But as you said, that's not you. So why don't you campaign the way you've been doing it all along? Just talk to people. Don't put on a fake smile. People will see through that, anyway. Be a curmudgeon, you're good at that. But you're a pretty sociable curmudgeon if you stop to think about it. Every time I go into the CC, you're talking to someone."

"That's different," Ed protested. "I'm not asking for their vote."

"It's no different. You're listening to people. You have listened to more people's concerns since the CC opened than Cyrus has his whole life. And people know that. Don't campaign. Just listen to as many people as you can without asking them for anything. Everyone already knows you're running for the Town Board. So let them talk. They'll think you'll do the same if you're elected. Listen to their concerns. And if you're elected, you might even get some of them addressed. And I guarantee you this — they know full well that Cyrus won't do anything for anyone but Cyrus."

"Isn't there someone else who could do this?"

"The deadline has passed. And I think you're perfect for the job. You're as honest as they come. Some people might say too honest, but that's a quibble. And you care about people. I've seen it. You told me before the CC was even a reality that you hoped it would benefit the community. Has Cyrus done anything like that? You want to help people. You have a passion for it. Maybe even more than helping yourself. There is no one else, and there's no one anyway who's better suited to this job than you. Please, Ed, we're counting on you. I think the vast majority of the community is counting on you. I have my ear to the ground in this town, and it looks like you have a lot of support. Hang in there, Ed. You'll be great. Oh, and I almost forgot. Kara and I are expecting you tomorrow morning at the library for debate preparation."

Edison said he remembered, and would see them at 9:30, then said goodbye and disconnected.

Still sitting in the dark, Ed put his head in his hands again.

"Oh Lord," he said into his lap. "If he only knew what kind of person I really am."

That night, Ed tossed and turned until he fell into a fitful sleep. And dreamed about sitting in his car waiting at a railroad crossing. The signal lights were flashing, and the bars had descended, blocking his path. He heard the loud tooting of a locomotive and saw the steam coming out from its top. It transfixed him. He stared at that steam and watched the locomotive barreling down the tracks. His car was first in line, and sat stopped a few feet in front of the bars, perpendicular to the tracks. As he stared at the steam and listened to the sound growing louder as the locomotive approached, he spotted out of the corner of his eye… a little girl who'd wandered onto the tracks. He lowered his window and shouted, but the little girl either didn't hear him, or was so intent on looking for something, maybe something that had rolled away from her. The locomotive was getting perilously close, and he jumped out of the car to try to get the little girl off the tracks. He shouted as he approached, trying to get the little girl to move off the tracks without him risking his life to do so, but she still didn't respond so he started onto the tracks himself, continuing to shout, and almost made it to her, when a hand grabbed him from behind, and stopped his forward movement.

"No, no, I'm almost there. Don't stop me, I can make it. No, no, no, oh my God, it's too late."

"Edison, wake up. You're having a nightmare again."

"What? No, oh my God."

Edison finally realized that he was in bed, and Brenda was nudging him gently to get him to wake up.

He was shaking, and tears filled his eyes. Sweat poured down his face, and he tried to wipe it away with his hand, but he couldn't stop sobbing.

"Don't worry, honey. It was just a dream. Everything is okay."

Ed blinked through his tears. "But I'm not, am I?"

18

"Tough night," Brenda said, stating the obvious.

"Yeah, it was." Ed stared down at his scrambled eggs. "I don't seem to be getting away from the troubles. They've just followed me to New York."

"Would going back help you deal with it better?" Brenda tried to keep her voice neutral. Although a part of her wanted to shout encouragement for that idea, she wanted Edison to make that determination on his own. Of course, she wasn't giving him her own reason for moving back, and she wondered why, given this terrific opportunity to do so. But she knew. If Edison moved back just for her, and the daily reminders of his malfeasance continued to torture him, he'd blame her. Edison dashed her hopes with an instant answer.

"Nah, I don't think that would help. You remember, I had nightmares there, too. And way more frequently. Maybe I'm getting a little better." He stopped. "Although last night, it didn't seem like it. Anyway, New Jersey isn't the answer." He looked back down at his eggs and picked at them before pushing the plate away and declaring he wasn't hungry. If Brenda gave a disappointed look, Edison didn't notice.

"I have to get over to the library soon. Debate prep."

Brenda felt defeated. Ed didn't want to go back to New Jersey. And if she was honest with herself, and put aside her personal interest in moving back home, maybe Ed had showed some improvement. He didn't fight with everyone; he didn't stare at the ground while speaking to people; and he'd spearheaded the CC. And now he was running for Town Board. No, Ed had a life here, and not much remaining in New Jersey. At least not in his mind. But his nightmares continued.

Brenda had a decision to make. And only three weeks left in which to make it. She thought about just turning it down. Being over seventy, how much longer could she do the job anyway? But college professors never retire. She could do it well into her eighties. Brenda had seen colleagues do just that. And she wanted to take the job offer, and would in a heartbeat if it wasn't for Ed. So she didn't turn it down, deferring a decision until the deadline got a little closer. At that point, she'd talk to Ed about it. He couldn't get out of the Town Board race now. There was no other candidate. But maybe… she couldn't believe she hoped this… maybe Ed would lose the election.

She sat at the kitchen table and sipped her coffee while Ed got ready to leave for the library.

"Want a ride, honey?" she asked.

"No, thanks. I'm going to walk."

He put on a sweater as she watched.

"Honey, it's pretty warm outside. I don't think you need that."

"It's cold in the library. I always freeze there."

"Why don't you just carry it, then?"

Ed pulled the sweater off. "Yeah, good idea." He gave her a little wave, opened the door, and left to walk to the library for the big debate preparation session with Stan and Kara.

Edison walked down his street and turned left. There were sidewalks going from his neighborhood all the way to the town, which was only a half-mile or so away. He strolled along, taking his time. It was still early, but the sun was glowing, and he silently thanked Brenda for urging him to carry his sweater. He held the garment sort of bunched up in his left hand while he walked. Wild flowers dotted the side of the walkway, and he idly watched the scattered blooms as he moved.

Upon reaching the edge of the central park, Ed noticed the wild flowers give way to a more organized set of flower beds of all kinds and colors. He looked at them with approval. The park looked gorgeous. His town looked as bright and colorful in the spring and summer as it seemed dark and white in the winter.

Reaching the library, Ed observed the book return box outside the front door, and muttered to himself.

"We need to move that inside, pronto."

He opened the door and Kara greeted him. "We've set up a sort of mock debate stage in the big reading room," she told him after saying hello. "Stan is in there already. I'll ask the questions, and he'll play Cyrus."

Ed sighed. "We're going to do this formally." It was a statement of resignation, not a question, but Kara answered anyway.

"We thought that would be the best way to prepare. Do you have a problem with it? We can do something else."

"No, no, it's okay. I'm just dreading the real thing, that's all. And this is doing it twice."

Kara looked at him for a moment. "You're not getting cold feet, are you?" Her tone was anxious, and Ed picked up on it.

"No, I'm all in. It's just not what I'm used to, that's all."

"We know, and that's why we're going to help you with it. But you know…I mean I think you know… that no matter what we do today, Cyrus will be awful to you. He's a nasty man."

"I know."

They went into the big reading room, rearranged to have a single table in front of two smaller tables set about six feet apart. Stan sat at one of them and rose to shake Ed's hand.

"Don't expect Cyrus to do the same," he said.

Ed nodded. "I've met him. Charming, he wasn't."

"Okay. Just one piece of advice. Don't try to out nasty him. Your, um, propensity for getting worked up is well known. He'll try to get you to erupt, to lose your cool. Don't let him. Be the picture of gentlemanliness, as best you can."

Ed gave a sort of bitter half-laugh. "That's your department," he said to Stan.

"You're quite capable of it, Ed. I've seen it, and so has Kara."

Kara nodded. "Yes, I have. Okay, let's get started." She assumed her place at the front table, and Stan sat down.

She looked at them both and said that the first part of the debate would be the moderator introducing herself, and laying out the ground rules. I won't read them here, but essentially you each get three minutes to give an opening statement, then the moderator will ask a series of five questions. Each of you will alternate being the first to respond to the moderator for three minutes, and then the other gets three minutes to respond. The moderator will permit absolutely no interruptions. At the end, they will give both of you three minutes for a final statement. Is that clear?"

Ed nodded. "I'll wing it on the statements today, but I'll work on refining them."

Kara smiled. "Great. Also, I've been told the name of the moderator. It will be Sharon Titus."

Stan whistled. "I didn't know that."

"Who is she?" Ed asked.

"Old Mrs. Titus. Or tight-ass as we called her. Way, way out of earshot, of course." He explained. "Mrs. Titus was my English teacher in sixth grade. Heck, she was everyone's English teacher. Kara had her, too."

Kara smiled. "Yes, I did. Cyrus did, too. It's a small school, even with Meeker Falls kids, and it was not like we had a half-dozen English teachers."

Ed looked at them. They were both in their fifties, so that made Mrs. Titus.....

Kara answered his unspoken question. "She's eighty-two. And sharper than any of us."

"Is she still teaching sixth grade?"

"No, she retired, but she still tutors, and is very active in community events."

"Um, what does this mean for me?"

"I think it's a good thing. She's strict, but smart and fair. And she won't put up with nastiness or disrespectful behavior. It's unlikely that Cyrus will try to challenge her. And even if he does, she's quite capable of smacking him down. My understanding is that, given the sizable crowd expected, we'll have microphones in front of you and her. And she can mute either of you." She looked at Ed. "Of course, neither one of you needs a microphone when you're angry. But I know Mrs. Titus. She has a way of shutting people up."

Stan started laughing. "The air-horn."

Kara laughed too. "Yes. I understand she has a new one."

"Is she for real?" Ed asked.

"She's a local treasure. And curiosity."

Kara sat back down and said to Ed, "Before we start, I want to ask you a basic question. Can you name the current members of the Town Board?"

"Um, uh, Rufus Winkle…" He looked at her in exasperation. "I don't know," he admitted.

"That's what I wondered. It's okay, but let's put in some time to fill you in on the basics so that Cyrus won't be able to paint you as an uninformed newcomer."

"I am an uninformed newcomer."

"Please don't say that. You're not that new, and you know more than you think. Okay, Rufus Winkle is the Mayor, and by statute is the presiding member of the five-member Town Board. He's occupied that role for twelve years, serving six successive two-year terms. Abner London has served on the board for ten years, and is very close to Rufus. Larry Percival has served for six years, and doesn't seem close to either of those two men. And Clarice Dunleavy, who is a friend of mine, dislikes both Rufus Winkle and Abner Landon. Cyrus Boone is close to both of them, and if elected as they originally expected, would form both a quorum and an unstoppable majority for whatever mischief they wanted to achieve."

"And I'm replacing Carter Cooke? Do you know why he resigned? And whose camp was he in? Although from that Town Board meeting I attended, I think I already know."

Stan spoke up. "And you'd be right. He was very much a buddy of Rufus and Abner. But he's very ill. And has four teenaged kids. I don't know how Lydia will get along without him."

"People will help. That's the place we live in. We may not like someone on a personal level, but when the chips are down, we're a single community."

Ed had lived nowhere but a big-city suburb, and he kept his skepticism to himself. He couldn't, for example, believe the community would rally around Cyrus if he suffered a similar misfortune. But these good people believed in the essential decency of people, at least in Standard, and he had no desire to puncture their belief structure.

So, he just thanked them for their insight, and they proceeded to a little more briefing, as a prelude to the actual mock questions.

19

The Mayor was concerned. That idiot Boone was blowing it. He could sense trouble. He hadn't kept his job by not having his ear to the ground, or to the pulse of the community. And Cyrus' pulse was almost nonexistent. Hell, he was on life support. Winkle ordinarily wouldn't care. He'd dumped people overboard when it was expedient to do so, but he didn't have that option this time. Cyrus was the only game in town for his purposes, and he had to stick with him. If only Cyrus had the personality to run in an actual election. Abner was completely reliable, and while he was as unctuous as an oil factory, he was also as smooth as glass in dealing with the public. He took a moment to rue Carter's illness. Not just because he and Winkle were friends and his illness genuinely saddened him, but because he was all in on their very special project. So was Cyrus, of course, but he was so abrasive, and had made so many enemies, that his election was in serious jeopardy. He almost seemed to enjoy alienating people. And he'd been so sure that the Town Board seat would be his without even lifting a finger, he'd failed to lay any groundwork for an actual fight for the position.

Rufus thought a long moment about Cyrus. He was a part of their project, for sure, but Rufus didn't like him much. And he disliked him more when, instead of even trying to make a show of reluctance to take Carter's place, or express any kind of dismay at Carter's illness, he'd shown outward glee at his good fortune. Bad optics, and hell, an awful guy. But thankfully, Rufus didn't need him as a friend, just a business partner. And he only needed one vote from him. Then he'd throw him out with the other trash.

Rufus was almost certain he could count on Larry Percival's vote. That said, he held the tiniest doubt. Rufus liked sure things. He had no illusions about Clarice Dunleavy. She'd never play ball. She harbored the quaint illusion that she served on the Town Board to do positive things for the community. Rufus had no problem with serving the people, if it also lined his own pockets. When the town benefited, so did he. No harm done. But he was not greedy. No, he was not. A little here, a little there, and pretty soon it added up to a lot. But this project was different. It didn't suit his small amounts at a time theory of government. It was a big score. He hadn't sought it out. They had approached him. And he had the votes all lined up with Abner and Carter on board. But then Carter got sick. And his condition worsened at the most inconvenient time possible. Now they were stuck with Cyrus. He sighed and picked up the phone.

"Cyrus, you're blowing it," he said into his phone, then listened to Cyrus' rejoinder.

"Show some tact, man. Any at all. If you pull any obnoxious shenanigans at the debate, old Tight Ass will smack you so hard you'll be debating in Meeker Falls."

He listened for a few moments, then nodded to himself. That asshole may actually pull it off.

"Okay, that's good. Maybe by the time of the debate you'll know more, but that should be enough. But wait until the end. And Cyrus… behave yourself until you get to that point. And even then, state the facts as if you're reluctant to say them, but you think the community should know."

The Mayor disconnected and drummed his fingers on the desk. He took a moment to think, and then shrugged. He'd just have to see how it played out. The debate was in two weeks, the election in three. He had no contingency plan.

***

Kara and Stan briefed Edison on the general structure of the town and county, and which things the Town Board handled, and which were the bailiwick of the County. Then they proceeded to some mock debate questions.

"I don't know what questions Mrs. Titus will ask. No one does. She might not even know yet. From what we know of her, she may wait until the actual debate to decide what to ask, so that no one even has a scintilla of a chance of stealing the questions."

"She always guarded her tests that way. At least it seemed like it," Stan offered.

"She abhorred cheaters," Kara agreed. "She'd point to the ground and say 'Cheaters go straight to Hades.'" Stan and Kara chanted it and then they both laughed.

"She was fond of the Greek classics," Stan reminisced.

"Yes," Kara agreed. "She might even spring something on you and Cyrus at the debate. You never know with her."

"I ran into her at Cleavon's last week and before she even said hello, she demanded to know which epic poem referred to Circe."

"That's our Mrs. Titus. She always wanted to make sure we learned. Still does. I assume you answered correctly?"

"Homer's Odyssey. Hard to forget."

Edison gaped at them. "She's going to quiz me on the classics? Does Cyrus know that stuff?"

"I bet he does. Impossible to leave her class without learning things. But no, I doubt she'll do that. You don't need that kind of knowledge to serve on the Town Board, and she knows that. She also reveres civics. I know she is aware of how important this election is to the library. She comes in all the time."

"Is she biased in our favor?" Ed asked it hopefully.

"She might secretly want you to win, but she'd never, never let that affect her role. She's as fair as they come." Kara paused and looked at Edison for a long moment.

"You're as straightforward and honest as she is. I think you'll do well with her. Leave the personalities out of it and respond to her questions honestly. If you don't know something, don't fudge. Just say you don't know, but you're ready to learn. People who claim to know everything are sententious asses, or outright liars. Usually both. But a willingness to learn. That's gold to someone like Mrs. Titus."

They proceeded to some mock questions, which Edison mostly handled well. Some things he didn't know enough about, and said so, kind of like his response to Howard's garbage collection question. Not ready to take a position. On the library issue, he didn't hedge a bit. He supported it without reservation.

Stan played a belligerent, pompous Cyrus, constantly belittling Edison, and interrupting him. Kara didn't use an air horn, but she stopped him from overdoing it, saying that it was unlikely Cyrus would overdo it, either, out of fear of Mrs. Titus' wrath.

The session exhausted Edison, but he thanked the two of them for their help. He left the library feeling worse that he had before they started.

As he walked, his mind swirled with conflicting emotions. He appreciated their efforts, but the whole exercise had just made him more nervous. He stopped for a moment and held up his right hand. It was trembling. He stared at it for a moment, and it gradually subsided. He lowered his hand to his side, and walked on for a spell, then spotted his nemesis, the park bench, and sat down. To his surprise, he felt comfortable there. He watched some children playing kickball in the park, and let his internal roiling subside.

Feeling better, Edison rose from the bench and began walking toward the CC, where he had made an appointment to meet Jack Smiley to go out to lunch. As he strolled along, he spotted something creeping towards him. As he gaped at the object, he gave an inward groan. He knew what, and who, was heading his way. Seeing nowhere to escape to, Edison gave a deep exhale, letting out the breath he'd involuntarily held. Then he shrugged with resignation. He'd avoided

Cyrus during his campaign stops at the Dump and at Pete's, but here he came on his golf cart, heading towards Edison at seventeen miles per hour.

Edison just waited for Cyrus to say whatever Cyrus had in mind. Edison had nothing to say to him.

But to his surprise, Cyrus didn't start yelling and cursing at him. Instead, he pointed a chubby index finger in his direction.

"You can still pull out," he said, his voice dripping with contempt. "Although, I don't care. I will get what is rightfully mine. You can count on it." His eyes took on a malevolent gleam. "I have a surprise for you, and I can't wait to deliver it." Cackling to himself, he put his golf cart in gear and drove away.

"Oh crap," Edison said aloud to himself. "Whatever he has in mind, it can't be good." Edison glanced at his watch, and his gait took on a more purposeful pace. If he didn't hurry, he'd be late. He'd just have to see what evil Cyrus had in store for him when the time arose.

20

When Edison arrived at the CC, he spotted Jack chatting with a few people on the low steps leading to the building. He waved as he approached, and Jack introduced him to the other people.

"I hope I can count on your votes for this fine man," he said, and shook each of their hands. Edison forced a smile and duly followed suit. They all filed away.

"See, nothing to it. Three votes in your column."

"What did you tell them?"

Jack studied him for a moment. "What they wanted to hear, of course."

Edison pressed. "And what do they want to hear?"

"That you're honest, hardworking, and will always listen to their concerns. And that only liars or politicians make specific promises unless they're damn sure they can keep them."

"Aren't you a politician?"

Jack laughed. "I'm glad you didn't ask me if I'm a liar. I'd have to take offense. But yes sir, I'm a proud American politician. Everyone needs a calling, and that's mine." Jack paused and looked Edison right in the eyes.

"But you're not. And not a liar either. And that's what I tell people every time I get a chance, like just a few minutes ago."

"Eddie, my boy, don't be like me. I'm the best there is at being me. And people around here don't want someone like me on the Town Board. They want someone like them. Now let's get some lunch. Bab's?"

Ed nodded. "Okay with me."

They strolled to Bab's Bistro, greeted Bab herself, who was standing near the entrance, and an attractive hostess who identified herself as Jenna seated them. She smiled and handed them menus.

"Franco will be over in just a minute to take your orders."

True to her word, a well-dressed twenty-something server approached and inquired whether the two men wanted cocktails to start.

Jack ordered dry martinis for both of them, and the server hurried off.

They chatted amiably about nothing in particular until the drinks arrived.

Franco brushed his long wavy hair off his face, then recited the lunch specials.

Neither of them expressed an interest in the specials, and Franco waited, pen poised, to take their orders from the menu. He jotted them down and walked away.

A busboy came a minute later and placed a basket of warm bread on the table, and departed, leaving them to have a private conversation.

"I'm hearing good things about your chances," Jack told him.

"People have been nicer to me than I expected," Ed responded. "But I don't think it's me. I think Cyrus isn't that popular in this town."

Jack stifled a belly laugh to avoid making a scene. "That's an understatement. He's genuinely disliked. Even detested by many people."

"So, I have a chance of pulling this off? With all those people clinging to their cherished traditions?"

Jack gave a long pause, studying Edison's earnest face. "I see I need to explain something to you about Standard. It's my hometown, you know. People do respect traditions here, but it has nothing at all to do with a history of the head of the Zoning Board being next up for Town Board. That's habit. The Town has always done it that way. And the truth of the matter is that very few people want to serve on the Town Board, so they've been complacent about a situation that's profoundly undemocratic. But if no one is even interested in running… well, no one is much worried about being disenfranchised. But to be clear, tradition is very important to people in this town. Like helping each other in tough times. Genuinely caring about one's neighbors. It's a small town. At some point, you get to know almost everyone here. You're still a newcomer, and you might have noticed that it takes decades to shed that sobriquet. That's a cherished Standard custom. But a harmless one. I'll bet you found everyone welcomed you to your new home and helped you get acclimated. That's the real tradition here. Citizens of Standard value hard work, family, pride in being lucky enough to live here, teamwork, appreciation of nature, and community, to list a few things. You have a leg up on Cyrus on most of those things, especially spearheading the creation of the CC, the embodiment of hard work, pride, and teamwork. You're not an ordinary newcomer."

"I have a lot to learn about this town," Edison said.

"You do. But despite your, um, not always sunny disposition, most people who meet you, like you. You're one of those naturals we in the politician business hate."

"You don't hate me."

"Nah, I like you. See what I mean?"

Ed nodded. And he understood a little better what made old-time Standard residents tick.

They sipped their martinis, then devoured the food when it arrived. Eschewing dessert and coffee, the two men paid the check, and walked out the door, where they shook hands and parted ways.

Edison ambled toward home, Jack's primer on small-town values ringing in his ears. As he reached the central park, he stopped to watch a family of birds congregating around a crook high in a tree, partially concealed by copious branches and leaves. Even with his poor vision, he spotted the nest and watched the birds for a while, thinking about how the townspeople valued nature. When they'd first moved here, he and Brenda had delighted in taking walks down the many nature trails sprinkled just outside the town. They lived amid such beauty, with many wooded areas, including right behind their house. They had only a short walk to lookout spots with remarkable views of the Adirondack Mountains, snowcapped in the winter, but green at this time of year. The two of them appreciated the wonders of nature, but it seemed like they were just going through the motions now. They rarely took the time to enjoy the natural gorgeousness of the Hudson Valley.

Edison watched the birds for a while, then strolled on. Cyrus was a long-time resident, but Edison couldn't imagine him communing with nature, or helping someone other than himself. And hard work? The man wouldn't even walk anywhere — it took too much effort.

Jack had told Edison he was likeable, even that he was a natural, whatever that meant. Edison didn't feel likeable. He knew he had a quick temper, and he knew, to the very core of his being, that outward appearances could deceive. Jack had clearly figured that it took a while to get to know the real Edison. That his agonistic temperament was just a facade. Edison knew better. He was exactly as he appeared, and also a careless, ignorant fool, and well… much, much worse than that.

Ed continued walking and wondered why closing the library mattered so much to those board members. It couldn't only be a cost-savings measure, could it?

As Edison continued to combine strolling and thinking, he didn't pay attention before crossing the road. A car honked at him, and he looked up. He refrained from extending his middle finger, because, well, he was totally at fault. So when he looked up, he intended to affect an apologetic pose, sort of half shrug and little wave, then stopped and waited for the owner of the familiar face to lower his window.

"Hey Dave, sorry about that."

"Lost in thought, are we?"

Edison hated the application of the plural pronoun to him, and Dave knew it. A few times, being barked at will do that to a person. Some people would stop, but Dave had no intention of doing so.

Edison glared at him, but the look didn't last long. "Yeah, I guess so."

"How was lunch with Jack?"

"Does everyone know everyone else's business in this town?" Ed demanded.

"Pretty much. Not much goes on without the gossip mill circulating it freely. Also, I was coming out of the CC just as you were leaving, and when I reached the street, I saw the two of you heading into Bab's."

Someone behind Dave gave a short honk, and they both looked back at a few cars backed up behind Dave's car. He made the left turn, pulled over, and told Edison to get in, and he'd drive him the rest of the way home.

Dave pulled into Edison's driveway and cut the engine. He unbuckled his seat belt, and reached into the back seat of his Buick Regal, which he'd been driving today instead of his pickup. Retrieving a file folder, he extracted a multi-page document held together by a single staple in the top left corner. He handed it to Edison and told him to check out the first page.

"What am I looking at?" Edison inquired as he scanned the page.

"It's an RFP."

"A what?"

"A request for proposals. The standard vehicle for a company to solicit vendors to bid on a job."

"And this means what to me?"

"It requests Dave's Electrical Contractors, Inc. to bid on a job in town."

"So? You get a lot of those. You're the only licensed electrical contractor in Standard."

"The only local one, yes. There are several state licensed ones that also can work here. That's a good thing, because I'm, well… semi-retired."

"I still don't get it."

"Two things. Check out the job. It's on page three."

Ed turned to the specified page and scratched his head. "A shopping center? In Standard?"

"Yes, and an enormous one. A big national outfit, Hellion, Inc. is evaluating our bucolic little town for a vast shopping complex."

"That's crazy," Ed said. "The Town Board would never approve it. It wouldn't even get past … the Zoning Board. Oh, shit."

"A big prize to the man with the sudden realization."

"If it's possible to get worse, let me point you to page four, which identifies the location for this lovely enterprise."

Ed turned to page four. He thought about the legal description. He had some familiarity with it because of the time he'd spent studying the layout of the town when he was looking for a permit for the CC. Dave waited patiently for reality to set in.

It didn't take long. "They're proposing to build in the exact location where the library is currently situated."

"Another prize. Yes, they are."

"Why would they ask you, of all people, to bid on a job that doesn't even exist?"

"That's two questions, really. Why me, and why a job that doesn't exist? I'll answer the first question. They must have a requirement in their bylaws, or believe it's good local politics to reach out to local business. They won't hire me, of course. It's just for show. I wouldn't take a job that involved razing the library anyway, but they don't know that. No, they have their own electrical contractor lined up, and it isn't me."

"And the non-existent job part?"

"I think you can guess the answer to that one."

"It's a done deal already."

Dave nodded. "Yeah, they must be pretty sure of themselves to send out RFPs. Not just to me. They need a lot of different vendors for a job like that."

"It will ruin our town."

"It will. But I'm sure they care about that as much as stepping on a bug. They think they'll make a lot of money. But there might be one thing they didn't account for."

"And what's that?"

Dave looked at him. "You."

"Oh great, now I have the pressure of trying to save the library, and the entire character of the town, too? I'm having a hard-enough time with the idea that I must actually serve with those weasels on the Town Board if I'm elected—even for a single vote on the library."

"It will be more than that vote. The shopping center project will need town approval, too. I hate to say this about anyone, and I do like Carter Cooke and hope he recovers, but his resignation was very fortuitous for this town. Because he was likely to vote for getting rid of the library."

"It's pretty clear that Mayor Winkle and Abner Landon are corrupt," Ed postulated. "Cyrus, too. What can we do about it?"

"Look, Ed, you can't say that, for one. There is no proof. No vote has even taken place that anyone can say improper. We can't call anyone a crook. But we can get you elected, and foil their scheme, and the plans of Hellion, Inc. to destroy our town."

21

Edison told Brenda about Dave's revelation as soon as he entered the house. After blurting it out, Brenda told him to sit down, gave him a glass of water, and told him to calm down.

"You're going to have a stroke if you keep getting worked up like that."

Edison complied with his wife's entreaty and took a moment to catch his breath. He hadn't realized that he'd literally run inside after parting from Dave.

"Okay, now tell me a little about your day. Dave's story makes a lot of sense, and we'll talk about it, but you've been out all day. How did everything go? Tell me about the debate preparation, and your luncheon with Jack."

Edison felt ashamed of himself. He hadn't even said hello, much less given her a kiss. And he hadn't asked her about her day at all.

"I think it all went pretty well, and I'll tell you all about it after I do this."

Edison rose from his chair, strode over to where Brenda stood with her hands folded across her chest, and opened his arms. She smiled, and they hugged. He kissed her after they disengaged, and went back to his seat.

"Before I tell you about my day, honey, tell me about yours."

Brenda smiled again. "After you left, I picked up around the house for a little while, then walked over to the CC, and met Debbie. We went to Fresh Bean for coffee."

"That's a new place, isn't it?"

"Yes, it opened last month. It's nice in there. Comfortable couches and seating areas. We sat in overstuffed armchairs with a little table between us. It was lovely."

"How's Debbie doing?"

"She's good, actually. And Fritz is doing a little better."

"Thyroid cancer, is it?"

"Yes. But Deb says the doctors told her there's every chance he'll recover."

"That's good."

"When he does, they're planning on going to Europe. They've always wanted to visit Rome. She's a history buff, you know, and wants to see firsthand some things she's read about."

"That sounds nice," Edison said.

Brenda brightened. "Really? Would you like to do something like that?"

"Um… er…sure."

"Don't overwhelm me with your enthusiasm, Ed. No one is forcing you."

"It's not that I wouldn't want to go to Europe," Edison protested. "It's just there is so much going on right now."

Brenda sighed. "Yes, there is. And there always seems to be something, even with the two of us retired. With you so busy with the CC and your run for the Town Board, maybe I should go back to work. I do miss teaching."

It was a giant, neatly telegraphed message to Edison, and he missed it by a mile.

"Oh, I won't be doing this stuff much longer. I might not even win the election. Even if I do, what amount of time will it take up?

And then if you want to take a trip, we can do it. And you're still teaching at the CC, anyway."

Brenda's face exhibited the frustration she felt, but Edison didn't notice. Nor did he seem to understand the difference between being a full professor at a university and running a book club. Both are good to do, but hardly the same thing. And more to the point, while Edison had tried just then to ask her about what was going on in her life, he hadn't pursued it, or shown genuine interest. He was just going through the motions, because he felt guilty for not asking. At least he did that. Lately, he hadn't come close to caring about her life. She didn't add "miserable backwater" in her head, because she didn't believe it. Standard was a nice town, but it lacked the vibrancy of her hometown. It wasn't even close. Her eyes wandered over to the kitchen shelf where the letter lay hidden. But she averted her eyes immediately when Edison told her more about his day. She listened with interest, and then told him he should call Kara and tell her about the hidden agenda Dave had identified. When he phoned her, she asked if she could put him on speaker so Stan could listen in. Ed assented and greeted Stan.

The two of them listened to Edison's report, and Stan erupted.

"Those conniving crooks. I knew they had a hidden scheme. And I just knew it involved money. They should be locked up."

Kara reacted more quietly. "It makes sense, if you think about it. And a part of me is glad it isn't a vendetta against me, or the library. It's just another crass money grab."

"No one would have a grudge against you, honey. Everyone likes you. Probably even the Mayor and his cronies. But they smell the almighty dollar, lots of them, and you're just in the way."

"I'm glad I'm not an employee of the town," Kara said. "Then they could just fire me to get me out of the way. Stan and I both work for the county, and the county runs the library. But it's on Town land, and if we lose that space, I guess I'll be working in Meeker Falls. Although not as a librarian, they already have one. As her assistant, I imagine."

"That might not happen. Edison will get elected, and will try to get the votes to keep the library right where it is."

Ed spoke up. "I sure hope so."

"We should do something about those crooks on the Town Board," Stan declared.

"We have no proof at all. We just have a big corporation reaching out to a local vendor about a project that isn't yet approved. Optimism isn't a crime. Even if they think the fix is in, it isn't a done deal. At least not yet. We can't prove the Mayor and his cronies have anything at all to do with Hellion. And if all goes right, we'll ensure they don't get the chance to commit a crime. Unless, of course, we can find proof of an already paid bribe."

"Anyway, keep campaigning, Ed. I think it's going well," Stan said. "And thanks for the information."

Brenda listened for a moment to Edison's side of his conversation with Kara, then left the room, half to give him privacy, although there was no secret about their discussion. The other half was to give her time to think.

Edison had pleasantly surprised her by impulsively hugging and kissing her, and even asking her about her day. But in an instant, it gave way to that maddening aloofness toward her, and her thoughts and dreams. She knew in her heart of hearts that without some dramatic change, the two of them would never take a trip together, to Europe or anywhere else.

Guilt drove almost everything Edison did, and the hug and kiss and feigned interest in her day was no exception.

Brenda had to admit something, though. The move to Standard accomplished its intended purpose. It had distracted Ed enough for him to build a new life for himself. He wasn't the same even-tempered, kind man he was before the troubles, and she knew he'd never be the same.

Brenda had friends and many things to occupy herself, and she guessed she'd built a new life for herself, too. But she couldn't help thinking that… she liked her old life better.

Brenda shook her head. No use pining about a life she'd left. Even if they returned, it wouldn't be the same. It never is. The old house was long sold, and that neighborhood had undergone a whirlwind of changes as well. What was the expression from the Thomas Wolfe book? "You can never go home again."

Standard was a pleasant town for someone like Edison, who no longer drove or had a driver's license. But until the troubles, the great State of New Jersey had issued him one. He'd passed the eye test every ten years as required, and for the life of her, she couldn't figure out how, at least the last time. His peripheral vision was shot, and that alone should have flunked him. But because he'd been such a moron and not seen an ophthalmologist, the glaucoma had affected his central vision as well. Edison hated doctors, and this time that antipathy had cost him dearly.

At first, neither of them noticed the onset of his visual impairment. Sudden is noticeable, slow change is not. And this was very gradual. But Brenda had observed it after a while, particularly when riding as a passenger while he drove. The number of near misses he had was staggering, but Edison always blamed the other drivers for their recklessness. Brenda tried to talk to him, and urged him to see an eye doctor, but Edison had shrugged it off.

New Jersey's every ten years vision test requirement for renewing a driver's license had delighted her. She'd accompanied Ed as he drove to the DMV, and even kept her mouth shut when Ed drove right through a stop sign, hoping that the State of New Jersey would put a stop to his driving.

She sat next to him while they administered the eye test. He almost missed when aiming his head to put his eyes into the two binoculars-like spots on the eye examination machine, but righted himself just in time. Brenda looked to see if the examiner saw the near *faux pas* and was sure she did. When the examiner told Ed to read the letters on Line 3, he paused for twenty seconds, then he slowly spoke each letter he viewed, almost like he was learning to read. And then he stopped. The examiner asked him whether that was all he saw, and Brenda noticed him ever so slightly tilt his head, and then he almost gasped the letter "A." Brenda saw the examiner give a slight nod as if he'd gotten that one right, but to her surprise, the woman again asked whether that was all Edison saw. Brenda saw Edison tilt his head a bit the other way and asked the examiner, "8 on the right?"

"Close enough," the examiner said, to Brenda's dismay. "It's a six, but I'm going to pass you."

Ed thanked the woman, and he and Brenda, struck dumb by the unexpected turn of events, followed Edison to the section of the DMV for obtaining a photograph and a shiny new driver's license.

Edison drove them back, narrowly missing a parked car, and muttering about careless people parking too far away from the curb.

Brenda was glad Edison didn't drive anymore. She wished he'd stopped much earlier, and so did Edison, but one thing was clear: Just because a state issues you a driver's license, it doesn't mean you're competent to drive. And examiners that "help" people pass a test they should fail are not doing either the driver or the public any good. And maybe doing a ton of harm.

22

A few days after the renewal of his license, Brenda again rode as a passenger while Ed drove. She hated sitting there, vulnerable to his poor driving, but had reluctantly gone with him to run some errands they both needed to get done.

As they approached the stop sign at the end of their neighborhood, Brenda tensed and held on to the arm-rest, and was gratified when he came to a stop. He looked first one way, then the other, and, satisfied that the coast was clear, moved forward, when Brenda, in absolute shock, grabbed his arm and screamed, "Stop!"

Fortunately, Edison obeyed, and a man on a motorcycle, who'd been proceeding from Edison's left, stopped short. From the car, Edison and Brenda could see him trembling. He remained stopped and Edison rolled down the window. For once, he didn't blame the motorcyclist. He just asked if he was okay, and the man, still quivering, gave a weak nod.

"That was too close," he managed. "If you hadn't stopped when you did… I don't want to think about it."

Edison was contrite and apologized. "I just didn't see you. I'm glad you're okay."

The man swaved him away. "I'm just happy to be alive. Please just go. I'm going to stay here for a while."

"Okay." Edison drove away, leaving the motorcycle rider shaking his head, as if in disbelief that he'd survived… the incredible carelessness of the driver of a lethal weapon — an automobile.

Brenda tried to talk to Edison about the near, terrible accident, but he waved it off with "I just need to pay more attention. No harm done."

Edison continued driving. He had a few fender-benders, with the same refrain "No harm done. I didn't hurt anyone. Just a few dents."

***

After Ed disconnected, he wandered into the living room, where he found Brenda just sitting. No magazine or book. Just sitting there. With some trepidation, he ventured an "Everything okay, honey?"

Brenda looked up, startled out of her not so fond memories.

"Oh, I'm fine, Ed. Just thinking about things, I guess."

She was glad he cared enough to ask. Oh, she knew Edison loved her. But their relationship had become… unequal somehow. His visual appearance rarely showed signs of his depression. His inward turmoil was another story. He kept busy, as a distraction from how he felt, which was awful. Living here was way better for him than New Jersey, and she knew it. But maybe not for her. And how to broach the subject of moving with someone who didn't want to move, or was better off not moving?

So she refrained from mentioning it once again. She just pretended to love Standard and to encourage Edison in all of his endeavors. And at this moment, it was his run for the Town Board.

"That's good," Ed said absently, not listening to her answer. "Kara and Stan agree that the hidden agenda for the library is awful, but acknowledge there's nothing much we can do about it."

"Do nothing about it, then. Just move on," Brenda said, hoping her tone wasn't as dismissive as it sounded in her head.

"That's good advice, thanks." Ed hadn't noticed. He never noticed. She needed to be more assertive about what she wanted. Now was as good a time as any.

"How about we take a walk, honey?"

"Ed looked at his watch, then at the television, then back at Brenda. She didn't jump in as she might have done in the past and told him it was okay, they didn't need to do it.

"Um, okay. Yes, let's take a walk. It's nice outside. Good idea."

Brenda didn't say what she thought, which was something approximating Don't do me any favors. She just smiled and agreed that it was a nice day. And the two of them walked outside and began their stroll.

Although initially reluctant, Edison immediately enjoyed the walk. He reached for Brenda's hand, and they strolled out of the neighborhood. He didn't need to inquire which way Brenda wanted to walk, because she gently pulled on his hand in the opposite direction of the town.

Up to that point, they'd said little to each other, and the walk seemed almost purposeful, like they were heading somewhere — to the grocery store, or to a restaurant for dinner. But both those things were in the opposite direction. As they walked, houses of varying colors, black roofs and matching black driveways faded into the distance behind them. They crossed the street, and walked a short distance to a well-trodden path, and left the roadway, which gave way to a sea of greenery. Blooming trees lined the pathway, with no structures of any kind obstructing their magnificence. The path upon which they walked seemed tunnel-like, as large leaf bearing branches overhung it on both sides. They encountered no people. It was as if the splendor of the Hudson Valley had magically appeared for their benefit.

Neither Edison nor Brenda spoke. It was almost a silent agreement not to break the special moment. Continuing to hold hands, they strolled along, just taking in the beauty.

The pathway gave way to a vast verdant meadow. They took in the saucy, but sweet smell of the greenery mixed with the many flowers they spotted. Brenda pointed at the many crocuses spread throughout the meadow, including several partially dug up, and chopped almost in half.

"I read somewhere they're like candy to a hungry rodent," she said, breaking the silence.

"I heard that too. Look at all the flowers! That pretty purple plant is a hyacinth, I think."

Brenda affirmed his guess, and pointed out the yellow and purple primroses, and a cluster of the yellow blooms of forsythia.

A dragonfly lazily passed before their eyes, and they watched it until it flew out of sight. Edison leaned down and picked up a dandelion puffball, and they both blew on it, scattering the seeds into the air, creating hosts of new yellow flowers in the days to come.

"We used to do that all the time when we first moved here, didn't we?"

Bren murmured agreement, and leaned into his side, grasping his arm with her free hand in a sort of side hug. They stood there for a while, just taking in the utter silence of the meadow. After a few minutes, they walked through the meadow to a break in the trees, where they re-entered the wooded border of the meadow and proceeded down a crooked path through the trees. They paused multiple times to gaze at the plethora of purple violets peppered along the path, or to examine an interesting moss formation. The expansive ferns almost obscured a small green snake apparently enjoying the cover of the leafy shelter. They stopped multiple times to catch glimpses of various birds —a robin here, a blue jay over there, a sparrow or two, and multi-colored woodpeckers, with their staccato drumbeat.

They were completely alone, and at one stopping point, Edison leaned over and gave Brenda a long, passionate kiss. One that he'd not given her in a long time. And he knew it. He'd neglected her, and he resolved to make amends for that. He stopped himself. Oh, shit. I'm doing it again. I'm doing things to make up for unacceptable behavior. No. Not with Bren. I'm going to do things because I want to do them with her. Because I love her. And because I want to be a good husband and a good friend.

"This is nice," he said to her. "Thank you for inviting me to walk today. I've missed it. I've missed you."

Brenda looked at him with a quizzical expression. "I haven't gone anywhere. I'm still here, honey." A part of her wondered whether he was aware of the letter, but she thought not. Something else was going on here.

"I just mean us spending quality time together," Edison hastened to say. "We used to do this all the time, and I guess one project after another has occupied me lately. We just haven't done this." He stopped and looked her in the eyes. "And I want to start it up again, even if it means giving up this stupid campaign."

"I don't think the two things are mutually exclusive, honey. We can do both. Now, no more talking. Let's keep enjoying this nature trail. You remember what's at the end?"

Edison smiled. He did. They continued along the trail, stopping and gawking at crumpled brush bearing the tracks of a large mammal, and speculating whether bears roamed the woods. Edison thought not, and that maybe it was from a beaver, dragging his wide tail. Along the way, an apparently abandoned bird's nest in the crook of a tree caught their eyes, and they stopped to consider its former occupant. Perhaps a bird of prey?

Their hands tightly clasped, they stepped over fallen limbs and small streams, and avoided stumbling over tree roots embedded in the path. As they reached the end of the trail, it opened up to a small landing, with metal bars preventing them from going further. And it was a good thing, too, because beyond that little landing was a steep drop of a several hundred feet or more.

Standing on the landing, still holding hands, Edison and Brenda looked out upon a spectacular view of the Adirondack Mountains, majestically appearing in the distance, with a slight cloud cover, which only lent a mysterious shadow effect on the peaks. The two of them gazed at the view in awed silence. People infrequently visited this little spot, although well-known to long-time residents.

Edison hugged and kissed Brenda again, and after a time, they turned around and walked back on the trail, retraced their steps through the meadow, and back through the trees to the roadway, and home.

23

When they returned, darkness had set in, and they had nothing prepared for dinner.

"Takeout?" Bren inquired.

Ed bowed to her in mock formality. "May I invite the lovely lady out to dinner at Thorsen's?"

Bren smiled. "Yes, you may. Has the gentleman made a reservation?"

Ed reached for his phone, punched in a few numbers, said a few words, and disconnected.

"Yes, the gentleman and lady will have a table ready for them at 7 p.m."

Bren glanced at the kitchen clock. "Great, plenty of time to get dressed." If this was a new Edison he was selling, she was a more than willing buyer.

Brenda put on a pretty dress and the string of pearls Edison had bought her so many years ago, and fixed her makeup from nature walk to going out to dinner at a fancy restaurant. As she looked in the mirror, she saw an older woman, but not an old woman. She had many years left on her. How she would spend those years was the open question. She was enjoying her day with Edison, and days like this made her view Standard in a more favorable light. If this little town did so much for Edison that he could enjoy times like this without turning sour and unappealing, she could see herself staying here for the long haul. But she couldn't help wondering if today was an aberration, and at the first sign of adversity, Edison would regress. She gave a little shrug and resolved to enjoy the moment. And at the moment, Edison appeared in the bathroom's doorway wearing his best suit, a regimental striped red tie on a snow white pressed white dress shirt complete with French cuffs and the gold cufflinks she'd bought him when he was still working. He'd combed the sparse gray hair running down both temples and sported shined dress shoes. He looked as handsome as the day they'd met, but much more distinguished.

And instead of tapping his watch and saying something like "Let's get a move on, here, can't keep people waiting," followed by a sigh, and the added "Like you always do." Edison didn't do that. He just smiled at her and told her how nice she looked.

It blew her away. What had happened to him? Again, she wondered if he'd seen the letter, and was trying to keep her from leaving him, like a guy buying flowers for one girl when he'd just spent time with another. But no, she was sure he hadn't seen the letter, and he sure wasn't having an affair. It wasn't their anniversary, or his or her birthday. So, what was it? She'd ask outright, but decided not to ruin this time together by raising a fuss.

Brenda finished up her preparation for their big date, and went downstairs, where she took hold of Edison's arm. They proceeded out to her car, where he opened the driver's side for her, and held her arm while she settled behind the wheel. He walked around to the other side, got in, buckled his seat belt, and off they went to Thorsen's, a fancy French bistro just outside of Standard. Still walking distance, but Brenda was not about to walk all dressed up and in heels. Edison didn't want to walk, either, and they drove the short distance and parked right in front of the restaurant. Walking in, an attractive, immaculately dressed, and supremely competent appearing hostess welcomed them. She took their name and feigned delight at having the Orwells gracing their humble eatery. Feigned, because the hostess didn't know them from Adam, but had clearly received impressive training to greet every visitor like they were old friends and honored guests. She accompanied them to a table covered in a white linen tablecloth with matching cloth napkins, and upon which sat pristine flatware and faux crystal goblets.

"Nice place," Brenda whispered.

Edison nodded. "It is, honey. And I don't think you need to whisper." He smiled. "I bet it's not a secret how nice it looks in here."

That impish smile. Brenda loved that smile, but hadn't seen it much since the troubles. Oh, how she hoped she'd see it more.

A tall, twenty-something server in formal attire approached and took their drink orders. Brenda requested a glass of dry sherry, and Edison ordered a martini. The server hurried off to fill the orders.

While sipping their *aperitifs*, Edison and Brenda chatted away, first about the day's nature walk, then the upcoming events at the CC, the next book choice for the book club, and the old days — the days long before the troubles, high school, college, almost everything but the more recent days in New Jersey, or the upcoming election. By silent agreement, they avoided both topics. The server gave them a suitable time to finish their drinks and scrupulously avoided imposing upon their quiet conversation, by lurking nearby, but out of earshot.

Spotting a break in the conversation by assessing their body language, the server swooped over to take their dinner orders, with Edison ordering steak frites, and Brenda opting for a leg of lamb, with fingerling potatoes in garlic lemon butter and French green beans with slivered almonds. After the server left, they continued to chat amiably about all uncensored subjects, and continued doing so between bites after the food arrived.

It was a lovely dinner, capped off by decaffeinated coffee and a chocolate *mousse* they agreed to split. The server obligingly brought two spoons, and they took turns dipping them into the goblet containing the sweet treat. A perfect evening, capping a perfect day. They both sat back and enjoyed a companionable silence as they sipped their coffees. And then, disaster struck. Brenda and Edison watched a man steer toward their table, and they both groaned at the sight of a person with the capacity to ruin their perfect day. It was none other than the ever-unctuous Mayor Winkle, second only to Cyrus Boone in undesirability.

The Mayor approached, hand extended. Edison didn't move at first, but after a slight kick under the table from Brenda, he rose. Brenda remained seated.

"Good evening, good evening," the Mayor boomed, causing other diners to look up, then pretend to ignore the scene about to unfold. They weren't about to miss this. But if they expected, maybe even secretly relished the thought of a confrontation between the two men, they were disappointed. Edison did not erupt. He extended his hand, and gave a mild response of "Good evening."

The Mayor shook his hand, then looked down at Brenda. "And this is the lovely Mrs. Orwell?" he inquired.

"Yes. Mayor Winkle, may I present Brenda Orwell? And I'd add brilliant to your characterization."

"Of course, of course. Quite so, quite so." The Mayor had a habit of repeating himself. He turned back to Edison.

"Big debate coming up. I hope you're ready. Cyrus has been around for a long time. He knows the ropes, knows this town intimately. He grew up here. You're from New Jersey, I hear. I know you're not one of those awful carpetbagger types. No sir, not you. But you can't possibly understand this town as well as him. Hell, I mean heck, Mrs. Titus was Cyrus' English teacher. She's known him since he was a little boy." The Mayor paused and leaned in conspiratorially, as if sharing the details of a secret code.

"Make sure you brush up on your Greek literature." He chuckled, and didn't explain. Just trying to psyche him out, Edison surmised. He doubted that the outcome of the debate would turn on his knowledge of Homer.

But Edison just contented himself with listening. He saw no benefit to arguing with the Mayor, so he simply nodded and murmured responses. If the Mayor wanted to send a message to the other people in the dining area that he was not born in Standard, so be it. They knew that already. And the Mayor was trying to provoke an outburst, to paint Edison as unhinged. Edison spotted that intention immediately, so he figured the best thing he could do was to not argue, just listen. And add, when the Mayor paused, a comment that he was looking forward to debating the issues with Mr. Boone, and that he expected that Mrs. Titus would have some excellent questions that would lead to a healthy exchange of ideas and positions on issues important to the town.

If his failure to provoke an outburst from Edison disappointed the Mayor, he didn't show it. He just expressed a wish for a pleasant evening, nodded to Brenda with an added "Pleased to meet you, Mrs. Orwell," and walked back to his own table, where several people awaited his return. Edison sat down and turned back to Brenda, but before he spoke, he looked over her head at the Mayor's table, and saw several heads leaning in for an apparently whispered conference.

"Well done," Brenda told him. "He was trying to get a loud, angry defense from you. You handled him well."

Edison nodded and thought for a moment. "I'm guessing that carpetbagger comment will be the first line of attack at the debate."

"Sure it will, but you knew that. And anyway, this isn't the place to discuss it. That man tried to ruin our wonderful day. Let's not let him."

Edison smiled. "A strict prohibition of political talk, at least until tomorrow."

Brenda made a motion as if zipping her lips. "Done," she agreed with a laugh.

Edison leaned forward. "It's been such a nice day. I've enjoyed spending time with you."

Brenda smiled at him. And wished, oh how she wished, that this Edison, her Edison, always acted like this. Things had changed between them since the troubles, but for the first time in a long time, Brenda dared to hope their life together might return to happier times. They wanted to linger over coffee and maybe enjoy *digestifs* of brandy or sherry, but they couldn't do so without viewing the smarmy figure of the Mayor at his table. So, Edison paid the tab, and feeling generous, left a more than adequate tip.

Spotting the size of the gratuity, Brenda raised her eyebrows, but said nothing. Maybe this was part of Edison returning to his former self. Once upon a time, he'd leave tips like that, when the service warranted it. Tonight's service certainly did, but Ed hadn't rewarded stellar service in a long time. Something had snapped in Edison after the troubles. It had changed virtually every psychic element of him. Happy to morose. Kind to angry and suspicious. Respectful to argumentative. And unlike today, generous to miserly.

All of this renewed Brenda's fervent hope that Ed was coming out of his... funk, to put it gently.

When they returned home, Brenda turned toward Edison after he closed the side door and pulled him into a warm embrace, something mostly absent from their lives. But Edison seemed better, so why not see whether she could coax him into getting naked and having sex right there on the living room couch? They used to do that back in New Jersey, almost never making it to the bedroom before disrobing wherever they were in the house. The floor, the coffee table, the couch, it didn't matter to them. They'd acted like kids well into their sixties, until... disaster struck, and Edison seemed to lose all interest in sex. Standard was a gorgeous town, but it was a celibacy zone as far as Edison seemed to view it. Brenda loved him, and she never cheated on him, although... once, she was tempted. She felt young, and had needs, but Edison was so wrapped up in guilt that he didn't even seem to notice.

But if she hoped this evening would be different, Edison doomed her to frustration and disappointment. He didn't wriggle out of the embrace, but he didn't return the hug either, or kiss her when they disengaged. Nor did he try to undo the remaining buttons on her blouse, even though she'd strategically undone almost all of them the moment she'd entered the house.

But Edison didn't notice, damn him. Their beautiful day forgotten, Edison gave her a vacant smile and sat down in his chair.

"Do you think I should come up with a catch phrase or something like that to respond to that carpetbagger thing that asshole Mayor Winkle mentioned?"

Brenda just stared at him. She opened her mouth, then closed it. She felt rejected, because that's what just happened. Edison couldn't even muster a simple kiss, much less a passionate response. For a few moments, Brenda felt old and ugly. But she knew better. She was barely seventy, and still very attractive, but the love of her life paid no attention to that at all. Oh, how she'd hoped their romantic day would continue, and would represent a turning point, but she knew now it was just another transient moment. Her gaze involuntarily went to the kitchen, where the letter lay hidden. And she wondered.

24

"Did you hear me, Bren?"

Jolted out of her deep thoughts, her husband's question momentarily disoriented her.

"What? Oh, sure honey, come up with something." She attempted to control her fury before saying to Edison, "Thank you for our wonderful day."

"Oh, yes, um, you too." Edison looked at his phone.

"Maybe I'll call Kara and ask her if she has any ideas."

If he expected a response, Brenda dashed that hope. She had already left the room. Edison didn't see her storm out. He checked his watch, which showed the time was just about 9 pm. He wondered if that was too late to call, but shrugged and tapped Kara's speed dial number.

Brenda went upstairs to her sitting room and plopped on her chair. She couldn't take much more of this. She had two choices. Stay with Edison in Standard, because she knew he'd never move, or leave him and go back to New Jersey by herself. But they'd sold their house. Their home. Their beloved home with the complete master suite on the first floor, oh so perfect for the two of them to live in. Brenda missed that home. She missed the big lawn, emerald green in the spring and summer; the beautiful red maple in the front yard; the pin oaks in the back; and the patio where they entertained guests, or just sat together sipping cool drinks in the summer. The working fireplace crackled year-round. They enjoyed just sitting on the couch watching, while reading magazines and holding hands. And sometimes the hand holding turned into something even more romantic.

Brenda sighed. That house, that life was gone. Someone else lived there now. It would look foreign to her if the new owners permitted her a peek inside. It certainly wouldn't feel the same. That's what happened in life. Things look different at different times, and people behave differently, too. Brenda wanted to turn back time. She wanted her old house and her old Edison back. She wondered if she had changed as well, and figured she probably had. But she knew one thing. If she moved back, her old home wouldn't have her or Edison in it. She'd need to find a place to live. And she badly needed a girlfriend to talk to about it all. She couldn't talk to anyone in Standard, but she knew whom to call.

She eyed the sitting-room door and craned her neck to position her right ear to listen. And she heard Edison on the phone.

She rose, closed the sitting-room door, picked up her phone and tapped the speed dial for her sister in New Jersey.

The phone rang a few times, and Bren reconsidered calling, at least while Ed was downstairs. But before she could disconnect, her sister Britney answered, a little breathless.

"Hi Bren," she panted into the phone.

"Um, Brit, did I catch you at a bad time?"

Her sister laughed. "The out of breath thing. No, I'm not in the middle of fucking Carl, don't worry. I don't want to wear the poor dear out, now do I? Anyway, if I was, I wouldn't answer the phone at all. I was in the garage and left my phone on the kitchen table. So, I ran to get it. I guess I'm just a teeny-weeny bit out of shape. What's up? Everything okay?"

Brenda chuckled. Teeny-weeny was an understatement. Britney had always carried a few extra pounds. But she was very attractive anyway, and very vivacious. She'd never had trouble finding boyfriends, including the last one, Carl, to whom she'd been married for over twenty-five years.

"I just needed someone to talk to," Bren started.

Her sister turned serious right away at Brenda's tone.

"What's wrong, honey? I know that voice. Is it Edison? Is he hurting you?"

"No, of course not. Ed's a sweetie, you know that. But he's not himself. He's… self-absorbed. Distant."

"He's depressed," Brit stated the obvious. "I know you both thought moving north would help. But it hasn't?"

Bren thought for a moment. "That's the thing. I think it has helped. Him, not me."

"How so?"

"He's found a new life here. He has the Community Center, and now he's running for the Town Board."

"Does he ignore you? Is he so busy that he has no time for you?"

"You know, I don't think that's exactly it. It's more… he's found a zillion ways to distract himself from how he really feels."

"Guilty."

"Yes. Ed hates himself. And everything he does is designed to assuage his guilt. He intended the community center to be a safe place for kids and adolescents. Keep them off the streets."

"No symbolism there," Britney said dryly.

Brenda gave a tight smile. Britney didn't need to see her to know her sister's face at that moment.

"And now he's running for Town Board."

"Why? Local town boards are the next worst thing after cesspools."

"He feels guilty." Brenda said.

"I'll bite. Why? How does that relate to ….?"

"It doesn't. It started as another reason for him to get down on himself. The Community Center has a small reading room. The Town Board wants to call that the town library, and use the library space for something else. It's clearly a corrupt town board that wants to use the property for some awful purpose. The librarian is our friend. Ed thinks it's his fault they're trying to eliminate the library because he thought a reading room in the Community Center was a good idea."

"That sounds crazy, the way you describe it. And his solution is to run for a position on a corrupt town board?"

"He thinks he can stop the corrupt members."

"Well, isn't that the way he's always been? Tilting at windmills, fighting the good fight. Honest to a fault and believing in good triumphing over evil?"

Brenda sighed. "Yes, that's my Edison. And I love him for it. But it seems so laser-focused now that it's more like an unquenchable thirst for redemption. That after this is over, he'll look for a different way to make up for what he's done. And how will this one end? He gets elected to the Town Board? And is serving alongside those crooks? That won't end well, that's for sure. And what's next after that?"

"And where do you fit into all of that?" Britney breathed it, more as a statement than a question.

Brenda sobbed out the answer. "Nowhere good."

"Don't cry, honey. We'll figure this out. Do you want to leave him?"

"I do sometimes," Brenda admitted.

"And you don't other times," Brit prodded.

"No. Sometimes Edison can be so sweet and thoughtful, just like he used to be." Bren told her sister about the day's events. How a special day had made her think he might actually turn a corner. That they could have an enjoyable life together in Standard. And then he'd rejected her obvious advances.

Britney gasped out loud. "Nothing? Did he push you away?"

"No, not exactly that. Preoccupied. He wanted to call the librarian and tell her the Mayor approached him at dinner."

"Let me get this straight. He rejected making love to you in order to call another woman?"

Brenda sighed. "It's not like that. Ed's not having an affair. Kara is committed to her husband. They act like teenagers around each other. No way she and Edison, who's much older than her anyway, are having an affair. But it was awful anyway."

There was a brief silence on Britney's part, then she ventured in a small, timid voice, "Are you having an affair?"

"No. I've never cheated on Edison."

Britney read the tentative end to Bren's sentence. "But you've thought about it."

"Yes."

"Oh, honey, I'm so sorry. You're not getting any, are you? We Haverford girls are very sexual creatures. That must be hell for you."

"It's not good," Brenda said. "There's something else," she added.

"What is it?"

"I received a letter." And she told her sister the contents and the deadline to respond.

"Have you decided?"

"No. But after today, I'm much closer."

"You can stay here as long as you want. We have plenty of room."

"Oh, I wouldn't want to impose. A night or two, that's all I'd accept. But thank you." She heard Ed plodding up the stairs. "I hear Ed heading up here, so I have to hang up. But thanks for listening."

"I'm here. Call anytime." And before she disconnected, she added, "day or night."

25

"**H**i Stan. Am I calling too late? Oh. I'm sorry. I'll try tomorrow. Oh, okay, thanks." Ed waited for a moment.

"Hi Kara, sorry to call so late, but I wanted to tell you Brenda and I ran into the Mayor at Thorsen's tonight."

Ed listened for a moment.

"Yes. It was good. No, not an anniversary or anything like that. Um, I don't think so, anyway. No, I'm sure it wasn't a special occasion. We just had a nice day together and thought we'd cap it off by going to an excellent restaurant. Um, no, we had no plans this evening, no TV or cards or anything like that. Our day is over now. Bren went upstairs. I think she's in her sitting room."

Ed listened to Kara's response to what he'd said. And although she didn't say it, he had the distinct impression she wasn't happy with the late call. And she was trying to tell him something, but for the life of him, he couldn't figure out what. But he didn't ask. He quickly completed his recitation of what the Mayor had said, apologized again for the lateness of the call, and disconnected.

He sat for a moment in his chair, trying to figure out what Kara was trying to tell him. And he didn't think it was only limited to the lateness of the call. Kara and Brenda were friends. Maybe Bren could decipher Kara's cryptic words. He rose and trudged towards the stairs, and proceeded, one step at a time. His back and legs both hurt. His regular walking and jogging never bothered Edison, but they'd had a long day. And he'd enjoyed it immensely. It reminded him of the better days… before…. Ed put those thoughts out of his mind. But he knew he couldn't eradicate the near constant feelings of guilt. Not for the first time, he wondered whether he should take Bren's suggestion that he see a mental health professional, like a psychologist or social worker. Someone independent to talk to. But he put that out of his mind as he reached the top of the stairs. Before going into the bedroom, he saw a light on down the hall in Brenda's sitting room, and walked there. He intended to peek in and reaffirm what a nice day they'd had, and expected to find a happy Brenda. What he found was his wife's beautiful facial features covered with smeared makeup, and freely falling tears, accompanied by quiet sobbing. She didn't look up, so she didn't see Ed slowly back out of the doorway, and pad silently to the bedroom.

Ed felt guilty as soon as he reached the bedroom. He knew he should have given a quiet knock, and consoled Brenda, but for the life of him he didn't know why she needed consoling. They'd had a perfect day together. What could be wrong? He justified his inaction by telling himself that he was doing her a favor by not intruding on her quiet moment. So, he shouldn't feel guilty, because he was doing the right thing. He'd just check in with her in the morning, to make sure she was okay. Maybe she'd just come out and tell him what was going on. That would save him a lot of trouble. Finding out the problem without having to admit he didn't know what the issue was. A good, sound plan. And even Edison knew, deep inside, that he'd just showed the worst kind of cowardice. He knew that before the troubles, he would have met the adversity head on. But he had little appetite for such things now. So, he said nothing about it to Brenda when she entered the bedroom. She'd washed up in the hall bathroom, so her tear-stained face had returned to normal.

They exchanged a few grunts, finished their evening ablutions, and went to bed.

***

Dave walked out of the Kelly's hardware store and almost bumped into the Mayor.

"Almost knocked you down there, Rufus. Bringing your royal Mayorness to Kelly's?"

"Funny man. No. I spotted you going in when I drove by in my Lincoln. So, I parked, because I wanted to talk to you."

Dave looked over at where the Mayor had parked. Right in front of a "No Parking at Any Time" sign. Classic Rufus. The law applied to everyone but him. The man had charm, though. Dave had to give him that. Dave sighed. It was never good if the Mayor took an interest in him. He might as well get it over with.

"What do you want to talk about?"

"You are friends with Edison Orwell, is that correct?"

Somehow, Dave felt like he was beginning his testimony in a courtroom, and the prosecutor had just asked him to admit commission of a heinous crime. Dave wanted to bolt, given the Mayor's sleazy demeanor, but resigned himself to just answering with the expected response of "Yes." He and Ed were friends. Dave waited for the other shoe to drop. It didn't take long.

"Your application for a variance to expand your business is still pending," he said. "It can go two ways. It can die, or we can approve it. Soon."

Dave laughed inside. He'd long since decided that expanding his business was a dumb idea, particularly so because of his semi-retired state. Maybe he wanted it five years ago, but they'd denied it so many times, he'd almost forgotten that Town policy resuscitated such applications every year, unless formally withdrawn. He'd just neglected to withdraw it. Now this yahoo wanted to use his burning desire for expansion to get… he knew the answer already, but he made the Mayor say it out loud. And he wished he'd had the foresight to turn on the recorder on his phone, but too late now. So, he braced for the Mayor's pitch.

"What about it, Rufus?"

"Oh, nothing. Just an observation. Just an observation. On another totally unrelated note, if Edison Orwell is your friend, convince him to withdraw from the race for the Town Board seat. You and I both know he doesn't have the temperament for such a position, and it would be a shame if a landslide loss humiliated your friend. I worry about his anger issues. He might react badly to a loss, and as Mayor, I need to guard against things like that."

Dave smiled at the Mayor. "And we all appreciate your benevolence toward us townspeople. We surely do. But you've met Edison. He's a hardheaded sort. He wouldn't listen to me if I told him to withdraw. I think you know that."

"That's a shame, a real shame," the Mayor said, and turned as if to walk back to his illegally parked car.

"I'm not done, Rufus."

The Mayor whirled around. "What?"

"I'd never ask him. I'm glad he's running, and I'm pretty sure we both think he'll win. And by the way, I don't give a shit about that variance application. You can tear it up and flush it into the sewer where you and your cronies live."

For the first time in a long while, the Mayor stood speechless as he watched Dave stomp off.

***

The next morning, Ed came downstairs and found Brenda sitting at the kitchen table. He grabbed a cup of coffee and sat down.

"Pleasant time yesterday," he offered tentatively.

Brenda, who'd been staring out into space, jolted, as if she hadn't seen Edison come into the room. She had, of course, but she intended to make Edison suffer today. He'd blown all the goodwill he'd engendered during the previous day by turning into a clumsy, oblivious, inconsiderate oaf after dinner. And the more she thought about it, the madder she became. He hadn't even initiated the walk. She had. He'd gone along only reluctantly, and that it had worked out well was more a reflection of him being a captive to her desire to spend quality time with him.

Her talk with Britney had made her even angrier today. Her distress last night was palpable, but Edison hadn't even noticed, much less inquired, what was wrong. And damn Britney. She'd hit the nail on the head. She'd been horny as hell last night and he left her completely unsatisfied. And an unwilling celibate since the troubles. Oh, they'd had a rare romp in the sack, but nothing like they once did. They'd mostly made love in the bedroom as they grew older. The floor, the coffee table and the couch were tough on the old bones, but now they'd stopped altogether. She couldn't take it much longer. She'd admitted to Britney that a couple of men had tempted her to cheat on Edison. A certain gentleman she'd met at the CC had shown obvious interest in her. And where she'd once shut down such amorous interest from men, she'd flirted right back. And she had a pretty good idea that if she gave the go-ahead... Brenda pushed the thought out of her mind. She wasn't a cheater. Either she stayed with Edison, or she didn't. And the temptation to accept the offer contained in that letter had grown exponentially. But it was time to confront Edison head on.

She looked up at him, and something in his demeanor caused her to pause. He knew something was wrong. And he hadn't the faintest idea what it was. The poor bastard was feeling her out, seeing if she'd reveal something to him.

She wondered whether he'd overheard her talking to her sister, but she could have sworn that she heard his footsteps after she completed that call. And suddenly she knew. He'd heard her crying. And he'd done nothing to console her, or to even find out what was wrong. He was worse than inconsiderate. He was a coward. An abject coward. Afraid to confront just a little adversity. And this man was running for the Town Board? If he was afraid to even talk to his wife, how could he possibly confront what those hostile, horrible men had in store for him?

Brenda decided on the spot that she didn't care about any of that. She cared about being married to someone who let her cry her heart out and didn't lift a finger to help. Ruling out an immediate confrontation, Brenda decided to proceed as if the two of them were through. Because, for all practical purposes, they were.

She looked at her watch. "Gotta run. Book club in a half-hour. I have plans after that, so I'll see you tonight. She got up and hurried out the door, leaving Edison with his mouth agape. She had no plans after the book club. But a certain Sam Williams had taken to attending the book club, and she had little doubt that plans could develop right after that.

Edison gazed at the departing form of his wife. She's angry with me, he thought. And was very upset last night. If only he knew why. He retraced his activities the previous day. They'd taken a walk and had a perfect day. Brenda seemed to agree with that. They'd gone to Thorsen's for dinner, and again, had an enjoyable time, at least until that asshole mayor had shown up. But they seemed to weather that okay, and had returned home. So far, so good. When they'd returned home, he'd said he wanted to call Kara to fill her in on the Mayor's interruption of their dinner. He'd obviously called too late, because Kara's responses were strained. And she kept asking whether he and Bren had any plans that evening, and he'd wondered… and Brenda had given him that warm embrace right before he called Kara… and oh, shit. And then he went upstairs, saw Bren crying and did nothing. Oh shit. He was a terrible louse, and an awful person. How could he be so stupid? Edison thought about whether he'd always been this tone-deaf and inconsiderate. And uninterested in sex. He didn't think so. Another gift from the troubles. He couldn't treat Brenda this way. Hell, he shouldn't treat anyone this way, much less the love of his life. He needed help. Professional help. He consulted the contact list on his phone and located the name he sought. Barnard Forstein, Ph.D. Bren had found Dr. Forstein for him, and had helpfully saved the office number on Edison's phone, but he'd refused to go. He hated psychologists. But he needed help so much that any reservations he had went right out the window. He didn't want to lose Brenda, and her leaving without talking about what had happened was a clear sign he was losing her. If he hadn't already. He picked up his phone and called Dr. Forstein's office and made an appointment. The doctor had an office in Meeker Falls, so Edison would either need a ride from someone, or take a taxi. He'd figure that out later.

26

When Brenda arrived at the CC for the book club she facilitated with Kara, she immediately noticed a tall, silver-haired man with a firm chin, slightly bushy eyebrows, a celestial nose, and dark brown eyes. As soon as he saw Bren, he flashed a toothy smile and perfect white teeth.

Bren's heart fluttered. For a moment, she felt like a schoolgirl in the presence of this handsome man. But she quickly recovered and returned his smile, and added a "Glad you could come today, Sam."

As other people filled the remaining seats around the table, Kara came in and sat in the seat Bren saved for her.

"I was running a little late this morning," she whispered.

She looked up. "Let's get started, everyone."

As they finished the session, Sam approached Brenda, ostensibly to talk more about the book they were all reading. Kara had to return to the library, and gave a slight wave as she departed. Everyone but Sam and Brenda filed out of the room. The door had springs on it, so it automatically closed, leaving the two of them alone.

In the past, Bren would have quickly exited the room without being rude, but continuing the conversation out in the lounge area of the CC. But not this time. Looking up at Sam to listen to what he was saying, she could see that he noticed she hadn't run away. He continued talking about the book, but placed a gentle hand on her shoulder. It was all Bren could do to stop herself from… she didn't know what. Sam's hand began moving, ever so slightly, and wandered down to her shoulder blades, continuing the soft caress while still speaking and pretending nothing was amiss. And Brenda couldn't stop him. Oh, she knew full well she could stop him by just asking him to stop, but she didn't want to. A kind, handsome man was paying physical attention to

her, and she wanted him to take her in his arms and kiss her, then un-
dress her right there in the conference room of the CC. She didn't care
if someone caught them, and cared less if anyone saw them. But Sam
had other ideas.

"Would you like to join me for lunch?" he asked.

"Yes," Brenda said in a breathy voice. Then she realized he had
invited her to dine with him, not make love with her a scant ten feet
away from dozens of people just outside the door.

"Great," he said. "I'm an excellent cook, or so I tell myself.
May I fix you lunch? Or would you rather go down the street to Bab's
Bistro? My treat."

Brenda looked up at his twinkling eyes, trying to read his moti-
vation. They revealed nothing, but only a fool could misunderstand the
difference between an invitation to a meal at a restaurant and one at a
man's house.

Brenda had a favorable opinion of Sam. She'd met him soon
after they'd moved. Many people in Standard knew and liked him. In
short, he was not a stranger, and Brenda figured she'd be safe in his
company. And she knew something else. If the meal turned amorous,
which she fully expected, she was all in.

"Please make me lunch at your house. Who could pass up a
home-cooked meal?"

"Excellent. Let's go."

They walked out of the CC and out to the parking lot, where
they boarded his Ford Explorer for the brief trip to the outskirts of
Standard. They pulled up in front of a cute, red painted ranch house
with black shutters, and a small porch in front. Sam dismounted and
walked around to the passenger side, where he helped Brenda out. She
almost missed a step, but Sam's muscular arms caught her, leaving
them a momentary half-embrace from which they quickly disentan-
gled. Brenda mumbled a soft "Thanks for catching me."

Sam offered his arm, and Bren took it as they walked toward a
side entrance to his home.

***

Edison went into the living room and sat down. Shifting to the left in his chair, then right, then back again gave him no comfort. Standing up and sitting back down didn't help, either. He touched his nose, then his cheek, then put his hand back down. Retrieving his reading glasses, Edison picked up his copy of *Field & Stream*, then adjusted his glasses. They seemed crooked to him, so he adjusted them again. Edison tried to look at the magazine, but it seemed more blurry than usual, so he put it down and picked up the TV remote. Flipping through the channels, Edison muttered about "10,000 channels and nothing good to watch," and turned the TV off. He sat there, staring into space, but only for a moment, before rising again and going to the kitchen to pour himself a glass of water, which he drank while standing in front of the sink. He stared out the kitchen window for a moment, then returned to his chair. Attempting again to read his magazine, Edison found it still blurry. He wondered if his eyes, so screwed up already from glaucoma, were getting worse. He decided they weren't, but it seemed hard to read, and he put the magazine down, and just sat there.

Edison knew full well what the problem was, and at least at that moment, it wasn't his eyes. He had that appointment with the head shrinker in two days, and he had to figure out a way to get there. His original idea of a taxi went up in smoke when he realized that he lived in a place where the only taxi was driven by a sole proprietor and sole employee, Zachary Ford. Zack was an octogenarian who purportedly drove taxis in New York City before retiring to the quiet greenery of Standard and operating a part-time taxi company. He also had the distinction of being the most notorious gossip in the county. If you rode with Zack, just be prepared to have the details of your ride disclosed to the entire town. And Ed surely didn't want his first visit to a psychologist to become common knowledge. At least not before the election. The election again. Ed was sick to death of the election. And he was sure it was the precipitating cause of tension between him and Brenda.

He was obsessed with it, and he feared the stupid local politics were driving the two of them apart.

The call he'd just received from Sheila Graves, a malicious petty gossip, didn't help his mood. She'd told him Brenda had left the CC with none other than Sam Williams. They'd gotten into Sam's SUV and motored off. Sheila speculated where they might have gone, but Edison just muttered, "Probably to the bookstore outside of town," and as politely as he could, hung up on her.

He doubted they went to the bookstore. He had a lot of horrible imaginings, mostly of the two of them entwined in a steamy bedroom scene. Edison tried to put it out of his mind. He trusted Brenda, didn't he? She was an honest and direct person and would never have an affair. Brenda wouldn't cheat. She'd leave him first. Ed sighed. What was she doing? Leaving with a man from a public place like the CC. She had to know its effect on the very active town gossip mill. Sheila would tell everyone, and within a matter of hours, the news would be common knowledge. And it might start out innocently, like a trip to the bookstore to pick out a new book club selection, but the story would morph into the most scandalous affair since King Edward VIII abdicated the throne to marry Wallis Simpson. Okay, maybe not that dramatic, but it was going to be embarrassing to Edison. And what about his chances at being elected to the Town Board? People would hold it against him, he knew it. Brenda's unthinking action might have just cost him the election.

Edison put his head in his hands. Oh shit, he thought. There he went again, thinking only of himself and the stupid election.

Brenda was the most important force in his life. She'd been there for him after the troubles began, and had stayed with him, supported him, and even uprooted her life to move to a place where he wouldn't have daily reminders of the horror he'd wrought. He'd visited sheer hell upon Brenda, and she'd not only endured it, she'd provided unselfish emotional support. For what? To be treated like crap by the beneficiary of her kindness. Ed felt awful. And he was even more ashamed. He reveled in feeling awful. Somehow, feeling bad for doing bad things was a comfort to him.

But he had to change. And he knew he couldn't do it alone. He hoped he hadn't already lost Brenda. He hoped she'd see his long-resisted appointment with a psychologist as a positive step. And he resolved to have a real discussion with her when she returned. If he'd already lost her, he'd do whatever it took to win her back. But he hoped, oh how he hoped, that she wouldn't leave him.

***

Brenda entered Sam's home and complimented him on how well-decorated it was. She ran her hand down the sleek quartz kitchen countertops, and gleaming stainless appliances. Wandering into the living room, she admired his tasteful arrangement of furniture and beautiful window treatments. It almost looked like it had a woman's touch, Brenda observed, and Sam laughed.

"It did. Darcy Quinlan."

At Brenda's blank stare, he added, "She's a decorator based in Meeker Falls. She designed the whole place."

"Oh. She did a good job."

"Thank you. I will convey that to her next time we see each other."

"Do you see her often?" Brenda ventured.

Sam chuckled. "Occasionally. But maybe not the way you think. She's 32 years old, and married."

It occurred to Brenda that she was married, too, but she said nothing. This nice, cheerful man was such a positive change for Brenda that more than ever, she wanted him to take her in his powerful arms and… what was she thinking? Okay, she knew exactly what she was thinking. Was she willing to take that step?

If Sam was thinking the same thing, he didn't show it.

"The cooking, however, is entirely mine."

Brenda jolted back to reality. "What are you fixing?"

"I thought a nice Chicken Piccata, roasted vegetables, and lemon garlic rice." He paused. "You're okay with garlic?"

Brenda assured him she loved it, and commented on how great it sounded.

"Great, I'll get to it, then. Would you like a glass of white wine while you wait?"

Brenda agreed readily. She wanted to fortify herself. Because she had every intention of letting this go as far as Sam wanted. The man was actually cooking for her. If she kept her nerve, she intended to make it worth his while.

Sam poured her a glass of white wine, and she sat down on the living room couch. She sipped her wine while Sam busily attended to their fancy lunch.

As it was an open floor plan, the two of them could carry on a conversation while Sam attended to preparing their meal.

"It's nice to have someone to cook for," he said.

"I believe you told me you were married once."

"Yes. Barbara. The love of my life. She passed away about ten years ago. Cancer."

"Oh, I'm sorry. That must be hard for you."

"It was. Not so much anymore. I was a mess for years. I owe my life to Dr. Newsom."

"He's…"

"She. A therapist. Clinical psychologist in Albany, where Barbara and I lived for thirty years."

"Do you still see her? If you don't mind my asking."

"I don't mind. Nothing to be ashamed of. Yes. About every six months, now. Back then, it was weekly."

Brenda almost said that she wished Edison would see a therapist, but stopped herself. She had no intention of mentioning him at all. Sam didn't seem to mind her being married, so she would not raise it.

"Good for you. Asking for help can be hard."

"Not so hard if it's life or death," Sam said.

"That serious."

"Yup." Sam looked at her. "I hope that doesn't diminish me in your eyes."

"Not at all," Brenda said. "I admire it."

She didn't say, "and it makes me want you even more."

"Enough about that. Let's talk about the book we're reading." He chatted on about the book, about literature, about music, about all kinds of things that Brenda used to talk about with Edison, but he'd shut down so much. She felt compassion for Edison. She loved him, too. And he'd suffered a terrible shock, one that she acknowledged would be hard to get over. But he'd caused it himself. This man had also suffered a terrible loss, but not one of his making. Unlike Edison, he'd worked to get better. Edison just turned it all inward, figuratively curling up in a fetal position on everything that truly mattered.

Brenda wanted Sam to stop cooking and come sit next to her on the couch. Once they finished the meal he was busily preparing, she expected him to move close to her. She clandestinely unbuttoned one button on her blouse, which Sam was sure to see when they sat down to lunch. She fidgeted on the sofa, and glanced at her wineglass, which she'd nervously drained.

"All ready," Sam announced, and Brenda sat upright. She was ready. Very ready. But they had to eat lunch first. That seemed to be the plan.

27

"The debate is the day after tomorrow. Are you ready?"

Edison couldn't concentrate on Stan's question. The phone call from that busybody had unnerved him. He could only think of Brenda and Sam together. He had paced in the house and couldn't sit still. When his phone chirped, he'd looked anxiously at the caller ID, hoping against hope that Brenda was calling him. He hadn't heard a word from her since that morning at breakfast, and all he could think of was that she'd left him for good, and that the next call he'd get was that she wanted to pick up her things to move them to Sam's house.

He didn't give a shit about the election, Stan, Kara, or anyone else. He knew he'd been a dope, and that he'd thought only of himself for so long, he'd forgotten that Brenda had feelings, too. And that she had needs that he hadn't satisfied… needs that that jerk Sam was satisfying at that moment. Edison had hated himself ever since the troubles, but he never understood until that moment that he had covered Brenda with his self-loathing, and that she'd likely tired of it. Of him. And he knew he hadn't done a thing to get over it. He'd refused to go to a psychologist. Refused to get help. It was a theme with him, he reflected. He'd also refused to get help for his deteriorating eyesight, telling Brenda he was just fine. And look how that had worked out. He hadn't learned a thing. He'd just retreated into himself, kidding himself with all these distractions. Like the election. Well, he'd deal with that right now.

"I'm withdrawing from the election," he told Stan.

"You're what? No, you're not. Many people are depending on you. You can't pull out now."

"I've decided," Edison told him. "It's no use trying to change my mind."

"What has gotten into you? Please, don't tell anyone yet. Think about it."

Ed sighed. "I have thought about it. I keep telling you. No harm taking a little more time to consider it, but I doubt it will change anything."

"I'll call you later," Stan said.

***

Brenda walked out of Sam's house. He'd offered to drive her home, but she'd declined, saying she enjoyed walking, and it wasn't very far from home. Sam lived on the outskirts of Standard, but the weather was pleasant, and the distance was not far. Besides, she needed to think about what had just happened.

She glanced at her watch. A beautiful, gold Cartier, with a single diamond, that Edison had given her for her fiftieth birthday, and which, fancy or not, she wore every day, even in the decidedly less formal town of Standard. She fingered it gently and noted the time. 3:15. She wondered what she'd say to Edison when she returned home. Would she tell him the truth? At the very least, she owed him that. And not because he'd once given her fancy presents. Because… she loved him. She still loved him. She wished he'd never caused her such… loss. Loss of her home, her old friends, her identity and status as an esteemed university professor. And loss of her true love. Because Edison was sure as hell not the same man she'd married and lived with for so many mostly happy years.

Brenda glanced back at the house she'd just left, and saw Sam watching her through his kitchen window. He waved, and she waved back, then strode purposefully away, down his driveway to the little cul-de-sac, and out to the main road, where she strolled slowly towards home.

***

Edison continued to pace around the house. When would she get home? And what would he say to her? Continuing to shuffle around, he went upstairs, then came back downstairs and into the kitchen and looked out the window. Returning to the living room, Edison sat down again. Picking up a magazine, he stared at it without actually reading the words, sighed, and put the magazine down again. He stared into space for a while, then stood up and went to the door. Opening it, he stepped out and gazed at the driveway, where their car still sat motionless. Realizing he'd left his phone inside, Edison momentarily panicked. What if Brenda had called in the few moments he was outside? He rushed back in and looked at his phone. No message. He sat back down and heard a sound at the side door. Brenda. Finally home. Ed panicked all over again. He hadn't figured out what to say to her. Was he angry? Hurt? Did he have any reason for either? He didn't know. All he knew was that Brenda had left the CC with a man from her book club.

No time to create a strategy. And what was he thinking? Create a strategy to say hello to his wife? What had happened to him? He trusted Brenda, didn't he? And if he didn't anymore … that was truly awful.

"Hi honey, I'm home."

"I'm in here," Ed said, then considered whether that sounded normal. He hoped so. He decided not to cross-examine her on what she'd done all afternoon. If she raised it, well, he'd just have to deal with it.

Brenda came into the living room, and they shared an awkward kiss and hug.

"I'm sorry I'm so late," Brenda said, hoping that she sounded normal. She had thought all the way home about how she would handle this, and decided she'd approach it head on, if Edison asked questions. If he didn't, well, she might just keep the afternoon's events to herself.

After the obvious tension in the room became apparent to both of them, their separately planned silence devolved into simultaneous blurted confessions.

"I made an appointment with the psychologist today."

"I spent the afternoon with Sam Williams. At his house."

"What?"

"What?"

Brenda spoke first. "I'll tell you everything, I promise. But tell me what changed your mind about… you called Dr. Forstein? Or someone else?"

"I have an appointment with Dr. Forstein the day after tomorrow. I was hoping you'd give me a ride, but I can take a taxi, if you can't, or don't want to drive me."

"Of course, I'll drive you. But why the change of heart?"

Ed looked at Brenda for a long moment. "You did," he said. He wanted desperately to reach for her hand. He wanted to feel her warmth in his palm, but he resisted. They both had stories to tell, and he needed to get through his part first. Then, he shuddered, endure her part.

Edison continued. "I mean the thought of losing you. I knew already that you left the CC in Sam's car. That busybody, Sheila Graves, called to tell me. I don't know whether the two of you… and it's not like we've… and I've been such a shit… I almost couldn't blame you if… but I hope you didn't… and I want to be a better, more loving husband."

Brenda listened to Edison pour his heart out, and she felt shame. Profoundly ashamed of her thoughts, but elated that she meant so much to Edison that he'd taken an affirmative step to fix what was wrong between them. Until that moment, she hadn't been sure. And she was relieved. Ashamed at what she'd done, but relieved at what she hadn't done.

"Nothing happened," she said, and observed Edison's relieved face. "But Eddie, I'm so sorry, but I wanted it to happen. I led Sam on, and I gave him every sign that I would have sex with him at his house this afternoon. I even unbuttoned a button on my blouse."

Brenda watched Edison's face fall, and she hastened to tell him the rest. "And he was willing. But after we had lunch, I lost my nerve. Lost my lust, too. I went to the bathroom, re-buttoned my blouse, thanked him for the lovely lunch, and skedaddled out of there."

"He drove you home?"

"No. He offered, but I told him I enjoyed walking. And I needed to think. I wasn't sure I was even going to tell you this, but we tell each other everything."

"I'm going to punch that creep in the mouth. You know I will."

"Please don't. For me, Eddie, please don't. I was as much to blame, maybe more so, than him."

Edison muttered something about only a creep would try to sleep with another guy's wife, but he stopped. He and Brenda had some serious talking to do. And if she wanted him not to punch Sam, he wouldn't. He'd find some other way to get even. But he didn't tell Brenda that. They needed to talk.

"I haven't exactly been the most amorous of souls lately, have I?"

"That's putting it mildly. Since the troubles, I don't think we've made love at all."

Ed hadn't realized it was that long, and he said so, but Brenda set him straight.

"And you've remained…"

"Celibate. And I'm not in the priesthood."

"No, you're not. That must have been…"

"Quite a hardship. But I love you, and kept hoping you'd come around. I never came as close to cheating on you as I did today. And

Eddie, I have to tell you, I decided today to not cheat, but I was fully prepared to leave you."

Ed's voice cracked. He couldn't help it. "Are you still...?"

Brenda didn't answer directly, and she hadn't told him about the letter yet. "Let's see what happens," she said. Brenda was terrified that Edison had made one appointment. That was a start, but only a start.

They talked for a long time after that. Brenda still didn't tell him about the letter. She wasn't sure why, but they talked about whether to stay in Standard or maybe move back to New Jersey. Ed told her he was pulling out of the race for Town Board, and she told him not to. If he won, and they decided to move away, he could get the library issue resolved, then simply resign, and let Cyrus and his cronies ruin the town all they wanted.

They threw together a makeshift dinner, then repaired to the living room as usual. But this time, Edison took her by the hand and invited her upstairs.

Brenda, who had several years of pent-up horniness, dragged Edison over to the couch, and they pulled each other's clothes off and made love right there.

28

The next morning, they lingered over breakfast.

"That was nice," Edison ventured.

"Mmm. Very. I missed you, honey."

Ed started to say he was sorry, but Bren reached over and put a finger over his mouth.

"Enough."

Edison got the message. More positivity. He had something to talk to Dr. Forstein about.

"You won't have to think of subjects to talk about, honey," Brenda said when Edison shared his thought. "You'll have plenty."

Edison knew she was right. But he was truly terrified to talk about the actual issue. What they called "the troubles," and his recurring nightmare. Which he hadn't had last night, come to think of it. And then he remembered.

"Oh shit," he said.

"What is it?"

"My appointment with Dr. Forstein."

Brenda got nervous. Was he backing out already? "What about it?" she asked casually.

"It's the same date as the debate." He fished out his phone. "I'll call Stan right now and tell him I'm pulling out of the race. No way I'm missing my appointment with Dr. Forstein. Cyrus can have the stupid Board seat."

Brenda reached over and pulled his arm down. "You can do both, honey. It's still forty-eight hours before your appointment. Let's see if you can push it back a day."

Ed hadn't thought of that. The truth was, he'd had enough of town politics already, and he was sure it was a strain on his marriage. But he reluctantly agreed, called the office and they gave him a fortuitously canceled appointment slot a day later. So he could do both. And it thrilled Brenda at which appointment he'd sought to cancel.

"Do you have any plans today?" Ed asked nervously. He didn't even know how to act around… the woman with whom he'd spent most of his life. He had no desire to monitor her activities, but she'd scared him. Brenda had made it crystal clear that the only reason she'd not consummated sexual relations with that guy … with Sam… was that she didn't want to cheat on her husband. He swallowed. But she could still leave him. Implicit in that sentiment was if he didn't shape up. And just a single night of long-overdue lovemaking, and making an appointment with a psychologist, wouldn't change much.

Brenda looked at him sadly. He's trying so hard, she thought. Over hard. He's not himself. She mentally corrected herself. He hadn't been himself for years. She'd scared him, and now he was overcompensating.

"Just a few errands, honey. I thought I'd do a little food shopping, then maybe lunch with Alyssa. She called me a few days ago and suggested we get together."

"Oh, okay. I thought maybe you'd like to take a walk today."

"Oh, okay. How about this afternoon? Study this morning. The debate is tomorrow, and you don't want to look unprepared."

Ed almost said how little he cared about the fucking debate, but he kept his mouth shut. Errands and lunch with Alyssa didn't sound like a pretext for seeing Sam, so he just nodded, and mumbled agreement that he'd look over his notes for the debate and see her later. He wondered, however, why she seemed to push him into preparing for the debate and the election, when all that trouble with her erupted after he'd spoiled their romantic day with a call to Kara. He decided it was just a timing issue and shrugged it off.

Brenda departed, this time taking the car, and Ed retrieved his notes and sat down at the kitchen table.

Almost immediately, he realized he had no pen or highlighter to use for margin comments and to identify parts he wished to emphasize, a process honed in a long history of making presentations when he was still working. He glanced over at the open cupboard, where Brenda kept a decorated cup containing assorted items such as scissors, pens and pencils, a little penlight, and even a pink highlighter. He rose and walked around the table in the cupboard's direction, and immediately tripped over Brenda's chair, crashing into the cupboard. The cup fell to the floor, spilling its contents. Several cookbooks also tumbled out. Ed cursed, and felt his bruised side, then bent over to pick up the mess he'd made.

He righted the cup, and redeposited the pens and pencils and other items, and placed the cup back on the shelf. Then he stooped to pick up the cookbooks, and when he did, a long business envelope dropped to the floor. He picked it up and looked at the return address. It bore the legend of the university where Brenda had served as a professor before they moved to Standard. The postmark was dated almost a month before. Ed stared at the envelope for a few moments, then put the cookbooks back on the shelf, took a pen and the highlighter from the cup, and sat down at the table with both his notes and the envelope in front of him.

He wished the contents had fallen out when the envelope hit the ground so that he could truthfully say that he couldn't help but see what the sender had written. No such luck. He had three choices. He could open it up and read the contents of a letter Brenda obviously wanted to keep from him, or he could show how much he trusted her by leaving it on the table, telling her how it fell out, and that he hadn't looked at it. The third option was to put it back in its hiding place and pretend it had never fallen out. He decided that curiosity or not, that

was the best choice, then immediately changed his mind. How could
he be sure he put it back in the right book? And it might not have been
in either book, just wedged between them. Ed hung his head in despair.
Why was he trying so hard to figure out ways to deceive her? But he
was dying to know what was in the letter. And the only way he'd know
was to read it, or have Brenda show it to him. And if he put it back, she
might never show him. He had only one choice, and he knew it. He
left the unread letter on the table in plain sight and hoped it wouldn't
drive him crazy until Brenda returned home — and that she'd tell him
what was in it when she did.

He turned his attention to preparing for the debate. He looked
over his notes, made a few adjustments, highlighted (in pink) a few
things, and then glanced every two seconds at the letter. They'd had a
long talk yesterday, and a congenial breakfast. He'd heard from
Brenda how she missed her friends and the environs of their former
home in New Jersey, and had even agreed to think about whether Standard or New Jersey was in their long-term future. They'd talked about
love and intimacy, and many other things, but not once had Brenda
told him about the letter sitting right in front of him. So he wondered
what else she was withholding? They obviously needed much more
than a single long talk.

Ed sighed and returned to his debate notes. After a while, he
decided he was as prepared as possible, and figured Cyrus was a dope,
anyway. Debating him would be like Muhammed Ali boxing… Sam.
Relishing that delicious thought for a moment, Edison pushed the
whole thing out of his mind. He left his notes and the letter on the table
and wandered into the living room and sat down in his easy chair and
picked up a magazine. He stared at that for a while, then got back up
and walked outside, headed… nowhere in particular. His feet took him
in the CC's direction, but he didn't want to go in, so he skirted that
street and walked toward the park. Eschewing his nemesis, the park
bench, he walked right into the park, where he spied some adolescent
boys tossing a football. One boy missed the throw, and it bounced off

his shoulder in Ed's direction. He smiled at the lad, picked up the football and threw a pretty good spiral the short distance. The boy caught it and thanked him, then turned back and tossed it to his friend. Ed congratulated himself that he still "had it," then felt his arm. He still "had it," all right. A sharp pain emanating from his rotator cuff. Sighing, he continued walking to the opposite edge of the park, then turned back toward home. He hoped Brenda would return soon. If they were going to fight, he wanted to get it over with. If they were going to have a long, honest talk, leaving nothing out, he wanted to start it as soon as possible.

Brenda, in fact, had gone shopping and had lunch with Alyssa. She didn't call Sam, and had no intention of doing so. She did, however, dread running into him, or inevitably seeing him at the next book club meeting. Not because seeing him would tempt her, because she knew it would, but because she wanted to see if Ed could return to his former self. And that would be the most attractive and appealing result for her. Thoughts of Sam would whoosh right out of her like air flowing out of a popped balloon. She didn't just want sex, she wanted love and attention. Ed's love and attention, sexual and otherwise.

Those thoughts filled her mind as she pulled into her driveway, exited the car, and retrieved the groceries from the trunk. She carried the two bags into the house, and it pleased her that Ed hurried out to help her carry them. She didn't need the help, but the effort was sweet, and she told him so. They walked together into the kitchen and dropped the groceries on the counter.

Brenda went to the bathroom, then returned and retrieved some ice from the freezer, then poured a glass of water and sat down at the table. And saw the letter sitting right in front of her. She looked up at Edison and just waited for an explanation. Of course, they both had something to explain. Edison started anyway.

"I didn't open it," he began. "I saw the return address, but I left it on the table without looking inside."

"How did you find it? Were you snooping?"

Ed felt a little annoyed by the comment. He hadn't been snooping. Snooping how? The letter was in a bookcase in the kitchen. It's not like it was in a hiding place, or in Brenda's underwear drawer. But he kept his mouth shut about that, which was the best thing to do. Instead of getting defensive, he just told the truth. He'd tripped over a chair and crashed into the cupboard, and two books fell out and the letter fluttered to the floor.

Brenda seemed satisfied with that explanation, and even noted that she hadn't exactly hidden it, so the snooping remark was unfair. But she didn't believe he hadn't read it. If the tables were turned, she would have. Maybe.

"And you didn't read it?"

"Nope. Didn't open it. If you wanted to share it with me, you would have."

This put Brenda squarely on the spot, and she knew it. Ed knew it, too. He stopped pretending he was so honorable, and let her off the hook.

"I wanted to open it. Truthfully, I almost did. Weighed the different ways I could do so without you knowing. Considered putting it back and pretending I'd never found it, but was afraid I'd put it back in the wrong book. I thought of reading it, and pretending I didn't. Nothing seemed like a better choice than to leave it in plain sight, explain what happened and leave it to you to decide what to do next."

Brenda laughed. "So you reluctantly decided the truth was the best option?"

Ed hung his head. "That's about the size of it."

"Don't feel bad, honey. It's me who owes you an apology. I deliberately kept this from you, even after our long, supposedly honest talk yesterday."

She pushed the letter toward him. "Open it and read it. I want you to. No more secrets."

Ed opened the envelope, unfolded the letter, and read it. He remained silent as he did so, then looked up at Brenda, who was eyeing him with obvious anxiety.

"Are you upset?" she asked.

Ed paused. He needed a moment to process what the letter meant. To him, to Brenda. To both of them.

"You're upset. I wish I'd just shredded that thing and you'd never found it." She put her head in her hands, but Ed slid his chair next to her and put his arm around her shoulders.

"I'm not upset. It's okay, honey. It's wonderful, really. That the university wants and values you so much, they'd make you such a terrific offer. You gave up so much leaving New Jersey. Your home, your friends, and the great respect you had every day as a distinguished professor. And by the way, a job you loved. I want you to take the job. Let's return to New Jersey."

Brenda looked at Edison in amazement. That was exactly what she wanted. But that was the rub. It wasn't what Edison wanted. Or even what was good for him. He'd made a life for himself in Standard. He was the architect of the CC and was even running for the Town Board. And it wasn't like she didn't have a life or friends here. She surely did. But no professorship, and as much as she had wanted to make it so, it wasn't home.

She turned and kissed him. "Thank you, honey. I know you're serious, and I can't tell you how much I appreciate the support. And I have been pining to return to New Jersey. I won't deny it. And this offer is amazing."

"So take it. We'll move back."

Brenda put a finger on his lips.

"Let's talk about it first. I think I can get them to extend the offer for at least a month. That will give us time to figure out what we really want. As a couple."

Ed liked the sound of "doing things as a couple." The last thing he wanted was to separate from Brenda. Not with physical distance, or emotional either.

"I'd have to go through with the election," he said morosely. "It's too late to find another candidate. I still think the best thing is to back out. That takes away any sense of obligation to stay here."

"By simply not fulfilling it. No, that's not you. Or either one of us. Do the debate, finish the election, win it, and do a few good things for the community. In the meantime, we can figure this thing out, and take steps to prepare if we decide to move away. Does that work for you, honey?"

Ed nodded. "The debate is tomorrow, and the election is a week after that. If they'll give you a month, it will give me three weeks on the Town Board to take care of the library issue. After that, I won't feel any obligation."

"Except maybe to the people who voted for you," she said dryly, but Edison seemed not to hear her. Or pretended not to.

29

"No, no, no. Stop! Can't you see the train coming? Oh my God, she's going right on the tracks. Either she can't see, or can't hear, or is just oblivious. Oh, my God, the train is coming fast. It will never stop in time, if it can stop at all. Oh, God, it's so close. I have to get there. I have to stop her, get her to safety. The seat belt won't budge. Something's holding me back. Oh, my God, why can't I move? I'm going to be too late. It's coming so fast, and I can't move. Oh, God, I can't help her. That locomotive is going to… oh God, why can't I move? I can't stop that train, and I can't stop that little girl. Oh God, please save that little girl, please, please… I'm just shaking, shaking, I'm not doing anything…."

"Wake up, honey. Wake up. You're okay. You're right here in bed with me. Nothing's happening. You're okay."

"But she's…"

"No one is here but us, honey. You're at home. You were having a nightmare."

"It was so real." Edison paused and tried to collect himself, but he was shivering, and couldn't stop. Sweat poured down his forehead and temples. He used his pajama sleeve to wipe it off, but as soon as he did, it came back.

Brenda looked at him, and gently stroked his arm, then glanced at the clock. It was 2:20 a.m.

"Why don't you get up and walk around a bit. Maybe get a glass of water, use the toilet, and wash your face. Try to get it out of your mind, so you can get some sleep. Big debate, tomorrow. Er, today."

Ed nodded and struggled out of bed and just stood there. His quivering had abated somewhat, and he felt a little better. He tried to think of something other than his nightmare, or the debate. Something, anything to distract him so he could sleep.

"Do you want me to get up with you for a spell, honey?"

"What?" Ed hadn't realized he was still standing next to the bed. "No, thank you. At least one of us should get some sleep. I'll wander around for a little while. Try to think of sports, nature, gardening… anything." He shuffled out of the bedroom and made a stop at the hall bathroom, where he washed his face and urinated. That done, he washed his hands, dried them on a hand towel that had tiny red flowers embossed on its side. He hadn't remembered them. Must be new, he mused. He wandered out of the bathroom and went downstairs, where he considered, then rejected, the idea of turning on the television. He paused in front of it, and rued the twenty-four-hour nature of modern television, remembering with fondness the days when television broadcasts ended at a decent hour, with the playing of the Star-Spangled Banner, and the static image of some arcane symbol. Of course, those were the days of vertical hold, and the even more bizarre horizontal hold, which more or less required you to turn yourself into a pretzel, twisting buttons on both the front and back of the black and white television, while trying to adjust the antennae to just the right angle so you could see programming on one of the seven, if you were lucky, channels that were available. Which you had to select using a dial on the TV. No remote control, no sir. Dial phones with short cords, and oh crap, what the hell am I doing? Reminiscing about… that? He needed to get a grip. And for the first time, he thought… maybe that psychologist could help him. Because he needed help, big time.

Mission to distract himself accomplished, Edison plodded upstairs, and, trying hard not to wake Brenda, slid into bed, and mercifully, fell asleep.

He awoke to the sound of an alarm blaring, and he tried to ignore it, sliding the covers over his head, and burying his face in the pillow. It was no use. The alarm was one of those that starts out soft, then gets louder and louder, until it literally annoys you out of bed. He reached over and tried to slam his hand on the snooze button, but missed, and hit the base of his palm on the nightstand.

"Shit," he said into the pillow. "Shit. That hurt."

He sighed, pushed back the covers and put a single foot on the floor, followed by the other foot, propping him up into a sitting position on the side of the bed, in which he was the only occupant. Brenda was an early riser. A glance at the clock revealed the time: 7:30. Although he didn't feel great, Edison was happy he'd slept at all. He got up and stretched his hands over his head, and twisted his body to one side and then the other, getting the kinks out. He went into the master bathroom, and washed his face and brushed his teeth, but remained in his pajamas as he plodded downstairs. Brenda took one look at his face and pointed to the coffeepot.

"Good morning. The coffee's a little old, but I think it's still okay. I'll brew a fresh pot for your second cup."

Ed nodded his thanks, poured a cup, and sat down.

"Rough night," she commented. It was a statement, not a question.

"Yeah. I wandered around for a while, then I guess I fell asleep."

"You were sound asleep when I got up. I figured I'd let you sleep until the alarm, even though you have the debate today. I was glad you got a little rest."

"Thank you." He didn't say that they both might be better off if he'd just overslept and missed the debate. Because his heart was sure not in verbally wrestling with that cretin, at least not at that moment.

"Finish your coffee, and I'll get a little breakfast ready while you shower and shave. We have to be there at 10:30."

"The debate is at 11:30," Ed pointed out.

"Yes, that's when it starts. And that's when spectators like me have to be there. Debaters report an hour before."

"How do you know… Kara."

Brenda smiled. "She called me this morning, and I promised to drive you there to make sure you showed up."

"She was worried I wouldn't show up?"

"She said Stan was nearly apoplectic. Seems you've telegraphed a recent lack of enthusiasm."

"I'm ambivalent. But I'll do my duty to God and country and the bucolic little town of Standard, New York."

"Keep up the humor. You'll need a fair dose of it to deal with the likes of Cyrus Boone and his merry band of awful cronies."

Ed chuckled. "I'm not the only jokester today," he observed. He took a last gulp of coffee, placed his mug on the table, rose and headed upstairs to primp and preen for the Great Debate.

***

Brenda dropped Edison off on time for the debate and assured him she'd be in the front row of the audience. Before he got out of the car, he turned to her and inquired if she had any last-minute advice.

"Just be yourself, honey."

Ed nodded and opened the car door, and Brenda added a final caution.

"But not too much."

Ed did a double-take to see if she was kidding and saw only a faint smile.

"Be yourself, but not too much," he whispered to himself, then hastily looked around to see if anyone was nearby who might have heard him. He saw no one, and entered the building, where various people bustled around, transforming the public hearing room in the Town Hall into a debate stage.

He didn't see Cyrus or the Mayor, but he saw Mrs. Titus, sitting quietly in a corner, reading something in a leather-bound folio.

Ed studied her for a moment. She was sitting, but Ed could see that she was a tall, big-boned woman. She had gray hair, and if he didn't know better, he'd have guessed her age at about seventy. He could see clear, sapphire blue eyes under her wire-rimmed reading glasses. Ed shivered involuntarily. A formidable woman, and not one prone to tolerating fake charm or bullshit. Ed mentally discarded his planned reference to Town Board Members' choices as akin to navigating between Scylla and Charybdis. She'd see in a moment that he was being too clever by half, and kowtowing to her to get better treatment. And he could see just by a glance that sucking up was a terrible idea.

He thought about going over and introducing himself, but as she seemed engrossed in her notes, he'd best leave her undisturbed.

Instead, he asked an official-looking person where she wanted him to go, and she directed him to a small room at the side of the main hall. None other than Edison's campaign manager, Stan Cornish, occupied the room. He sat at a conference table, looking at some notes.

Spotting Edison, he rose and extended his hand. They shook and sat down. Stan explained the layout and ground rules, asked him if he felt ready, and nodded approvingly when Edison answered in the affirmative.

"Don't let Cyrus get under your skin," he warned. "He'll try, for sure, but just smile at him, and keep your composure. And stick to the facts, no insults. Mrs. Titus will shut that down in a second, and she won't be happy. No interruptions, either. Even if Cyrus says something horrible about you, do not interrupt. Take a page from Ronald Reagan, and say something like, 'there you go again,' and flash a sunny smile, and debunk it. If you can manage contradicting him cheerfully, all the better, but please don't go into one of your rants. This is not the time or place for it, okay?"

"Do you think many people will show up for this thing?"

Stan stared at him. "Are you kidding? Everyone in town will be here. There will be so much overflow they set up a separate room with a television monitor to insure enough room for everyone to see and hear what's going on. This has never happened before, it's both a curiosity and the social event of the season, maybe the decade."

"Brenda said she'd be in the front row. Given the crowds, do you think she'll be able to do that?"

Stan got up and opened the door a crack, then returned with a smile on his face.

"She's already there. Sitting right next to Kara. Early arrivals."

Ed was relieved. He wasn't a public speaker. He'd done small presentations, but this was different. Having a friendly face in the front row helped calm his nerves.

"From what I understand, Cyrus has ticked off many people in this town. Do you think he'll have much support in the crowd?"

"Oh, he'll have support. Loud, vocal support. Don't worry about that, just stick to the program. Answer the questions, listen with at least the appearance of interest in Cyrus' answers, stay calm and don't worry."

"Brenda told me to be myself, but not too much."

Stan laughed. "Good advice. You're a nice guy, Ed. Let people see that."

Ed shuffled in this chair. "Let's get on with it."

30

Stan looked at his watch. "I have to take my seat. Someone will be here momentarily to get you."

Edison sat by himself. He crossed his legs and
leaned back, then sat up straight, with his feet planted on the floor.
Wondering if he had donned his glasses unevenly, he adjusted them.
He was nervous, but consoled himself with a self-reminder that he was
smarter than Cyrus, and more refined. Cyrus would lose points for every scabrous word that came out of his mouth. He was unappealing,
both visually and with every spoken word. And he bore the scars of his
well-known corruption. Cyrus was the epitome of and the tool of an
undemocratic electoral system. This fired Edison up and he was ready
to go. When the organizer called him, he strode out to the debate stage
to loud applause and cheers. He smiled at the crowd and stood at his
designated podium. Facing him at a small table was Mrs. Titus, who
sat with her back to the audience.

His warm reception pleased Ed, and he turned to watch Cyrus
enter.

Cyrus waddled out of the room on the other side of the hall and
received loud applause and raucous cheers. His reception was much
louder than Ed's, but Ed reasoned it was only because his supporters
were louder.

Mrs. Titus remained seated while the two men took their
places. But before she could say anything, Cyrus walked over to Ed's
side with his hand extended, taking Edison by surprise.

But he recovered quickly and took Cyrus' ham-like mitt in his own and they shook. Cyrus closed his hand in an iron grip, but Ed expected this, and vowed not to show a scintilla of pain but to plaster a fake smile on his face.

Cyrus returned to his podium, and they both waited for Mrs. Titus to speak.

The venerable woman cleared her throat and introduced herself. She laid out the ground rules, and emphasized that she wanted a clean, fair debate. No interruptions, no personal attacks. She said she understood that emotions always ran high in these types of competitive events, but she would not countenance any departure from decorum. When she asked them whether they understood the rules and the admonition, they both answered in the affirmative.

"So stand up straight, Mr. Boone."

His reaction was automatic. He assumed a better posture.

Ed's glee was short-lived.

"You too, Mr. Orwell."

Ed straightened up, and tried not to show his chagrin.

"Opening statements, gentlemen. By random drawing, you speak first, Mr. Orwell."

Ed started. "Thank you, Mrs. Titus, and the organizers of this event, who have worked tirelessly to set up this great forum for the exchange of views in a truly democratic way. And thank you to the audience, the good people of Standard, who have come here today to take part in a great process." Ed turned to Cyrus. "And thank you, Mr. Boone, for your participation."

"I stand here before you to ask for your vote on Election Day. Immediately upon moving here, the people of Standard universally welcomed my wife, Brenda, and me. Folks made us feel like we were part of something special, the close-knit, small town life where we all help each other. We laugh together, smile together, and weep together. That's the life we chose. And I'm truly happy to give back, and to take part in the first actual election for a Town Board seat. To be part of the destruction of an undemocratic patronage system of choosing members of such an important body as the Town Board is both my privilege and my pleasure, and I take great pride in my small role in restoring our cherished right to vote for the people who run our town. The choice of whom to vote for is not as important as your right to make such a choice. Thank you."

"Hi everyone," Cyrus began, to cheers and waves from the audience. "Good morning, Mrs. Titus."

"Those were some fancy words from my esteemed opponent. Words that contained no vision for this town, which is not surprising, because he's not from here. He's a visitor. He hasn't toiled in the tough jobs all board members before have fulfilled prior to becoming honored members of our Town Board. Our cherished tradition…" he turned to look at Edison… "at least before now, mandated unglamorous service to our community, to give valuable experience in meeting the challenges facing this town — things like my particular area of expertise — zoning. The Town Board will have to decide the extent to which our fine community desires to balance expanded business zoning against desire of new residents like my opponent who come here to live. Those new residents clamor for special privileges like trash pickup right in front of their homes, as opposed to what townspeople have done for generations—hauled trash to the Town Dump, which is one of my favorite meeting places, by the way." Cyrus looked at the crowd. "Don't you all agree?" Cheers.

"We already have trash pickup for the businesses in town. No one is arguing with that, of course. Another issue for the Town Board to consider will address the location of the Town Library. Thanks to our own State Senator Jack Smiley, we have a state-funded community center that also houses a library. So no need for two, when we can put the funds to pay for that old library building to better use, maybe even lower taxes. Heck, maybe we can sell that building and make a tidy profit to put in our town budget. There are other issues that I am eager to help the community resolve once I'm elected to the Town Board, and I am sure my former teacher, well, everyone who is actually from this town's former teacher, will get to those issues, today. My opponent calls this a restoration of democracy and even describes our traditions as a patronage system. I ask you good people this question. How can that be so if he is standing next to me, running for office in an election? That no one prior to him had the unmitigated gall to skip the hard work does not make the process wrong. It might, however, say a lot about the candidate. Thank you, and God bless you, and God bless the Town of Standard."

Mrs. Titus cleared her throat and adjusted her glasses.

"Both candidates know I will ask five questions, all chosen by me. I have not shared those questions with anyone. I reiterate I will tolerate no interruptions. Each candidate will get a three-minute opportunity to answer each question. Be succinct. After long experience, I have found that anything more than the allotted time creates an exercise in tautology. I will give both candidates three minutes for a closing statement. By random drawing, Mr. Boone will receive the first question."

"What is your position on universal trash collection?"

Cyrus smiled. His grin looked a lot like a sneer, but Ed was sure he intended it to appear genial. After all, he hardly intended to glare at Mrs. Titus.

"Thank you, Mrs. Titus. As it was no doubt clear from my opening statement, I am opposed to it. The expense of such an endeavor could either bankrupt our town, or bankrupt our fine citizens through oppressive taxes, in order to provide big city service to people, many of whom, like my opponent, became used to such luxuries before their recent arrival in our more modest, more traditional town. The Town Dump has served all of us nobly for uncounted generations—going all the way back to my great-grandaddy's time."

"Mr. Orwell?"

"Thank you, Mrs. Titus. I have spent some time studying this issue. That's what I do, and who I am. I consider all sides of an issue to make informed decisions. And I will tell you this, many people whose families have lived here for generations have grown tired of lugging their garbage to the Dump. They don't want their taxes to sky-rocket, either, but they harbor no fondness for hauling trash in the middle of winter, when no one is congregating at the Town Dump to socialize. So, if we can do it without breaking our budget, or increasing taxes, I'm for it. Perhaps a system of user fees for those who choose to use the service might end up costing the town nothing. Anyone who wants to avoid the fee and use the Town Dump will be free to do so. Thank you."

"The next question will begin with Mr. Orwell. What is your view of the relocation of the library?"

"I oppose it, in the strongest possible terms. The library provides extraordinary value to our community. Calling a bookshelf in the CC a library is like saying ten bucks in your wallet makes you a bank. They are not even close to being the same thing. No one intended the Community Center, which I am proud to have played a part in creating, to replace the library. How could it? They serve two different purposes. One is a place of reading, of learning, of study, of discovery of talented authors, of researching a science project for school. Its massive collection of literature and research materials dwarfs the meager collection of bestsellers in the Community Center. The tremendous librarian in our Town Library, Kara Cornish, has helped countless people, young and old, discover new authors, research difficult issues, and discover a latent love of books and reading. She is irreplaceable. It's absurd to think that the Community Center provides any of those services. Kara and I viewed the decision to place some library books in the Community Center as a win-win for both places. The concept was that it would simultaneously provide a few books for the CC's reading room, while piquing people, young and old, to go to the library. The two were always, and still are, perceived as two distinct entities performing separate functions. They are not the same, and no one should ever, ever see or treat them as the same thing. They have peacefully co-existed ever since the CC opened, and should continue to do so. And that our schoolchildren will have to go to Meeker Falls to find an adequate library, after they sell our very own building to some developer, who will profit at the expense of our own citizens, young and old, shakes me to my very core. A few bucks in the Town budget is not worth the great loss our community will suffer."

"Mr. Boone?"

"My opponent refers to a few bucks in the town budget. That statement is a perfect example of his unfitness for the Town Board. As he took pains to say about trash collection, budgetary decisions are essential. Maintaining a library costs a lot of money. Paying to fix the ever-crumbling structure of that old building is expensive. Our town is small, and balancing the budget is always an issue. My opponent may not realize that, being new to this community, but our Town Board, led by our long-time public servant, Mayor Winkle, has done a remarkable job of keeping costs down and taxes low. As newcomers arrive in our town, they seem to want more and more services, so consolidation of resources is always on the table. The creation of the CC, after Jack Smiley's Herculean efforts, has created a place to save a boatload of money, and create an asset to sell to add to the town's coffers. That's a true win-win. The town benefits, and the existing library remains in the CC. No waste, no duplication of services. Everyone wins."

Ed was boiling over inside. He'd underestimated Cyrus, who seemed more focused and… coached than he'd expected. He'd figured that Cyrus would hammer Ed's newcomer status, but Ed hadn't expected to be deprived of credit for being the architect of the CC. Surely everyone knew that, didn't they? Maybe not. He'd better do a better job of taking his deserved credit.

31

"The next question is for Mr. Boone. How would you balance the imposition of town taxes against the need to provide services for residents? As a corollary, do you favor more services? Which ones?"

"If we sell the library, we will have a lot more money to spend on necessary services, and reduce taxes at the same time. Talk about hitting the jackpot. The creation of the Community Center by our own Senator Smiley made that possible, by allowing for the consolidation of the library and the CC, leaving a valuable asset to liquidate for the benefit of all our citizens. Things like putting an elementary school right here, so our kids don't have to go to Meeker Falls. I don't support it right now, but heck, maybe we'd even have money for my opponent's pet project, trash collection for him and his neighbors."

"Mr. Orwell?"

"I agree. We need to keep taxes as low as possible. We're not in a big city. But selling off our valuable resources is not the answer. Nor is providing new services we can't afford. As I've stated before, things like trash collection must be revenue neutral. The users of those types of services must pay for them. My opponent and I agree that having an elementary school in our town is a wonderful idea, but we can't eliminate one educational resource in order to fund another. I'd need to study the issue before taking an affirmative position on any additional expense, but I wonder just how much money is being needlessly spent on school buses and related costs to carry our children to elementary school. If we had a local one, the kids could walk to school, with sig-nificant transportation savings. That's the thought process I would bring to the Town Board. Snap decisions based on no information are not the way to govern. Review the facts, asses the costs and weigh them against the benefits. That would be my approach."

"He'll study an issue to death, but not decide anything."

A few titters from his cohorts in the audience.

"Mr. Boone! Keep silent until it's your turn. I won't warn you again."

"Sorry, Mrs. Titus." He made a motion of zipping his lips.

"The next question is for Mr. Orwell. What is your view on ex-panded zoning for business?"

Edison hadn't studied this issue other than viscerally, but he plunged ahead. "I think we should handle zoning issues on a case-by-case basis. I don't want to equivocate here, but it would be irresponsi-ble to just say, 'Let's create more business zoning.' It's not always a good idea, but in some places, it might make sense. The Community Center, for example, is on the site of an abandoned, dilapidated old house with overgrown weeds. The refurbishment of the area into a re-source for all people of Standard shows how the addition of non-resi-dential property can benefit everyone. But attracting new business should never come at the cost of limiting available housing for new families, or young people who want to stay here, rather than move away because of the lack of places to live. And we don't want to de-stroy the fabric of Standard by creating more and more business zones, or enterprise zones, with their accompanying tax breaks. Attracting business for its own sake is not good zoning policy. So, I advocate a reasoned approach to zoning."

"Mr. Boone?"

"Well, that was a muddled, murky mess of a policy, wasn't it?" Cyrus rubbed his hands together, as if in glee. This was his perceived area of expertise, and he planned to show it. At least that's what it looked like to Edison, who'd glanced over and watched the performance.

"Unlike me, my opponent doesn't know sh… a single blessed thing about zoning, as that confused, once again, indecisive statement shows. I've run the Zoning Board for three years. I know for a fact that we need more business zoning in this town, and we can do it and still leave more than adequate housing for our young people to stay here, and even our newcomers like my opponent. We've granted many zoning variances, and all were well-reasoned, and resulted in allowing our thriving business community to flourish. I have to wonder, however, about my opponent's actual view on zoning. He doesn't say, he just tells us he'll think about it. That's nice. The rest of us are doing the hard work, and he's just thinking. And his choice of the Community Center as an example of a good use of zoning policy? That property, which he has a personal interest in, mind you, was in a mixed-use zone already, and had been for a long, long time. He wouldn't know that, being a newcomer. And don't you wonder a little about his ethics, using something he has a personal interest in as an example?"

Ed was furious, but he'd resolved to stay complacent. But the king of corruption calling him out on an ethical issue was galling.

"The last question is for Mr. Boone. What are your views on schools and educational resources in our town?"

Cyrus tried to smile, but it came across as baring his teeth. Not a good look. And he made it worse by trying to suck up to Mrs. Titus.

"Education was a lot better before you retired, Mrs. Titus."

The comment elicited a few groans from the audience, and it fell flat. The venerable teacher said nothing, and didn't crack so much as a faint smile. She just stared at him, waiting for his response to the question.

"Um, yes. We have a stellar educational system in this town, and a great board of education running it. We have a middle school and a high school, and some fine teachers, but no elementary school or kindergarten. If we sell the library, we can have those schools here, too."

"Mr. Orwell?"

"My opponent seems uninterested in education. All he can say is that we need an elementary school here, and I couldn't agree more. But we also need to support our teachers, both financially and in a community active way. We need to keep parents involved, we need to help kids with homework, with their science projects, we need to encourage our kids of all ages to read, and to value reading. And the teachers, and the parents need to be supported, with places such as our town library, a veritable treasure, with a trained librarian like our own Kara Cornish, who connects with our youth and adults alike. Our library is a valuable educational resource, not a mere pawn to a financial game. We can't just sell the library like it's a big, expensive hunk of cheese. It's part of the soul of this community, and it's helped countless people in all walks of life. There is no education without reading. And a place that offers such extensive resources to all citizens free, in a tradition tracing its origins beyond Benjamin Franklin to ancient Egypt, should not be callously shoved aside just because a few books are available at a community center. All our education demands we keep this valuable resource."

Mrs. Titus cleared her throat.

"That concludes the question-and-answer period. The candidates now have three minutes each for final statements."

Edison thought about his performance and figured he'd done pretty well. Cyrus surprised him by being more prepared and knowledgeable than Edison had thought. Cyrus had almost appeared human, and certainly didn't show himself as the dolt of Ed's experience. He'd taken some shots at Edison, and had tried mightily to goad Edison into an angry response, but Edison hadn't taken the bait. Edison figured he'd won the debate, not because he'd been smarter or more knowledgeable, or a better debater, but because he'd shown restraint and thoughtfulness, and that he cared. Someone had clearly coached Cyrus to project the same thing, but his essential nature wouldn't permit it, so Ed thought he appeared pandering and insincere. It was hard to know how other people reacted, but he'd hear that soon enough. For now, all he needed to do was listen respectfully to Cyrus' closing statement, which probably was as canned and rehearsed as his own. Vote for me because I just showed I can do a better job than the other guy. What more can one say?

Mrs. Titus had just requested Cyrus' last statement.

"Mr. Boone?"

Cyrus looked out at the crowd, then turned to Edison for a moment. Ed thought he spotted a sinister-looking gleam in Cyrus' eye, but dismissed the notion as Cyrus turned back to the audience.

"Mrs. Titus, ladies and gentlemen. I hope what you just heard clearly showed me to be the better candidate to represent the good people of this town as the next Town Board member. I have the very experience that is lacking in my opponent, am decisive on the important issues facing our beloved town, and I know those issues so well, because I am a lifelong resident and homeowner here. I have worked tirelessly for the people of this town, know our complex zoning issues like the back of my hand, and have worked well with the other members of the Town Board for a lengthy period. My opponent is a newcomer who is simply trying to grab power. He wants to go right to the top without doing a lick of the hard work other Town Board members have done before moving on to their earned seats on the Town Board."

Cyrus paused and made an exaggerated turn toward Edison. He extended his index finger and pointed it right at Edison.

"Not only is this man a newcomer, he came here to escape from his arrest record in another state. Is this who you want as a Town Board member? He has the last word here. Let him deny it if he can, but I assure you he won't. Thank you."

32

The crowd erupted. It seemed like everyone was jabbering to his neighbor, creating a cacophony of voices that even Mrs. Titus had trouble silencing.

Edison couldn't help it. He lost all control of his mouth, which hung agape. His throat constricted, and he doubted he could speak at that moment, even if he wanted to. But he didn't want to. Leaving was his only thought, not only the podium, but the town, the state, even the country. He eyed the exit, but he couldn't move. Frozen in place, Edison stared out into the sea of faces that were now waiting for a denial, an explanation, anything. All the awful memories flooded into Edison's brain. And one thing congealed in the scattered remnants of any cogent thinking: Cyrus was absolutely right. He had an arrest record, and he ran away from it to the town of Standard. He couldn't deny a thing, and he felt ill-equipped at that moment to explain. Finally, he looked down at the front row and spotted the two shocked looking friends, Stan and Kara, sitting next to Brenda's kind, understanding, and sympathetic face. Brenda shifted in her seat, and looked ready to whisk him away, but she didn't, and somehow that gave him the strength to speak.

"Mr. Orwell? Did you hear me?"

"I'm sorry, Mrs. Titus. I was distracted."

"I'll bet you were," a voice said in the audience, but the speaker quickly shut his mouth at a stern glare from Mrs. Titus.

Edison took a deep breath and spoke. His voice sounded stilted to him, so he was sure it did to everyone, but he couldn't help that. He needed to give a short *spiel* and get the hell out of here. Edison knew his chances of winning the election had evaporated, and he doubted he could still live in Standard. Well, Brenda would get her wish to go back to New Jersey sooner than either of them thought. Edison gave a flicker of thought to moving to another state, maybe Florida. He haltingly went through the first part of his prepared statement, then stopped and stared straight at the audience.

"I know the only thing you want to hear at this point is about my arrest in New Jersey, which occurred within a year prior to our move to Standard. It is an intensely personal matter, and I will not share the details in this forum. All I can hope is that you respect my desire to maintain my privacy. Thank you."

The crowd erupted again, and Edison could hear multiple people say, "He didn't deny it. I wonder what horrible thing he did?" And much more like that. Ed strode in as dignified a manner as he could to the exit door, and out to the foyer, where he found Brenda, who had rushed out to meet him. He took her hand, mouthed "I'll call you" to Stan and Kara, and escaped out to the car before the crowd descended upon him.

"Let's get out of here," Edison said, and Brenda dutifully put the car in gear and eased it out of the parking space. Once underway, he looked over at her concerned face, and ventured a, "How bad was it?"

Brenda pursed her lips before responding. "Bad."

"Now we know what surprise Cyrus was saving for me," Edison said, with a resigned sigh.

They said little else until Brenda pulled into their driveway, stopped the car, and turned off the ignition. Then she turned and looked at Edison.

"I thought you were having a stroke up there," she said. "When that awful man said that, I could see you almost convulse, then you froze, as if your whole body had turned into a marble statue. I almost ran up there, but something seemed to pull you out of it."

"Something did," he said.

"What?"

"You." Edison wriggled out of his seat belt and leaned over to give Brenda an awkward hug and kiss. "You're right, he said. Not about the stroke, thank God, but about my shaking, then freezing. He took me by surprise, the asshole. He did exactly what he intended. But back to the point. I looked at the front row of the audience, and first saw the shocked looks on Kara and Stan's faces, then I found you. I saw your look of concern, and an overwhelming sense of calm came over me. I guess your warmth melted my frozen vocal chords, and I could focus, albeit poorly."

"It was better than my running up there and trying to carry you out," she said through pursed lips. "Let's get you inside. I'll fix you a nice cup of tea and when you settle down a bit, we can have a productive talk. Okay?"

Edison nodded. "Okay. But I'll tell you right now that I'm withdrawing from the race."

Brenda held up a hand, palm facing Edison. "Not now. No hasty decisions. Let's get inside and talk."

Ed nodded, opened the car door and staggered towards the side entrance. Brenda caught him, and took hold of his arm, as they went into the house.

The moment they closed the door behind them, Edison's phone exuded its musical tone.

"I hate that tone," he said. "But I don't know how to change it." He let it continue until it went into voice mail. Then he glanced at the caller ID. Stan. Shrugging, Edison put the phone back in his pocket, without listening to the voicemail. He had a good idea of its content and had no intention of talking to anyone but Brenda at that moment. He'd call Stan back later. Maybe.

As promised, once inside, Brenda fixed them cups of tea. When Ed sat at the kitchen table, Brenda shook her head and pointed to the living room.

"You need to sit back and rest for a bit. I'll bring your tea."

Ed gave a nod that served the joint purposes of thanking her and acknowledging the wisdom of her direction.

He walked into the living room, and plopped down on his recliner. Pulling up on the lever on its side, raised the footrest, along with his weary legs. He tried to think productively, but was overcome with a bemused wave of… what was it? Anger? Embarrassment? Self-loathing? Self-pity? Maybe all of those things. And maybe one other thing. Was he disappointed that he'd have to withdraw from the race? Did he want that job? He just shook his head, not as an answer to any of those questions, but in abject confusion. Brenda was right. He needed to settle down before figuring anything out. He managed a forced smile when Brenda arrived with two cups of tea, one of which she placed on a coaster on the little table next to his chair. She sat down with her own cup. When Edison opened his mouth to speak, she shook her head, then said, "Finish your tea, then close your eyes for a little while. Then we'll talk."

Edison was in no position to argue the point, so he finished his tea, then put the cup down and closed his eyes. He knew there was no way to get his roiling brain to cooperate in a nap, but he tried to do it, anyway.

When he woke up, he glanced at the clock on the mantel. 3:30 pm. Brenda was not in the room, but he heard her in the kitchen talking to someone, presumably on the phone.

When she was done, she went into the living room and found Edison awake. In response to his inquiring look, she said, "That was Kara. She called to see how you were, and I told her you'd call her and Stan back later."

"She didn't ask what it was all about?" Ed's tone was one of amazement, but Brenda put that notion to rest.

"Of course she did," Brenda said. "It blew her and Stan away."

"What did you tell her?"

Brenda gave him a long, pensive look. "I told her you'd call her and Stan later today. Look, Eddie, it's your story to tell, in whatever way and to whomever you wish. You know my view. They're your friends. I think you should have told them a long time ago. Mo and Dave, too. And honey, I mean this with love, so please take it that way. It's been terribly hard for me to have what amounts to a gag order, preventing me from telling a story that has affected me profoundly."

Edison hung his head. He knew Brenda loved him. But he'd done nothing to reciprocate it. He hadn't fully appreciated how little he'd given to her and how his secrecy affected Brenda until he feared she'd leave him. Oh, what a terrible person he was to push the love of his life into making such a dire threat. He corrected himself. Not a threat. A promise. Shape up, or I ship out. Not in those words, but in her actions. I've got to fix this, he thought. I simply must. Or I lose everything. Forget about the election, the Town Board. I have to fix this with Brenda.

"I know," he said. "I've made it hard for you. And I'm going to fix it. I won't object if you tell anyone you want about what happened."

"Thank you, honey. But I think it has to start with you."

Ed's shoulders drooped. "It's hard for me to talk about."

"I know. You have an appointment with Dr. Forstein tomorrow. I'll drive you there. If he wants to speak to me, too, I'll already be there. When you call Kara and Stan back tonight, why don't you just tell them you'll explain soon, and would appreciate them giving you a little time. If they ask you about the election, give them the same answer. Don't decide that right away."

"I want to quit that stupid race right now. Don't you want me to?"

"If you asked me yesterday, and if I gave you an honest answer, I'd have told you yes, and that we should move back to New Jersey."

"What changed your mind? And won't it be impossible to live here now?"

"Oh, nothing has changed my mind. We still need to talk all of it over, but I'll be damned if I'll let the likes of Cyrus Boone and his cronies decide for us. He's an appalling person, and so are his cohorts. As for it being impossible to live here, I think that's up to you. You made a mistake. A whopper of a mistake, to be sure. And I don't think you've processed it well, or dealt with it in a healthy way. Maybe your psychologist will help. As for the views of the residents of this town, how many of them do you think have made mistakes or done things they're ashamed of?"

"Not the one I made," Ed said, a bit too stubbornly.

"Maybe not. Maybe so. I don't know the answer to that. But we both need to get things on a healthier footing, or it will be hard to live in either Standard or New Jersey, or anywhere else, for that matter."

Ed called Stan and asked him to put it on speaker so Kara could hear as well. And he told them what Brenda had suggested, that he needed a little time, not more than a day or two, and that he'd appreciate their kindness in giving it to him. They asked the same question a few different ways, but received the same answer. Stan pressured him on how he needed to get a reasonable explanation out as soon as possible, or he'd lose any chance in the election. Ed stuck to his guns, along with profuse apologies for the inconvenience, and Stan finally gave up with ill-concealed disgust.

Ed hung up and turned to Brenda. "Great, now I'm pissing off my friends. I should have just told them what happened."

"Maybe. But you've waited this long. Talk to Dr. Forstein about it. It's possible he'll have advice for you. Maybe not, but you might as well see."

33

"You can start by not calling what happened 'The troubles,'" Dr. Forstein told Edison after the first few minutes of introductory discussion. The opening conversation comprised Dr. Forstein asking Edison to tell him what was going on in his life, and Edison, to his surprise, volubly pouring out his problems, all of which he said resulted from the troubles.

"We in the shrink business aren't big on euphemisms," Dr. Forstein added with a smile. "And it's entirely up to you, but you can call me Barney. Many people are more comfortable with that."

Ed thought about it. "How about Dr. Barney?" he asked.

"Sure. Dr. Barney it is."

Edison couldn't help it, he liked this guy. He wasn't sure he was ready to tell the entire story, but asked if everything was confidential.

Dr. Barney nodded, briefly covered his mouth with his left hand, and again flashed that genial smile.

"It's hard to talk about," Ed stammered.

"Tough things often are."

No sympathy, but somehow open and kind. Like the guy had heard many awful things, and was prepared to hear Edison's story, even if he was a convicted criminal. Ed sighed. Not that far from the truth. But somehow, he got the story out. Dr. Barney said little, just gave encouragement for him to keep going. And to Edison's surprise, he did. It took a while, with many stops and starts, and a host of meandering off the topic, but he told Dr. Barney what had happened.

Dr. Barney thanked him for sharing what had to be difficult for him to talk about, and Edison, already exhausted, wanted to get out of there right away. He anxiously told Dr. Barney that. The therapist glanced at his watch, and told Edison that they still had about ten minutes left in the session, but that they could stop right then, and start the hard work in the next session, or they could, as Dr. Barney put it "scratch the surface today, and get into it more next time."

Ed just stared at him. "That wasn't the hard work?"

Dr. Barney gave a soft chuckle. "My mistake. Of course, that was hard, and I didn't mean to suggest otherwise. In fact, my getting that much in only forty minutes might be a record. All I meant was that the events you described must affect your life now, or you wouldn't be here. You've identified one cause. Let's see if we can get to how it's affected your life."

Ed nodded. "One question."

Dr. Barney smiled. "Only one?"

Ed managed a wry half-smile. "Okay, I have about a million, but I'll only ask one. Or two."

Dr. Barney waited.

"You said one cause of my problems. You think there are others?"

Dr. Barney raised and spread his open palms to his sides. "Don't know. I just met you today. You've described something that has affected your life, something that happened in New Jersey. I haven't heard what brought you to upstate New York, or any of the other surrounding circumstances of your life. And how could you have told me? You've just met me. You said you had another question."

"How long will this take?"

"I can't give you an answer to that. A lot of that is up to you. If you're willing to work, I think we can make a lot of progress. You've already shown a desire to get better by just coming here, and even more so by telling me a very hard thing to share. So, we're already making progress."

"Progress is good."

"Yes, it is. Okay, our time is almost up, and you said you wanted me to meet Brenda."

Ed nodded. "She's in the waiting room. She drove me here. I don't drive anymore."

Dr. Barney raised his eyebrows a little, but said nothing. He let Ed lead him out to the waiting room, where Dr. Barney and Brenda exchanged a few pleasantries, after which he returned to his inner office, and Edison and Brenda took their leave.

"How did it go?" she asked as they drove home to Standard. And then, "Only if you want to tell me."

"I told him what I did in New Jersey." Edison said.

"On your first visit to a psychologist, you told a complete stranger about the troubles?"

"Yeah. I surprised myself, but it just came pouring out, like an exploding pressure-cooker."

"Did you give him details?"

Ed nodded. "He wouldn't accept what he called a 'euphemism.' Said that therapists aren't fond of them."

"You seem to like him," Brenda ventured, with obvious caution.

"In a decent guy who maybe can help me kind of way, I guess so."

"So you're going back?"

Edison looked over at her. "I need help. I know it. So yes, I'm going back. But I don't know whether we'll even be here for much longer."

"Let's just take it a day at a time, honey, okay?"

"I have to tell Stan and Kara something. Mo and Dave, too. Soon."

"You could tell them the truth," Brenda suggested.

Ed sighed. "It was hard enough telling Dr. Barney, who keeps things confidential."

"Honey, the word is out, thanks to that cretin, Cyrus Boone. And maybe in a toxic way, he did you a favor."

"That asshole never did a good thing in his life."

"I don't mean it that way, and you know it."

"Oh, I know. I'll come up with something to ease their minds."

"The police arrested you. No one charged you with a crime, and you certainly don't have a criminal record."

"Thanks to that lawyer you hired." Ed didn't say it appreciatively, but Brenda said nothing. They'd been down that road before, and she knew full well that Edison hated lawyers. She also knew that she'd been right to get one for him, or he might be in jail right now. Ed had wanted to go to jail for what he did, but Brenda wouldn't let that happen without a fight, and she'd won.

"Maybe so, but you can ease your friends' minds by telling them the truth."

Ed just sat there sulking.

"I can't believe your therapist would think it a good idea to bottle it up inside like a state secret."

"We didn't get into that."

Brenda decided not to take it further.

Their route home took them past the town square, then in the CC's direction. As they approached, they saw a car barreling toward the parking spaces in front of the building. From their vantage point, they could see it was going way too fast to be parking. The car slammed into, and over the concrete parking stop, up the short steps all the way to the front door, where it crashed and came to a stop.

"Look at that," Brenda screamed, and stopped the car a short distance away. Parking on the side of the street, the two of them hurried to the scene.

Upon their approach, they spotted a gathering crowd, all gawking at the crumpled car. Edison hung back while Brenda continued on to find out what happened. He wasn't yet ready to face the crowd. If he ever would be.

"Is anyone hurt?" Brenda asked.

"No one but the driver, thank God. And he looks okay, maybe a little shaken up, and has some bruises and scratches. Probably should go to the hospital to get checked out."

"Who is it?"

"Harry Crutch."

"What happened?"

"He said he didn't gauge the distance to the end of the parking area and stepped down a little on the gas pedal. He guesses he hit the gas too hard, and well… we all can see the result."

Seeing nothing she could do to help, Brenda headed back to the car in which Edison sat. He'd decided that if they needed his help for any reason, Brenda would come back and tell him. In the meantime, he didn't want anyone to spot him and ask inconvenient questions.

Brenda reported the exciting events to Edison, who just nodded, as much to himself as to Brenda.

He didn't stay silent for long. Once underway again, he muttered, "At least the lucky bastard didn't hurt anyone. Maybe he'll learn."

"Like you did?" Brenda said and immediately regretted it. "I'm sorry, honey, that was uncalled for."

"No, it wasn't. I take full responsibility for my pigheadedness."

"Yes you do, honey, yes you do," Brenda said, thinking that Edison taking responsibility for his mistakes wasn't the problem. It was dealing with the aftermath healthily. And she hoped his therapist helped him with that. Helped them as a couple. Brenda had been seeing a therapist herself for several years, but Edison had resisted. Until now.

She pulled into their driveway, and they entered the house.

After they settled themselves, Brenda asked Edison if he was going to call his friends.

"I'm tired now. I think I'll wait a little while."

"You can't avoid them forever," Brenda pressed.

Edison sighed. A part of him wanted to do just that. Pack up and move away, and never have to deal with it. He looked around him. How did that work out? He was sitting in a house in Standard, New York, more than a hundred miles from the scene of the… troubles. And it was like he'd never left. And he'd behaved today like a poltroon. He lacked the courage to face the crowd, and now he evidenced the same craven attitude towards his friends. Edison shook his head in disgust, picked up his phone, and punched in Stan's number. He owed him an explanation, and he was going to give him one.

Stan asked Edison if he could put the call on speaker so Kara could hear, and Edison told them the truth, precisely what had led to his arrest, only that, but no less. And they were supportive. Stan asked him why he hadn't just said that at the debate, instead of creating the impression that he'd done something worse, and Edison felt he had to say "I don't think there is anything worse," and he hurriedly ended the call as graciously as he could muster. The calls to Dave and Mo went about the same, and his friends rallied around him in support. We all make mistakes, that kind of thing.

"Feel better getting that off your chest?" Brenda asked.

"Not really. It's just making me think about it."

"Well, think about it this way. You made your friends feel better."

"Oh, I doubt that," Edison said. "They now know what kind of person I am."

"I think they already knew. Or they wouldn't be your friends. Maybe now they'll have a better understanding of your, um, mercurial nature."

Ed didn't think so, but he was too tired to argue. He wanted to take a nap, and Brenda encouraged him to do so. She had some puttering to do around the house, but would try not to disturb him.

Edison fell asleep almost the moment his head hit the pillow. The day's events exhausted him. Unburdening one's soul was enervating. He wanted nothing more than to stop thinking about it. But his mind kept chugging along even after he fell asleep. A little girl, a desperate attempt to help her, an oncoming train, it's whistle madly blowing, a little girl trying to retrieve her ball, not seeing the train as it barreled down toward her, Edison crying out "Watch out, watch out, the train, it's so close, oh my God, it's so close, it can't stop on time, it can't stop, please, please get out of the way, the train, it can't stop in time… I can't stop. I can't stop. Oh my God, what have I done?"

34

Edison was trying to get to the little girl's side when Brenda woke him up. Edison couldn't stop crying, couldn't stop saying, Oh, my God, oh my God, look what I did. That poor sweet, innocent little girl, oh my God.

Brenda took him into her arms and tried to console the inconsolable Edison as he sobbed into her shoulder. He did that for a long time until he stopped. He had no tears left. Brenda sat him down on the chair in their bedroom and said she'd make him a cup of tea.

"I'll come downstairs with you."

"Why don't you wash your face first and then join me in the kitchen?"

Ed nodded and dutifully went into the bathroom and threw some cold water on his face. It felt good, so he did it again. He looked at himself in the mirror. His face looked like a dried-up prune. He felt bad, crying like a baby. Afraid to speak to people, even his friends. What had he become? Not the man he used to be, and not what he wanted now. He hoped Dr. Barney could help him, because he was a wreck. But there were a few things he could do on his own, and he resolved to do them. Right away.

He went downstairs and found Brenda making them tea. She placed one cup in front of his chair and one in front of hers. They sat down, and Edison immediately apologized.

Brenda waved it away. "No apology necessary."

"It seemed so real."

"A lot of things stirred up today," she said.

Ed nodded. The understatement of the year.

"I'm going to face those people," he said.

"Good for you. I know it's hard, but I don't think avoiding people will help."

"I know it won't. But I have an idea about how to do it without some kind of press conference."

Edison slept a dreamless sleep that night, and in the morning, he and Brenda began their stroll to the CC.

"You look determined," Brenda remarked as they walked. "Care to share what you have in mind?"

"I'm hoping Harry is there," Edison responded.

Brenda stopped in her tracks, and took Edison's arm to keep him stopped next to her.

"Tell me you will not go off on him again."

Ed pulled himself up ramrod straight in a mock show of dignity. "I intend no such thing."

"Then… why do you hope he's there? He might not be, you know. He might be recuperating, or too embarrassed to show his face."

"Maybe," Ed said. "I can do this without him, but I'd rather have him there. He's not the type to be embarrassed, anyway. He probably looks at it as funny. That's the read I get on him from our limited interactions. Other than my ripping his head off that time, we've mostly had cordial relations. And you said that he didn't seem very injured, just shook up. But I don't need him for what I want to do today."

"Which is?"

"Show some courage for a change."

"Eddie…" Brenda began. "You're not…"

"Timid? No, I'm definitely not that. But I need to do something, and I'm resolved to do it. Today."

Brenda didn't press him on it, and when they reached the CC, Edison charged right up the low steps, made a mental note of the damaged front door, and plunged inside. And was pleased to see none other than Harry Crutch, holding court in the lounge, telling his story and laughing at his "Whoops," as he called it.

When people saw Edison, they literally swarmed around him, with multiple inquiries of what crime he'd committed, how long he'd served in prison, and other similar inquiries. Harry and the few people around him stopped talking and looked in his direction as well. Edison raised his hand, promised he'd get to them in a moment, and asked if the crowd could part and let him have a brief conversation with Harry.

Harry held his hands in front of him, palms facing Edison in an exaggerated show of defending himself, and people laughed.

"No yelling, no screaming, and no profanity, I promise," Edison said in a quiet voice. His tone caught people's attention, because they stopped talking, and Edison went over to Harry and sat down. People crowded around, wondering what Edison would say or do, but not wanting to miss a single word.

"I just want to tell you a story, Harry. And bear with me, because it's difficult for me to tell this one."

Harry's eyes darted to the exit. He didn't want to hear this, no matter what it was. But there were too many people around, and escape, alas, was not possible. He sighed loudly, as if telling Edison to get it over with already. He looked up, as if asking for divine help in avoiding what was sure to be an unpleasant experience. But God was on Edison's side, it appeared, because no celestial help came to Harry's rescue, and Edison began his tale.

"I know a man…" Ed stopped. "As you know, I have terrible eyesight. I suffer from glaucoma, and while that's bad enough, I pretended it wasn't a problem, and didn't seek medical help until after it had progressed. You know that because I told you the first day I met you."

Harry gave a reluctant nod. He remembered all right.

"Glaucoma attacks peripheral vision first, but can, and did in my case, dramatically affect my central vision as well."

He looked at Harry. "Yours, too."

Harry didn't affirm it, but didn't deny it, either. He sat stone-faced.

"You were at the debate," Edison continued. He looked around. "All of you were." A few nods and affirmations.

"Cyrus told you all that I had an arrest record. That is absolutely true." Lots of murmuring in the crowd along with shouted questions, which Edison ignored. He held up his hand in a request for silence.

"I'm just telling a personal story to Harry."

"Could you get on with it, then?" an annoyed Harry looked ready to bolt.

Ed's face fell, and his shoulders drooped. He regarded Harry with the profound sadness he felt, and the other man said nothing more.

"I ignored my impaired eyesight and kept on driving. Had a few close calls, but justified them to myself repeatedly. One time…" he searched for Brenda in the assembly, found her, and said "Brenda can confirm this, one time, she literally grabbed my hand to make me stop, because if I had just charged into the intersection without seeing that guy on a motorcycle, I would have killed him. He was coming from the left, and I never saw him. Thank God she stopped me."

"So, why were you arrested?" An impatient voice. "If you stopped in time…"

"They wouldn't have arrested me. And I wasn't. There was no cop there, anyway. No, get this —- I kept driving. Think about that. I kept driving, even though Brenda had saved me from killing a man because I couldn't see well."

"Edison, please get to the point. I'm dying here."

Edison looked at him for a long moment.

"No, you're not. You're uncomfortable. So am I. I told you this was hard for me to tell. When you do awful things, you rarely go out and tell a bunch of people about them."

"So, what happened?" People were getting impatient. They wanted to know all the juicy details, so they could tell… everyone in town.

Edison took a deep breath. "I kept driving. Brenda tried mightily to get me to stop, but I didn't. It was too inconvenient, too much of a loss of independence, all those things. So… one day, I was driving home from getting a haircut, and…" Ed's voice cracked, and Brenda came over to sit next to him.

Edison gave her a grateful look. "I never saw her. Not until… oh my God… the second before I drove right into her. That poor little girl." Ed was openly sobbing, and he didn't care. His secret was out. And he didn't care about that, either.

Harry looked like he wanted to run away, but Edison wasn't looking at him anymore. Brenda tried to comfort him by putting an arm around him. He let her do that, but he shook his head when she suggested that he'd told the story, and maybe it was time to leave. Accepting a proffered tissue from someone, Edison blew his nose and said he had a few more things to tell. The girl hadn't died, but her condition was grave, and he understood she'd have permanent injuries. He didn't go into detail. He told how he'd called 911 and an ambulance and a police cruiser arrived at the same time. The police officers had questioned him at the scene, had determined that he had neither been drinking, nor texting on his phone, that he'd had his seat belts on, and had no evidence of drugs or liquor in his car. They examined his license and registration, both of which were in order. After completing their on-the-scene investigation, one officer remarked it was a terrible accident, and that it must be hard for him.

"Hard for me? I hit that little girl. It's hard for her." Edison had almost demanded to be arrested, and the officers obliged.

But he had committed no crime. He was a duly licensed driver, had not been driving under the influence of alcohol. They had an argument that the law might extend to visual impairment, but it wasn't like Edison wasn't wearing his glasses. And he'd passed the eye exam when applying for a license. That the lady giving him the eye exam at the DMV had told him that his vision was "close enough" for her didn't matter. He was a licensed driver who had a terrible accident. And the police, who hadn't wanted to arrest Edison in the first place, wanted no part in arguing with the lawyer Brenda brought. So, he'd gotten off scot free, with an arrest, but no conviction, not even any charges being brought. But the little girl was in the hospital, fighting for her life, because he'd been a stubborn mule. The little girl's parents had threatened to sue, and were none too happy about no charges being brought. Edison's lawyers had told him he actually had an outside chance of beating any such lawsuit, and he'd fired them on the spot. He'd accepted avoiding imprisonment, but there was no way on Earth he'd avoid responsibility. And no way he'd oppose that little girl. He advised her family attorneys that a lawsuit was unnecessary. He'd consented to a judgment requiring the turnover of all of his personal assets, keeping only his pension.

Brenda favored paying something, but not giving it all away, and she held onto her personal assets and half the proceeds of the house, but she'd consented to the sale, and they had moved to Standard. The assembled crowd hung on every word. They had questions, but most of them thought better of asking. Harry clearly expected Edison to lower the boom on him, but Edison just rose, took Brenda's proffered arm, and they walked out of the CC.

35

Edison spent much of the day fielding phone calls, almost all supportive. His friends, who Edison had called the day before, called him and told him they'd all heard already through the active Standard grapevine what he'd told the assembled CC crowd. They were predictably supportive, but what surprised Edison was the sheer number of Standard residents, many of whom he knew only casually, that had called him to tell him in different ways how tragic the whole situation was, but that they thought he'd handled it as honorably as possible.

Many people told him how they knew someone who they wished would stop driving, be it fathers, mothers, friends, relatives, or strangers. Others told him they'd tried to speak to Harry afterwards, but that he'd stormed out of the CC right after Edison left, and spoke to no one. They liked Harry. He was an affable fellow after all, but all agreed he shouldn't be driving, at least not far. One person with an unknown number called Ed an asshole and hung up.

Clara Bingham, his elderly neighbor from down the street, told Edison he shouldn't be too proud of himself. After all, Edison had done a terrible thing. And that poor Harry Crutch, such a nice man, not like Edison at all, had only run into a door and hurt no one. She had a sister who'd done much the same thing, that accidents happen, and that her sister could drive just as well as she could. She was just old, not blind. Edison assured her he wasn't proud of his actions, much to the contrary. He hated himself for what he did, and he fervently hoped no one made the same mistakes he did. Everyone is different, he acknowledged. He had just told his own story. He'd made no comment at all about anyone's age. But he said, as gently as he could, that sometimes, as he had not done in his own case, people should listen to their loved ones' advice about things they might not see or accept themselves. Mrs. Bingham gave him a cursory agreement and rang off in a hurry.

He had a few calls like that, but most people seemed to accept his story at face value, without trying to analyze it or him. A few people told him they personally could never, ever have told such a personal story in public, and that he'd been brave to do so. But, at least a few wondered whether he'd just done it because Cyrus forced him to, and that he'd only told the story because of political reasons—he so desperately wanted to get elected.

What could Edison do? He denied it and gave the candid response that he wasn't so sure he'd even stay in the race.

"Oh, I didn't mean that, Ed," said John Cartwright. "You should definitely stay in. Otherwise Cyrus Boondoggle will be our next Town Board member. That's what we can expect, a guy who digs up dirt on someone, finds their vulnerabilities, and uses it for political gain. The way I figure it, you outfoxed the fox."

"I intended no such thing," Edison said, and John laughed.

"Okay, if you say so." Edison could almost see John's conspiratorial wink, and he hung up in disgust.

He wanted to withdraw from the election and just move back to New Jersey, but Brenda told him to stay in. They'd work something out.

"How can I stay here?" he asked. "The whole town knows about that poor little girl that the pigheaded, stupid jerk gravely injured. And I'll lose the election, anyway."

"We ran away from unpleasantness in New Jersey," Brenda said. "Is that what you want to do again? What do you think Dr. Barney would say about that? Or do you want to run away from him, too? Do you think one session was all you need, that you're cured?"

Edison was confused, and he said so. "Don't you want to move back to New Jersey?"

"Not for that reason," she said. "Only if it is the right thing for us to do, with no impetuous pack up and clear out of town, like we did last time. Let's weigh our choices this time, that's all I'm saying. And this is very important — I don't want you to let that awful Cyrus Boone win."

"I don't either," Edison admitted. "But that ship might have sailed, don't you think?" Ed didn't wait for an answer. He wanted to give Brenda an answer to her question about Dr. Barney.

"Regarding Dr. Barney…" he began, and saw Brenda's chin set. "I am not cured. I may never be cured. But I like Dr. Barney, and think he can help me. I certainly intend to continue seeing him if we stay here. But he's not the only psychologist in the world. I'm sure they have them in New Jersey."

Brenda gave a faint smile. "Yes, they do, and Eddie… I'm glad you want to keep going to see one."

"Want to? No way. Need to? I'm sure of it."

"So, what are you going to do about the election?"

Edison sighed. "I guess I'll let the chips fall where they may."

***

Election Day arrived, with much town fanfare. People had hung red, white, and blue banners all around town. You could hear the sounds of brass bands playing American classics blasting from downtown. The sounds grew louder as you neared Town Hall, where organizers had carefully set everything up for the greatest local election of anyone's memory. A fight to the figurative death between two political gladiators in an epic battle. Or so it seemed to a good deal of townspeople, who were determined to turn the election into an extravaganza.

As Edison and Brenda neared Town Hall, they heard an exuberant high school band version of *Stars and Stripes Forever*. Clearly, the Board of Education and the band director had seen this as a real-life civics lesson. Not some nebulous national or state race involving amorphous candidates, but something close to home, and affecting their own lives.

Edison gave an awkward wave and tight smile, and he and Brenda entered the Town Hall to cast their ballots. Edison didn't want to vote for himself, because he was ambivalent about the election, but he was damned if he would vote for that asshole. Brenda had told Edison she was voting for him, and that, despite reservations about staying in Standard, she wanted him to win.

So, they both stopped at the place to sign their names, with Brenda taking extra care to make sure her arthritic hand wrote out a signature that matched the one on which she'd registered to vote. That accomplished, election workers ushered them to separate curtained voting booths. Standard still had the old-style mechanical voting machines. Edison had to take a moment, peered nervously around him, then pulled a lever, which closed the curtain behind him. Squinting through the reading part of his progressive glasses, Edison viewed two names listed in alphabetical order. He took extra time to make sure he was moving the correct slider before pushing it in the desired location, signifying a vote for himself. He peered at it to make sure he hadn't made a colossal mistake, gave a deep sigh, and again pulled the lever, registering a vote for Edison Orwell, and simultaneously opening the curtain. The people at the registration desk remained stoic, and all-business, so he eschewed any wave or comment, and walked out to the foyer, where Brenda was waiting for him.

"Brace yourself," she warned. "I can see a crowd outside, even from here. Are you ready to give a little speech?"

Ed nodded. "Not much to say, but I'll manage a few words if anyone wants to hear from me."

They walked outside, and as forewarned, a large crowd had assembled, just beyond the one hundred feet marker, designating the legally permitted distance from a polling place. There were many cell phone cameras raised, snapping the pictures of the candidate and his wife, and an assortment of cheers and catcalls. The crowd was taking a local election seriously, which, while unremarkable in many places, was unique in Standard. And its denizens were determined to make the most of it, with unprecedented pageantry. It looked to Edison like an even division between his supporters and detractors, both in number and in their location in the group. His supporters were on the left side of the loggia, and the boisterous supporters of Cyrus Boone stood on the right side. Edison mentally discounted any subliminal meaning behind the placement, and gave a simple wave, which elicited cheers from his supporters.

"You're going to win this thing," one yelled. "Good luck," said another. "Speech," cried a third, and others followed suit. The right side of the group stood sullenly as Edison gave a brief thank you to the voters, how he appreciated every single person who voted, whether for him or his opponent, and left it at that. His supporters booed when he mentioned his opponent, but it was mostly good-natured. The same was true of Cyrus' supporters. They stayed silent, rather than shout over him. Standard didn't have a large population. Everyone knew each other. And few people wanted to have their neighbors as enemies. There were a few rotten apples, of course. You couldn't avoid them anywhere, but Standard was mostly a kind place, and any acrimony resulting from the election would no doubt dissipate in a short time. Life would go on.

As Edison and Brenda began walking home, they encountered none other than Cyrus Boone trundling along at seventeen miles an hour on his golf cart. Edison doubted he'd picked up a golf club in his life, and maybe didn't even know that his transport had an alternative sporting purpose. They expected a nasty comment from Cyrus as he passed by, but he surprised them by not saying a word. Instead, as he approached Town Hall, he raised his fat cudgel of an arm, and waved to his supporters, who obliged him with cheers. Neither Edison nor Brenda looked back, although they quickened their pace as they walked home.

Brenda spoke first. "What are you thinking?" she asked, and immediately regretted the generality of the question. "I mean about the crowd and the whole fanfare."

Edison took his time answering. "I don't know what to think," he said. "It's a pretty big deal for a local race. I guess I started it, but... I don't know... it's creating some very high expectations, like the winner of this little town election will somehow be transformative. It's a Town Board seat, not the Presidency of the United States."

"I guess Tip O'Neill was right," she replied. "All politics is local. At least our fellow townspeople think so."

Edison grunted. "I just hope people don't expect too much. If I'm elected," he hastily added.

"You know, honey…" Brenda began. "Judging from the relative sizes of the two sides… and wasn't that freaky how they assembled on two sides of that small area… it's going to be close. And I think you're going to win."

"I just hope that if I do, I don't let people down. We're even thinking about moving away. How's that for being a politician? Offer one thing, then walk out on them if it's expedient."

Brenda knew he was right. If he won, they needed to stay, at least for a while. But if they did, she'd lose that professorship. She needed to decide quickly which she valued more — Edison or her professional career. She couldn't have both. And that the decision was hard hurt her heart so much she wanted to cry. But she didn't. She just offered the same, tired, "We'll work it out, honey." Kicking the issue down the road seemed the best course at that moment. After all, Edison could lose the race, and the decision would be much easier. But maybe not. She wasn't sure Edison wanted to move back to New Jersey under any circumstances.

36

"When will we hear the election results?" Brenda asked after they finished dinner.

Edison looked at his watch. "Polls close at seven. It's 7:10 right now."

"How fast can they count?"

"Nothing to count. They're mechanical machines. I guess they'll have to add the sums of the two voting machines together, but somehow, I think Mrs. Titus can do that."

Mrs. Titus was not only a retired schoolteacher and debate moderator, she also served as the town's Supervisor of Elections.

"And Kara told me Cyrus and I would get phone calls telling us the results the moment they're available. They will report the outcome in the morning Bugle."

"Our beloved town newspaper. I'm sure they're delighted to have actual news to report," Brenda said, without malice.

Ed nodded, without focusing on what Brenda said. He was thinking about how he felt about the imminent result. Would he be happy if he won? Edison wasn't sure he would be. He'd only run for one reason, and things were… complicated right now. Oh well, he thought, even if he won, it didn't mean he'd have to serve the full two-year term. He could just take care of the library issue and move on. They only needed one more vote on the Board to stop the closing of the library, and how long would that take? They scheduled it for a hearing in just a couple of days, at the next Town Board meeting. He'd cast his vote and resign as soon as it was… well… politically acceptable. He gave an unvoiced sigh of relief at that idea.

Edison's phone chirped. He looked at the caller ID, then up at Brenda.

"This is it," he said. He tapped the answer key and put the phone to his ear. He listened for a few moments, thanked the person for letting him know, and disconnected.

Brenda studied his expression for some sign, but Edison maintained a poker face. And he was good at that. Keeping a straight face. He was an excellent poker player, too. Mo told her that once. At present, though, Brenda wanted him to stop play-acting and get on with it.

Edison gave a little chuckle and put her out of her misery.

"It wasn't even close," he said.

"Eddie… for the love of…."

Edison cut her off. "I won. By a lot. I guess people hated Cyrus more than they disliked me. I was the lesser of two evils candidate. And I'm happy I beat the son of a bitch."

"Me too," Brenda said. "Congratulations! I'm proud of you, honey."

Edison thanked her, but he knew the elation would soon fade for both of them, as they confronted the reality of the invisible, but all too real forces pulling them in different directions.

Brenda saw the consternation in his face, and said, "We have time to figure it all out, honey. One thing at a time. The Town Board meeting is in two days. You can cast your vote and save the library. After that, we'll talk. Okay?"

"Okay."

At that moment, his phone chirped again. He looked at the caller ID, and it was Stan who offered his congratulations. They spoke briefly, then he put the phone on speaker, and Kara offered her congratulations as well. Stan told him not to expect a concession call from Cyrus, and Edison assured him he didn't. They disconnected, but his phone chirped again and again throughout the evening, with friends, neighbors and acquaintances, and people he didn't know at all, all offering their congratulations and good wishes. Senator Smiley called and wished him well, teasing him he now had joined the ranks of politicians like himself. He also heard from another consummate politician, Mayor Rufus Winkle, who offered his enthusiastic congratulations, said that he was sure Edison would be a "marvelous" board member, and that he looked forward to working with him. Edison listened to a bit more disingenuous crapola, said a hasty goodbye, and disconnected. He felt ill talking to the unctuous guy he'd have to associate with regularly. And that thought almost made him retch.

He went into the living room and sat down heavily. He was bushed. Totally exhausted. Brenda took one look at him and told him to go to bed. He fell asleep as soon as his head hit the pillow.

***

Edison woke up feeling a little better. If he'd dreamed at all, he didn't remember it. He went downstairs and grabbed a cup of coffee. Spotting him sitting there, Brenda sat down.

"How's my favorite politician doing today?"

"I'm not a…" he stopped when he spotted the merriment in her eyes. "I'm okay. Slept pretty well for a change."

"It's the second Wednesday of the month. Are you going to make your usual call?"

"Yeah. I hate to be a bother, but I can't help it. I want to know what's going on."

"Maybe it's time to think about letting it go. It's out of your hands. Why continue to torture yourself about something you can't control?"

"I don't know. Maybe there is something more I can do."

"Like what?"

"I don't know, give them more money or something."

"You already gave them almost everything you own, your house, your savings. Everything except your pension."

"I know, I know. But…"

"You have to know."

Edison nodded. "But I'll talk to Dr. Barney about it."

"Good idea."

Edison made his call to the rehabilitation hospital where his victim was undergoing treatment. The first time he called, the hospital told him nothing. He wasn't on the HIPAA list, so no way, no how, he'd get anything. But Edison, being who he was, found a work-around. He located someone who knew someone, who knew a temporary nurse who would violate Federal law to give some very limited information. But only on a specified day each month. And this was the day.

His usual updates usually comprised not yet walking, and varying optimism and pessimism about her chances of someday becoming ambulatory. Ed knew she'd had a few operations, and his last report suggested hopefulness that she'd need no more. But that she had a long road ahead of her at the rehab before she could even think about returning home.

This time, he received very different news. Or lack of it.

"She's not here anymore," the nurse told him.

"Was she discharged?" he asked. "I thought there was almost no chance of that happing soon."

"I know. All I can tell you is that she is not at this hospital. Gotta run."

Ed disconnected. And the parade of horribles took over his brain. Was she dead? Oh God, no. He caught himself. No one had said that. He sat down and put his head in his hands. He'd hoped that she'd get better. That she'd be able to live a normal life, however his crime had interrupted it and caused her such pain.

Brenda tried to console him. "You know nothing at this moment. We'll figure out a way to find out what's going on. And I think we'd hear if she passed away. And we can check that easily by searching the obituaries in the New Jersey papers. So let's do that, okay?"

Edison looked up. Brenda read in his pathetic expression a request that she perform the search for him, because he wouldn't be able to bear having the ugly truth pop up on the computer screen. She patted his shoulder, retrieved her laptop, and performed a search.

Before she keyed it in, she looked over at Edison and said, "Even if this turns up nothing, Britney lives near there, and can dig around and get information for us. We have it covered, don't worry." And she returned her gaze to the computer.

Edison stood up, then sat back down. He crossed his legs one way, then re-crossed them the other way. Then he uncrossed them and sat straight up. He adjusted his glasses, then took them off and blew on them, then picked up a tissue and cleaned them off before reseating them on the bridge of his nose. He raised his shoulders and sighed loudly. Brenda looked up at him and raised her index finger.

"Eddie, please settle down over there. You're making me as nervous as you look."

Ed did his best to remain still, but the waiting was killing him. He didn't want to check himself, but he didn't want the process he'd delegated to Brenda to take forever, either. He was in agony, and the waiting time seemed interminable. It frightened him that the little girl had died. Not that her condition wasn't awful already by his malfeasance, but that it would mark the end of any hope for recovery. He didn't want to admit it, even to himself, but he had hoped that there could be some sort of fairy tale ending — the little girl had suffered, but pulled through in the end. And Edison wondered — was the exorcism of his own demons dependent upon that storybook outcome? And he became ashamed of himself again. The only thing that mattered was the little girl, Sarah Jean. He didn't matter one bit.

Brenda shook him out of his reverie. "There's nothing here, Eddie. Not a single obituary referencing a little girl, much less, um…yours. So, it's unlikely Sarah Jean died. There's another reason for her leaving the hospital, we just don't know what. Maybe she unexpectedly made a full enough recovery to go home."

Ed doubted that, and said so. Brenda nodded. She didn't think so, either.

"More likely, she moved to a different facility," Brenda offered with a hopeful look. "There's only so much we can find out on the internet. I'll call Brit and ask her to get Carl to ask around. He's a pharmaceutical sales agent. He knows many people involved with healthcare. And he's a bulldog. If anyone can find out, it's him."

Ed nodded his assent, and Brenda made the call. When she hung up, she turned to Edison and said, "She's on it. And she's sure Carl can ferret out the information we need."

Edison impulsively rose from his chair and gave Brenda a hug. She felt warm and comfortable, and he didn't want to let go. He wanted so much for the little girl to be okay, and maybe, just maybe… he'd be okay, too. Standing there, holding Brenda, one thing was crystal clear to him — he'd do anything to keep her by his side for the rest of their lives. If a move back to New Jersey would do that, they'd move. Brenda loved her sister, and Brittany lived in New Jersey. Talking on the phone was one thing — being nearby was another. Brenda had an enticing job offer there as well. Edison could almost see the invisible forces pulling her back… home. Edison was a little better at seeing Standard as home, but he had zero desire to stay in Standard without Brenda. And he frankly didn't care a whit about his newly minted membership on the Town Board.

"There's nothing more we can do right now, so you might as well get ready for the Town Board meeting," Brenda said, patently not reading his thoughts at that moment.

"What? Oh, yeah, I guess so. But aren't we going to talk about maybe moving back to New Jersey?"

"We are, and we will soon. But don't you want to do what you set out to do and save the library?"

"Yeah, I guess I do." He reached over to the side table, opened a drawer, and retrieved a manila folder containing a Town Board member briefing for the upcoming meeting. But he wasn't worried. After all, a favorable vote on the library issue was all but certain. Mayor Winkle and his crony, Abner London, were certain to vote to close the library. But Kara's friend, Clarice Dunleavy, was equally certain to vote against, and Larry Percival already had signaled support for the library. So Edison's support for the library would carry the day, and it would save the library. And after that, it mattered little if he stayed or left. But it would matter. It would matter to Mo and Dave, and to a host of other people who'd had to live so long under corrupt leadership. But Edison didn't want to think about that at the moment. First things first. Save the library, have a serious discussion about his desired joint future with Brenda, and deal with the rest later.

37

Edison spent the days prior to the big Town Board meeting in something close to normal fashion. He had coffee with Mo at Pete's Eats, spent time at the CC, watched a ball game at Dave's house, and tried to tune out the cacophony of voices, telling him what they wanted the town to do. He hadn't contemplated what Town Board membership meant. The sight of so many people with their hands out looking for favors as if he was their ticket into some secret cabal disgusted him. But finally, the big day arrived. Edison's very first Town Board meeting. His induction as a legislator. Sitting two seats away from the man occupying the big chair, and looking down, literally, upon the townspeople he had sworn to represent, with honesty, fairness and dignity. Just like the Mayor, who'd taken the same oath and crapped all over it.

Mayor Winkle called the meeting to order, noted the existence of a quorum, gave a perfunctory welcome to the newest member, solicited and received the waiver of reading the minutes, and called on the bailiff to announce the first agenda item.

After a few routine board matters, the bailiff called the matter of the "Library Relocation," the Mayor's euphemism for saving money by facilitating "repurposing the property."

"Okay, the Mayor began, "we've already heard all the public comment we need at the prior meetings. The local ordinance requires no more, and I think people will just be repeating themselves at this point. Does the Board agree? If so, we can proceed directly to a vote."

Uh oh, Edison thought. Winkle is way too eager to get to a vote. He wouldn't do that unless… the fix was in.

"I think we need to hear more from the community," he said.

"I agree," Clarice Dunleavy said quickly. She'd obviously seen the writing on the wall as well.

"Anyone else?" the mayor inquired. Abner London remained mute. Larry Percival cleared his throat and said, "I think we've heard everything already, and anything more would be a waste of time. Let's get on with it."

"Very well," the Mayor said. I will treat my suggestion to proceed directly to a vote as a motion, which has carried three to two."

"Bailiff, please take a roll call of the voting on the pending motion regarding the Town Library."

"Regarding the motion by Vice Mayor Abner London to relocate the Town Library to the Smiley Community Center, as described further in the document attached to the agenda for this meeting, and in order of time served on the Board, as set forth in our Town ordinances, I call on Edison Orwell. How do you vote, sir?"

"Nay," said Edison.

"Clarice Dunleavy."

"Nay."

"Lawrence Percival."

Edison and all eyes in the gallery turned towards Larry Percival. Everyone knew he was the deciding vote here. And while he'd signaled support for the library, he hadn't voiced a firm commitment. And the Mayor seemed awfully sure of himself. So they got to Percival somehow. Edison held his breath and listened.

"Yea," said Larry Percival.

The crowd, mostly library supporters, collectively groaned. It was over. The library was dead. And Edison had run for office for nothing. He didn't even wait for the last votes, but they came anyway.

"Yea," said Abner London.

"Yea," said the Mayor.

"The motion carries. The Building and Works chief is directed to begin the process of relocation immediately, with its completion within thirty days."

Edison abhorred the sleazy local politics, but he stayed through the remaining items on the agenda, and the adjournment at its conclusion. He didn't want to face Kara, but he and Brenda ran into her and Stan as they departed.

"I'm sorry, Kara."

"It's not your fault. None of it. It's that corrupt Mayor and his cronies. They just do whatever they want."

"I tried…"

"Edison, please. You did everything a friend could do. Running for office? We all knew it wasn't something you wanted to do. But you did it anyway. And you might have succeeded. None of us could know that Larry Percival would shift gears like that."

"The Mayor got to him somehow," Stan said through clenched teeth. "If I, or anyone else, can turn up any evidence of a bribe, or public corruption, we can get a state investigation. But no one's ever been able to do it before. Who knows? Maybe this time they got so greedy they made a mistake. I'd like to throw out the whole corrupt lot of them."

"Maybe I'll just retire," Kara said, with a tiny tremor in her voice.

They all stopped walking and looked at her.

"Oh honey, you love being a librarian."

"Yes, but we all know that the CC is not a library. And a reassignment to that big place in Meeker Falls? I'd be a third or fourth wheel there. And I don't want to commute, anyway."

"Just think about it for a bit. Maybe we can figure something out," Edison said. But for the life of him, he couldn't think of a thing. Curse those greedy assholes. Look what they'd done to a quality person like Kara.

When they returned home, Edison and Brenda sat down in the living room. All they could talk about was Kara's predicament.

"Who are the developers that the Mayor is in bed with?" Brenda asked, out of the blue.

"I don't remember. Dave knows who they are, though. Why are you asking?"

"Just a scintilla of a thought on how to help Kara."

"I'm in favor of whatever you're thinking. Should I call Dave?"

"Yes, please."

Edison called his friend, and Dave readily provided the name.

"Terrible result today. What a bunch of crooked weasels."

"I expected it from Winkle and London. But Larry Percival?"

Dave just laughed at the comment. "Larry Percival is only principled when there's no issue. He would side with Clarice before you came along, because he didn't want to offend Kara and Stan, and he knew taking a sort of weenie position would offend no one. I'm maybe supporting, he seemed to suggest. But when he was the deciding vote, there was no way he'd cross the Mayor and Vice Mayor. Your arrival forced him to take a position, and choose who could do him the most good, or harm. That's our Larry Percival. He'll support you to the extent it won't cost him anything."

"What a guy," Edison said.

"Yeah. I saw you talking to Kara after the meeting. Is she okay?"

"No. She's not. She's talking about retiring."

"Ooh, not good. She loves being a librarian. She was born to it. Is the information about the developer somehow related to that? Do you have some sort of scheme cooking? If so, I'm in."

"Not me, Brenda. She has something in mind. But I'm not asking yet. She'll tell me in her own time. And I'll tell her what you said."

They chatted a few minutes more and rang off.

Edison reported the results of his chat with Dave, and Brenda nodded her thanks. She was thinking of something, and he'd let whatever idea she had percolate for a while.

He changed the subject. "As I'm no longer needed to cast a vote to save the library, having failed miserably in my effort, I'm free to resign anytime. Should we talk about a move back to New Jersey?"

Brenda looked up absently. Her mind was somewhere else.

"We should, but not right now, honey. But soon."

Brenda was not so sure anymore that she wanted to move. Oh, she missed her former home, missed her friends, missed her sister. But in some ways, she'd become accustomed to a less frenetic, quieter, more congenial, small town life. But one significant thing was missing, and no substitute existed in Standard, or even Meeker Falls. That full professorship at a quality university. The provost had dangled that tantalizing opportunity to return to the academic life she loved. A life that she'd involuntarily left. Her departure was voluntary in one sense, she supposed. But how could she not move when Edison so much needed to leave the daily visual reminder of his colossal, almost criminal, blunder? So, she'd resigned from her position at the university. And everyone, including the president and board of trustees of the university, knew precisely why one of their most popular professors had left. And given their current offer, they hadn't held it against her.

But the more Brenda thought about Kara's plight, the madder she became. Her friend, one of the most decent people she'd ever known, a woman who loved her work, loved promulgating reading, and adored the young avid readers she'd helped start on that grand adventure that books represent, was going to retire. Just because a few crooked local politicians wanted to make money.

Ed had tried to stop them and had failed. Now it was her turn. Ed played by the rules and came up empty. She intended to fight dirty.

38

First step, getting a strategic item to run in the local newspaper. Starved for actual news, the Bugle would jump at printing any juicy gossip item they could get their hands on. They adhered to strict journalistic standards, though. Oh, they'd publish any wild, crazy theory or speculation, but they'd put it in the loosely titled "Heard Around Town" section. If someone heard it around town, it didn't, strictly speaking, have to be fact, have attribution, or be anything other than someone heard it somewhere. The items inevitably became the topics for discussion all around the news-starved town.

Brenda casually started the rumor the very next time she went to the CC, and before long, folks had repeated it dozens of times. And, as expected, a Bugle reporter heard it and printed in the morning Bugle two days later.

The rumor that she'd started had the distinct advantage of being true. And it resonated with the townspeople for two reasons. One, because they were fully aware of the corruption on the Town Board, but hadn't thought it affected them much. And two, because people in Standard universally liked and respected Kara, and no one, other than the corrupt officials themselves, wanted her to lose her job, or even to have the library close. Blinded by greed, the Mayor and his cronies had grossly miscalculated the blowback.

But Brenda knew it wouldn't change much, because the Town had already scheduled the demolition of the library. The Mayor and his cohorts could just weather the storm, and collect their payday, with nothing stopping them.

She and Edison held a council of war, and Brenda explained her idea. She needed Edison's help.

"I'll call him, but I don't know if he'll go for it," Edison warned.

"I know, honey. But we have to try. It's the only way. Two things we know about corporations in America. They don't like adverse publicity, and they don't like government scrutiny."

Ed made the call, and to his surprise, Jack just laughed.

"You're too late, Ed."

"What? Too late for what? You won't do it?"

"Not only will I do it, I already did. What those assholes are doing to Kara is despicable. And while I like the Meeker Falls library, I prefer my old one. And Kara, Stan and I go way back. Those goons have gone too far this time. Everyone knows they get kickbacks, but they never amounted to much. People kind of viewed it as a charming aspect of small-town government. This time, it's big money, or so I've heard. And it's hurting a lot of good people. But the boys and girls in the Attorney General's office will get to the bottom of it. You can be sure of that."

Such investigations take a long time. But just the announcement of the "inquiry into the workings of the Standard Town Board" solved the immediate problem. The developer, fearing adverse publicity, terminated the contract. That didn't change the Town Board decision, but it delayed the closing of the library, because the developer was the one that had contracted to demolish it. So, a state of limbo existed. And there was only a single way Edison saw to fix it. He needed to have a talk with Larry Percival. Larry had to change his vote. If he committed to doing so, they could call an emergency Town Board meeting, and reverse the vote. And Larry, he knew, cared a lot about what people thought of him. Edison called Larry and invited him to coffee at Pete's.

"I know what you want to talk about," Larry told him. "And I have a lot to say about it. But let's not discuss this at Pete's. Too public."

"Okay. You name the place."

"Right here in my kitchen," he said. "I'll brew some coffee, and we can talk. And not just about…um…my recent vote. I can tell you some things that might help a new board member deal with the malediction of some of his fellow members."

Edison wondered about that. It didn't seem to him that Larry had steered the proverbial boat well himself, so he might not be his best choice of a coxswain. His thoughts flew to Clarice as more suitable for that purpose. If he stayed on the Board, and he and Brenda didn't move away.

But he accepted Larry's offer, and they agreed on a time. He'd hear Larry out, and hopefully, convince him to change his vote.

Later that morning, Edison sat at Larry's kitchen table, waiting for the drip coffee maker to finish percolating. He looked around at the decor. The room was bright and cheerful, with windows lining two perpendicular walls. The bright yellow paint contrasted well with white window frame paint and pretty blue chintz curtains. Someone had drawn back the curtains, flooding the room with light. Hitchcock chairs surrounded he round oak table at which he sat. One of which was currently covered by Edison's butt. Pretty placemats sat on the table, and Larry set a mug of his requested black coffee on the one in front of Edison. He sat down in a chair opposite Edison and took a sip of his own coffee. Spotting Edison looking around at the room, he made a self-deprecating comment.

"All of this is Doris. I couldn't interior design to save my life."

"She's got quite a flair," Ed observed.

"Yeah, she does. Lot of bright colors and soft fabrics."

"You do a good job on the outside of homes, though." Larry's company built and painted houses.

Larry smiled. "Yeah, between the two of us, we got it covered."

Pleasantries dispensed with, Edison dove in.

"Listen, Larry ..." he began.

Larry interrupted him. "I know what you're going to say. I've regretted that vote almost since the moment I cast it."

Ed was a little flummoxed by Larry's statement and told him so.

"Then why on Earth did you vote that way? You seemed supportive of the library at the initial meeting." Ed threw caution to the winds. "Did you get a kickback?"

"No!" Larry said it so vehemently, Edison thought he was about to get punched in the face. Larry was a big, muscular guy, and Ed stood no chance against him.

But he followed his statement with an enormous sigh.

"I might as well have," he said, rubbing his temples with his palms.

If Larry confused Edison before, he left him bewildered now.

"Just tell me what happened. Please."

Larry looked up and took a deep breath.

"You haven't seen many LP Construction trucks lately," he said.

Edison hadn't thought about it much. You notice presence more than absence, but now that Larry mentioned it, he hadn't seen many of the distinctive box trucks with the big red LP logo. He nodded, encouraging Larry to continue.

"We're not doing well," he said. "Financially," he added, unnecessarily. "With the economy the way it's been, and the competition from the big guys, a medium-sized operation like mine has trouble competing. Bidding a job is a nightmare now. There are so few jobs, and the competition so fierce, I've had to bid lower and lower, until I come so close to a losing proposition if there's a mishap, and I mean anything. A guy gets sick and can't work, the weather sucks, delaying a job. Anything can reduce the already slender profit to nothing, or... even cause us to lose money."

Edison could see what was coming, but he didn't push. He let Larry tell his story.

Larry paused and looked Edison straight in the eyes.

"No one needs to tell me what way I should have voted. I hurt people by putting my self-interest above the welfare of the town. I know I wounded a truly fine woman. Kara didn't deserve this. Those other two are just out to line their own pockets. Cyrus would have acted the same way. And Ed, I know you were trying to do the right thing by running for office. But you put me in an impossible situation. My family or the good of the town. If Cyrus had won the election, those three would have decided the matter on their own, and I could just cast an unimportant, non-deciding vote. I wouldn't have pissed off two people who can help my business. And now, even any subcontracting work on the new buildings that were contemplated on the library property is... well... gone. I might have to close up shop."

Edison felt bad for him, but not responsible. Which was a bit of a surprise to him because assuming blame for everything bad that happened had become a reflexive state for him. His sympathy for Larry had limits. Another nice man who the forces of evil seduced. He saw no other way. And maybe sometimes that's true. But often there are many other paths to explore before giving in. Before selling your soul. He thought of Dave, who envisioned a large expansion of his electrical contracting business. But when those awful people rebuffed him, Dave found another way. A smaller business, with no debt, self-set hours, and a good living. If he had expanded, he would be bigger, but not happier.

Edison kept his thoughts to himself. "Tough situation," he muttered.

Larry looked grateful for the perceived support. "Yeah."

"Um... so what's next?"

"What do you mean?"

"I mean, are you going to remedy your mistake?"

Larry stared at him. "I just told you what a tough decision I had to make. I gave a rationale. And you seemed to acknowledge how difficult it was."

Edison tried to keep his temper in check. It wasn't easy, but he held back. It would help nothing if he just ripped the guy. So, he changed the subject for the moment.

"You told me you could give me advice on how to deal with the Mayor and Vice Mayor."

"I just did. They control the town. Our townspeople have lived with it for years, with not much complaint."

"So… your advice is to just go along with them?"

"Well, you can vote a different way if it affects nothing."

"Does Clarice do the same thing?"

Larry guffawed. "Clarice does whatever Clarice wants to do. And gets outvoted every time."

Ed controlled his growing anger. Larry was not giving advice. He was soliciting Edison to not put him in the position of taking a difficult position on a matter of importance. If Ed consistently voted with Clarice, Larry would have to cast the deciding vote repeatedly, clearly not the position Larry wanted for himself.

"I have a pretty good idea of what you're asking," Edison said.

"I haven't asked you for anything."

"Not overtly. But I see the writing on the wall. I hoped to get you to support a motion to revisit the vote to close the library." Edison stood up. "Thanks for the coffee, and the elucidation of your position. I particularly enjoyed watching your crocodile tears. I know you feel so bad about what you did to Kara."

As he headed for the door, he turned around.

"We will get the motion to revisit the vote to close the library on the agenda for the next Town Board meeting, if we can't get an emergency meeting scheduled earlier. And once again, I expect you'll be the deciding vote. And I intend to ensure you're always the deciding vote." He didn't wait for an answer as he closed the door behind him.

Steaming with suppressed rage, Edison stormed out of Larry's neighborhood, which wasn't far from his own. He hoped he didn't run into anyone while he blew off steam, and luckily, he didn't. Calming himself while walking down his street, Edison entered his house. He hoped Brenda hadn't gone out so he could debrief her on his unsuccessful visit and was pleased to find her puttering in the kitchen.

39

"We have a little time," Brenda said when Edison told her about his conversation.

"How so?"

"They have no developer now. The immediacy of their situation disappeared the moment the developer pulled out."

"Maybe, but what's stopping them from closing the library anyway? Those two are vindictive as hell. The Board has already voted. They can go right ahead."

"With what money? Wasn't the developer going to pick up all the costs?"

Ed thought about that. "I'm not sure we know that. We suspect it, if only because the Board didn't vote to authorize any funds for it."

He slapped his head. "I just considered what I just said. We never voted to allow any funds for the consolidation of the library with the CC. Those two nimrods didn't think they needed any money, and they sure as hell didn't want to tell townspeople how much money they'd have to pay to eliminate their library."

Brenda smiled.

"You already figured that out, didn't you?" Ed accused, then chuckled. "Can't get anything by you."

"So, we have at least a little time. They can't complete their plans, but sure can make it difficult for Kara. And they will."

Ed looked at her. "You have an idea."

"I think so. It revolves around money."

Ed snorted. "Most things do." He paused. "Hey, you're not planning to bribe the Mayor, or either of those other two?"

"No bribes. Let's not add to the corruption. I think those three won't last forever in their current positions, given the State investigation. We can't wait for that. But the current absence of funding to move the library got me thinking. People in this town don't hate the library, and they all love Kara. But they liked the idea of cost savings due to a consolidation. Cyrus didn't get votes just from his close associates."

That development project was an open secret. People might not have known about the kickbacks, but it's hard to keep the magnitude of such a project secret in this town. The possibility of new affordable housing and the influx of business that would come from the project contemplated on the library land appealed to some people. And some of them value that over a library, particularly if they bought the idea that a consolidation with the CC would preserve it, save money, and bring in well-paying jobs. We don't think that would preserve the library, but some people do. And if you believe, as some people do, that everyone wins in that scenario, why wouldn't you support it?"

"So, we've lost already. If we don't have righteousness on our side, what do we have? They'll just find another developer, raze the library, and a sizable chunk of the population will cheer."

"Maybe not."

"So what's your idea, anyway? Out with it."

Brenda explained, and Edison smiled.

"I bet it will work. It will appeal both to the Mayor's greed and his desire to look magnanimous. He'll get a face saver, the town will get a popular development project, the purists who want no change to Standard will get the project moved from right in town to just outside the town, and it will save the library. And... I'll be able to resign from the Town Board."

"Do you want to do that?"

"I do if we want to move."

Brenda took a moment to look at him.

"Is that what you want? You've built a new life here. New Jersey is just a place of terrible memories."

"No, it isn't," Edison replied after a moment's thought. "We were both born and raised there. I played Little League baseball there as a kid, went to college and met the love of my life there. We have friends in New Jersey I've known since I was five years old. My hometown and I are both named after Edison. If people ask, I proudly say I'm from New Jersey." He paused.

"I'm… we're only here because a whopper of a bad thing happened there. I did the absolute worst thing in my life in New Jersey. And a little girl paid the price. I have nightmares about it. And the thought of revisiting the site where I did that makes me ill. But… we can move back to New Jersey, and I don't have to visit that place. And I want you to be happy. You have a wonderful job opportunity, and I don't think you should pass it up. And where you go, I go." He stopped. "If you'll have me, that is."

Brenda said nothing. She just took Edison's hand and pulled him to her in a warm embrace, which they held for a long time.

When they disengaged, Edison said, "Does that mean we're moving?"

"No. It means I think you're a dear, sweet soul, and I love you. Whatever we do, we'll do together. A decision on moving has to take a back seat to getting this library fiasco resolved. Then we'll decide. Okay?"

"Okay."

"First thing we need to do is find some undeveloped property outside of town. We'll need to attract a developer at some point, but that can wait. But when we do, we need an honest one, and one that takes the character of the town into consideration. And the way we'll do that is up to you, or rather Senator Smiley."

"Jack will love the idea. Whether he can pull it off, well, that's another story. He's not a miracle worker. But all this will take time, and I'm not sure we have time. When does your offer expire?"

"In a couple of weeks at the outside. They need to plan their scholastic year. But this is more important. And I'm not sure I want to return to that kind of grind. I'd love to teach, but not twice a week for lectures with full-time preparation and administrative duties. It will be a ton of work. But they need a full-time professor, not a part-time guest lecturer. So, I'm not at all sure I want to move back. But we don't need to get a development project going. We just need to start the process, so the Mayor abandons the library as a source of payola."

***

"I don't know if I can help with that," Jack said with a small shake of his head.

"Why not? You found money for the Community Center. You justified it by addressing urban blight, as I recall."

Jack laughed. "One of my finest moments. But in that case, you were fixing up an old decrepit house on a property overgrown with weeds, and simultaneously created a valuable town resource. As much as I'd like to take credit for my legislative acumen, that one was a pretty easy sell."

Ed sipped his coffee. They were sitting in a corner booth at Pete's, out of the earshot of nosy patrons. The spot served as Jack's Town of Standard office.

"I'm sure it took a lot more than that," Edison said. "And your efforts were and are much appreciated. What's different this time?"

"Tighter budgets, for one thing. Coupled with a legislative distaste for subsidizing private projects."

"Okay, state seed money is out. You know the problem. Any suggestions?"

Jack took a sip of his coffee and a bite from his apple cider donut. Then he looked at Edison.

"Do the townspeople want this kind of development?"

Ed sighed. "Some yes, some no. Bren speculated that many people voted for Cyrus not because they liked him, but because they knew about the development project and welcomed it."

"Brenda's a smart woman," Jack said. "Look, I think you're on the right track with this. As you know, I have my ear to the ground. Always do. It's how I get re-elected. And it's true that some people, maybe even a lot of them, want expanded business in this town. But even more so, they want expanded affordable housing. They want their kids and grandkids to be able to afford to stay here, but without enough decent affordable homes and apartments, they'll move away. Without enough good jobs, they'll go where they can find work. So, when I asked whether people want this type of project, I kind of already knew the answer. They want it. But not in the middle of their beautiful, quiet, traditional town. They want the benefits, but not at the expense of ruining what they have."

"You like the idea of a development project outside of town? But you said there was no funding for it."

"I like the idea. And I know just the property."

"Where? And please don't say that beautiful undeveloped stretch of land on the west side of the town. You know, the one with the nature walks, the rolling hills, the fabulous greenery, and that fantastic mountain view."

"Perish the thought. The government should designate it as a national preserve. Hmm. Maybe I can help arrange that. But back to the point. I'm referring to the old Gibson landfill."

"I'm not familiar with that," Edison admitted.

"It used to be the Town Dump. Before your time. Almost before my time, it was that long ago. What you know as the Town Dump is a transfer station. It has an area for direct disposal of waste, too, but not like in the old days, when people came and dumped everything in a big hole."

"Is it even suitable for development?"

"It is. Certified by the state DEC years ago."

"So why hasn't anyone developed it?"

"The public has shown very little desire for big, expensive development projects in the general environs of Standard. It seems like that's changing now. And there is some additional expense to reclaiming the land. And that's where I think I can help."

"But you said there was no money."

"There isn't. But there are tax breaks galore. And a tax break for developing affordable housing and new business on a former landfill? I can harness lots of support for something that doesn't look like pork."

"How long will that take?"

"It will take time," Jack admitted. "But dangling the strong possibility might just get a developer interested. And all that's needed here is for the attention to be shifted from the library property to the Gibson property. The development doesn't even need to start. And I have a few ideas about which legitimate companies might be interested. I can help with that. But you have the uphill battle, and you'll need to do your part."

"What do I have to do?" Ed asked, but he had a good idea of what, and he wasn't sure he could pull it off.

"Get the Town Board to change its focus from the library to the Gibson property."

Ed bowed his head and rubbed his eyes, while Jack looked on with amusement.

"You're enjoying this," Ed accused when he looked up. "I've already tried to get that vote changed. I worked hard on Larry, but got nowhere."

"You approached the wrong person. Larry's useless. Approach Winkle. And I'm enjoying the sight of you learning just how difficult the life of a politician can be. Lots of arm-wrestling and hand-wringing. But if you can help the people who elected you — well, it's a great feeling."

"What do I offer him?"

"Nothing right now. He has no incentive to change the vote. He may have no developer, but he may hope that once he gets the library moved out, he can find one. Maybe that's true, and maybe not. Right now, it's his only option. But once I issue a press release stating that I will be actively seeking a reclamation and development grant and tax break regarding the Gibson property, Winkle's eyes will shine with dollar signs. And he knows we are friends, so he'll believe he needs you. If his library project is dead, and the Gibson project is alive, which do you think he'll prioritize? And the best way to curry favor with both of us is to change his vote, and leave the library alone."

"I'll be damned. It sounds so… plausible. We need a developer. And you said your press release would mention a community grant along with a tax break, but before, you told me, no money was available."

"I have no doubt that at least a few developers will show interest. And don't be surprised if Winkle has one. It's his way of making money. And the press release will say I'm seeking a grant, and I will certainly try to get one. I just doubt very much I'll get it."

Edison muttered something about "politics," then said, "So what do we do about a Winkle developer?"

"The state will pick one. It may even be one that Winkle thinks he can make money from. But he'll need to be damn careful with all those eyes on him. And if his developer does a good job, it doesn't matter much except that graft is bad and illegal."

"Except that."

"A part of politics and life, my friend."

Jack shifted gears, and they chatted about other things for a while. Edison mentioned Brenda's desire to continue teaching, but maybe only part-time.

"If only there was a job like that teaching here. I'll bet Brenda wishes Standard was a college town."

"How many problems have I solved for you?" Jack asked with a grin.

"Um, too many, I guess."

"Nah. Not enough. Why don't I add one more?"

"Huh?"

"Do you know how many campuses the State University of New York has?"

Edison didn't.

"Sixty-four. And one of them would be delighted to employ a part-time adjunct professor with Brenda's qualifications. SUNY-Albany or SUNY-Binghamton might be the best bets, but not the only ones."

Edison thanked Jack for his suggestion, and they continued chatting. Jack looked at his watch and rose, as did Ed. They left a tip and paid the cashier on the way out. Their respective roles determined, they left the diner and parted company.

40

Brenda liked the idea. With Edison seeming to get better, or at least trying to, and with a simple plan to resolve the vexing issues with the library, things might just turn around for them. Maybe they could have a good life in Standard after all. There was just one thing. Sarah Jean. Brenda hadn't heard from Britney. And oh, how she hoped her sister bore good news.

Brenda shrugged. Nothing she could do about that. They just had to wait. She said it out loud, but she was alone.

"Talking to myself. Oops, there I go again."

She busied herself updating her resume, and putting the finishing touches on it, then located all the contact information for the various SUNY campuses. Following their individual directions, she fired off e-mail submissions to three — Albany, Binghampton and New Paltz. The last one was a geographical stretch, but there was no harm in trying. She could feasibly get there once a week. But she hoped for Albany. That done, she shut her laptop and returned it to the shelf. She hoped she'd receive a positive response from one of them before she had to respond to the folks in New Jersey. It would make the decision easy. Or so she thought at that moment.

Jack made his announcement a week later. His press release detailed how he was on the verge of securing a significant tax break for the development of the Gibson landfill, how the property had sat unused for too long and was an eyesore. It was the Senator's belief, the press release said, that development of the property could provide far-reaching benefits to the community, including housing and well-paying jobs. Also, its prime location would not adversely affect traffic in the Town of Standard. The press release also stated that companies seeking to develop the property should begin preparing their bids, because the Senator expected approval of the tax breaks within a matter of weeks.

Edison read the advance copy of the press release that Jack had sent him and smiled. Jack's word was money in the bank. He rose, stretched, scratched his belly, and announced, "Time to approach Mayor Winkle."

"Good luck, honey."

Ed picked up the phone and punched in the number for the Mayor's office. He didn't have the private line, and he wanted to give Rufus the idea that he was controlling the situation. And meeting him in his own office was the best place to let the Mayor think he was in charge. So, he spoke to the Mayor's appointments secretary, who put him on hold, and checked to see if the great man could spare a few seconds for a lowly Town Board member, or at least that's what Edison supposed.

Apparently, the Mayor had assented, because Ed was given an appointment later in the day.

Arriving at Town Hall for his appointment, Ed entered and proceeded down a long hallway to an office at the end of the corridor, which had a door with a window bearing a gold-lettered "Office of the Mayor."

Ed opened the door and entered the outer office. A young woman with a pleasant expression looked up at him from the desk at which she sat.

"Mr. Orwell, please sit down. The Mayor will be with you in a moment. He apologizes for making you wait at all, but he just received a phone call, which unavoidably delayed him."

Ed sat down. The power games had started. He'd sit in his chair for hours if need be, but the Mayor surprised him by appearing in the side doorway leading to this inner office.

"Eddie, welcome! Sorry about the delay. Damn phone calls interrupt everything. Come in, come in!"

Ed got up and did as he was told. He'd heard that the Mayor was smooth and could convince a freezing man to give him his coat, but he hadn't experienced it himself. Their pre-election restaurant encounter was nothing like this. He followed the Mayor to his office, where an enormous oak desk occupied a central spot in front of a bay window with a marvelous view of the countryside in back of Town Hall. In front of the desk were two guest chairs, and the Mayor's chair was tall-backed and higher. The epitome of power seating. Ed had expected this. Even welcomed it. But the Mayor didn't sit down at his desk. He motioned Ed to a small seating grouping with a leather loveseat, three chairs, and a coffee table. The Mayor sat down on one side of the loveseat, and Ed plopped down on one of the side chairs. The two men sat only a few feet apart.

"Much more comfortable to chat with a fellow Board Member," the Mayor said. He pointed to his desk. "That's not for us. It's for dealing with town business like vendors, lobbyists, journalists, or, he crossed himself, God forbid, lawyers. I was delighted you wanted to meet with me. We haven't exactly had an uncomplicated relationship up to this point. I thought of reaching out to you, but God bless you, Edison, you extended the first olive branch."

Ed didn't think of it that way, but what the hell, he could go with it. He smiled back and cleared his throat.

"Mayor Winkle," he began.

"Call me Rufus. You're a fellow Board Member, not a constituent."

"Okay, Rufus it is. You know that keeping the library open is near to my heart. I haven't been shy about saying so."

Rufus laughed. "I wouldn't use the word shy, no. More like shouting it every chance you get. Look, Ed, I'm going to save you a lot of hemming and hawing. The library project is dead. If you came here looking to change my vote, you got it. The library stays. I fully support your motion to reverse the earlier vote."

Ed looked at him in amazement, and Rufus laughed.

"Surprised you, didn't I? Look, Eddie. I never saw much sense or political benefit in continuing to beat a dead horse."

Ed thought that was a terrible expression, but kept his mouth shut. He knew what Rufus meant, and it benefited him. Sometimes silence is the best choice. Not one that Ed was accustomed to, but true.

Ed waited for the other shoe to drop, and Rufus wasted no time getting to the point.

"Your friend, our illustrious State Senator, just announced forthcoming tax breaks for the old Gibson property. I want in."

Ed just stared at him. The guy's *chutzpah* was legendary, but Ed hadn't seen it up close before.

"You know I have no control over that," he said. "And I doubt even Jack Smiley does. It's an open bidding process as I understand it from reading the same press release you did. Not only that, but the Senator only said he intended to seek the tax breaks, not that they were a done deal."

Rufus just smiled at him. It wasn't a toothy smile, just a glimmer, with the corners of his mouth turning up ever so slightly. Ed read it as a knowing smile from a man who was used to the political process and was dealing with a neophyte.

Rufus leaned in, glanced at the door and in a conspiratorial voice, almost a whisper, said, "If Jack Smiley wants tax breaks, there will be tax breaks. If he wants a particular contractor, he can exercise a significant influence on who the State chooses. The problem I have is that he hates me. So, any contractor I honestly think is good, he will move heaven and earth to keep from getting a contract, even if they're the lowest bidder."

"Oh, I don't think he's like that," Ed protested.

Rufus just continued his infuriating, knowing smile.

"Well, I certainly don't have any say over the matter," Ed said.

Again, the knowing smile. "You have more than you think," he said.

"Let me get this straight. Your support for the library is conditional on my trying to influence Senator Smiley?"

"No, no, no. I meant what I said. The library project is dead. There is no *quid pro quo*. I'm just asking your help in getting all contractors who bid on the Gibson job a fair consideration, even if I endorse one of them for a project in my town."

"Our town," Ed said.

"Our town," the Mayor agreed. "Look, Ed, I'm just asking that if there is anything you can do to get me treated as fairly as I'm treating you right now, to please do it. I want nothing else, word of honor." He raised his hand, palm facing Ed, to emphasize the solemnity of his word.

Ed stood up. "I certainly hope the State treats all parties fairly," Ed said. "I support that ideal without reservation, and I have no doubt the people who decide will treat everyone fairly."

"All I'm asking, all I'm asking."

The Mayor rose, extended his hand, and they shook. The Mayor put his hand on Ed's back to guide him to the door, gave him a slight wave as Ed walked down the hall and out of the building. Reviewing the interchange in his mind gave Edison an overwhelming desire to take a long shower. He was happy it saved the library, but the thought of that slimy character continuing to rule over Standard gave him a turmoil of emotions, but primarily anger and sadness at the same time. Jack was his friend, but he was a politician through and through. And to Ed, that was not a compliment. He'd correctly predicted the Mayor would cave, and the reason he would do so. Ed had approached that obsequious asshole, Larry Percival. That guy would do whatever Rufus told him. Rufus was the power broker, and he would dump anyone overboard to get what he wanted.

As he walked, Ed wondered. Would Jack do the same? Ed sighed. He probably would. He doubted Jack was as sleazy as Rufus, but he hadn't ascended to his current perch — in the conversation for a future run for governor — without getting his hands a little dirty. Not criminally, but in hard fought, bare-knuckled skirmishes that weren't characterized by good sportsmanship.

To be fair, Edison had sought Jack's political influence on multiple occasions.

Ed gave a slow shake of his head and tried to stop thinking about politics. When he returned home, he greeted Brenda with the good news about the library, and she held out her arms and gave him a big hug. "You did it, honey! Congratulations! Did you call Kara?"

"Not yet. I wanted to tell you first."

"Well, call her right now."

So he did and received effusive thanks.

He disconnected and said to Brenda, "I'm going to take a shower."

"Tough meeting?" she asked.

He looked over his shoulder at her. "He agreed right away, surprisingly enough. But he's a slime-ball just the same, and he's still in charge of our town. I just feel dirty right now, so I'm going to wash away any remnants of mayoral detritus. I'll tell you what happened later."

41

As soon as Edison went upstairs, Brenda's phone chirped. It was Britney. She had news about Sarah Jean. The little girl had a crisis and they moved her from the rehabilitation center to the hospital. She had a brief stay in intensive care, but had "come through it" and was resting comfortably. The doctors were optimistic that she'd be just fine, and back at the rehab center, where she'd made remarkable progress, in short order. Just a blip on an otherwise steady progression towards a more normal life.

Brenda told Ed the news when he finished his shower and returned to the living room.

"She didn't die. I was sure she had."

"I know, honey. But it looks like she'll be back to complete the long road to a normal life. Just an unpleasant, scary episode. Not good, but Brit said the doctors are optimistic that she'll be fine at some point."

Ed was glad she didn't die, of course. And even more so that her condition had apparently improved so much. But it wasn't like he had a happy ending to cheer his soul. He had caused so much misery, so much pain and suffering, to a little girl, no less. And her poor family. The grief at what he'd done washed over him like a toxic rain. He'd deprived her of a sizable chunk of her childhood. Years she could have been playing instead of lying on a hospital bed being poked and prodded by strangers. Maybe, just maybe, she could still have a full life ahead of her. The event had justifiably condemned him to a tortured life of grief, sadness, and self-loathing. And the thing he hated most was that people in town now treated him as some kind of sympathetic creature. Like something awful had happened to him, and people felt bad for him. Nothing had happened to him, and no one, no one, should look at him that way. But they would do it, anyway. Human nature.

Ed exuded a big, resigned sigh. At least other things were looking up. They'd saved the library, securing Kara's job. Brenda seemed to want to stay in Standard, and he had become part of the fabric of the town. Brenda's job prospects as an adjunct professor at SUNY were promising, and she seemed happy with the idea. He had a psychologist he liked, and knew that he had a lot of work to do, but he felt he had a positive attitude about it. He lived in a lovely town with a wonderful wife and had good friends and a seat on the Town Board. Okay, maybe that last was not a positive. And Sarah Jean seemed on the mend after a brief scare, and would soon be back at the rehabilitation center. Things were looking up. But he felt weary. He yawned, stood up, stretched, and ran his fingers through the sparse hair on his temples.

"You know," he said to Brenda. "It's been an exhausting day already. I think I'll stretch out upstairs for a nap."

Brenda smiled at him. "You do that, honey. I'm going to check my email, and do a few searches to see which SUNY campus I prefer, assuming I get a choice."

"You'll get a choice, honey. They'll be falling all over themselves to get you."

His compliment pleased Brenda. Edison hadn't given many in the past few years.

Ed went upstairs and stretched out, fully clothed, on their bed. He fell into a dreamless sleep in seconds.

After Edison went upstairs, Brenda walked into the kitchen and sat down. She flipped open her laptop, but before she could even check her e-mail, her phone chirped. She checked the caller ID. Britney.

"I just spoke to her," Brenda said to herself out loud. "I wonder what she wants."

She answered the call and listened to her sister's concise statement.

"What? How?"

Her sister elaborated on the news, and Brenda blurted, "Oh God, no."

Listening to her sister for a while more, Brenda thanked her and rang off. She didn't want to talk anymore. She needed to think. And try to figure out some advance damage control. But she knew, just knew, what would happen next. And she dreaded it more than anything else. She got up and fixed a cup of tea. That usually calmed her nerves, but nothing could help. Some things in life are inevitable. And this was one of them. The only hope was to mitigate somehow the effect of the news she'd just received. She tried to distract herself. She opened her email and stared blankly at it. Nothing registered. She was awake, but not seeing. A single thought pounded through her head. How to stop this speeding bullet? She kept pondering that question until… oh no, she heard Eddie's footsteps on the stairs.

Brenda panicked. She wanted to run out of the house before he came into the kitchen. She eyed the door with longing. But that would solve nothing. She had to tell him. But what Edison might do scared, terrified her.

Edison walked into the kitchen and Brenda looked up at him.

Her face was ashen, with worry lines he knew well, but hadn't seen lately. Her eyes, those beautiful eyes, exhibited an almost blind terror. What could lead to that? And then Brenda told him.

"Sarah Jean died, honey. She went into cardiac arrest. The damage to her body was just too much for such a little person to handle. It came as a complete surprise, because they thought she was doing much better."

Ed let out a gasp. He couldn't breathe. His throat constricted so much that he couldn't speak, even if he wanted to. He couldn't comprehend, either. She was okay, then suddenly she was dead. Because he killed her. He killed a sweet, innocent little girl. All he could hear in his head was "you killed her, you killed her," over and over.

Brenda saw those glassy eyes, but had no idea how to provide comfort. Ed was near catatonic, but not tottering. He stood fully erect, but his mouth was open and slack-jawed, with a stunned expression on his face. No words came out. Brenda took a few steps in his direction, hoping to hug him tight, but he suddenly turned and bolted for the door.

Brenda called out to him to stop, but Edison ignored her. She suspected she knew where he intended to go, and headed for the car to try to stop him. She didn't like her chances on foot. Edison walked everywhere, jogged frequently, and was surprisingly quick on his feet. He didn't sprint, but he could walk very fast and jog at a brisk pace.

By the time Brenda exited the neighborhood, Edison was not in sight. She pulled over and parked the car on the side of the road. She crossed and headed for the entrance to the nature trail.

Ed was determined to give himself the death penalty. One that the law refused to impose. He saw it as almost an even exchange. A life for a life. But he knew it was no such thing. He was old. Sarah Jean was a mere baby. Ed had a brief life left in him, and the way he felt upon hearing the little girl had died, well, he died with her. But Sarah Jean had a long life ahead of her, and Ed extinguished that with his abject stupidity, and self-centered, and reckless behavior.
Ed spotted the railing in front of the spot upon which he and Brenda had stood looking at the beautiful landscape, with the mountains high above and in front, and the deep canyon and river below. He felt a brief pang of regret, and an overwhelming love for Brenda, the love of his life always and forever, but even that couldn't stop his galactic im-

pulse to end it all. He willed himself to move quicker, and got up a head of steam before launching himself over the railing and plunging to his death. As he went over the railing, he heard Brenda's voice calling to him. "No, no, no, Eddie, no!"

Dear Reader:

Online reviews are much appreciated, so it would be great if you took a few moments to write a review on Amazon.com, BarnesandNoble .com, or any other review site. Thanks!

Just click on the link (or type it into your browser), choose which of my books you wish to review, and scroll down to where it provides for a review.

www.amazon.com/author/ericsmall

Eric Small

Ordering Information:

At Amazon.com, Barnesandnoble.com, and other online booksellers.

Out of Sight: *www.amazon.com/author/ericsmall*

Brazen Gambit: http://www.amazon.com/dp/0998859206 http://www.barnesandnoble.com/s/9780998859200

A Tale of Two Freddies: http://www.amazon.com/dp/098859231 http://www.barnesandnoble.com/s/098859231

Three Faces of Jennifer: https//www.amazon.com/dp.0998859265/ https//www.barnesandnoble.com/w/1137607647

Contact Information:

Middletown Publishing Group
St. Augustine, Florida
mpubgroup@gmail.com

About the Author

Eric Small is a retired government attorney living in Florida. He is the author of three previous books: *Brazen Gambit; A Tale of Two Freddies*; and *Three Faces of Jennifer*, all set in Middletown, New Jersey. *Out of Sight* is a novel set in the fictional upstate New York town of Standard, New York, and represents a divergence in both subject matter and locale.

www.ingramcontent.com/pod-product-compliance
Lightning Source LLC
Chambersburg PA
CBHW021149310726
48971CB00002B/555